Clare Stephens is a Sydney-based podcaster, screenwriter, editor and digital content creator. She's the former editor-in-chief at *Mamamia*—Australia's largest independent women's network—and has produced some of the site's most viral content. Her writing has appeared in *The Age, Sydney Morning Herald* and *Brisbane Times*, and she publishes a weekly newsletter on Substack. She is also a writer and producer on the Binge series *Strife*—seasons 1 and 2. *The Worst Thing I've Ever Done* is her first novel.

PRAISE FOR

The Worst Thing I've Ever Done

'*The Worst Thing I've Ever Done* is a riveting debut: thoughtful, compassionate, nuanced and so very topical. I couldn't stop thinking about it after I turned the last page. Clare Stephens keeps you on the hook—and doesn't let you off!'

Liane Moriarty, author of *Here One Moment*

'As compulsive as any app. Clare Stephens creates a cautionary tale for our times, full of wit and nuance.'

Jane Harper, author of *Last One Out*

'Clare Stephens has written the kind of debut that feels both urgently contemporary and quietly profound. *The Worst Thing I've Ever Done* is sharp, insightful and deeply compassionate— a compulsive read that dares to ask what happens when we become the object of the scrutiny we so casually dish out. With elegant prose and unflinching honesty, Stephens marks herself as a striking new voice in Australian fiction.'

Sally Hepworth, author of *Mad Mabel*

The Worst Thing I've Ever Done

CLARE STEPHENS

Atlantic Books
Australia

This is a work of fiction. Names, characters, places and incidents are products of the author's imagination or are used fictitiously. Any resemblance to actual events, locales or persons, living or dead, is entirely coincidental.

First published in 2025

Copyright © Clare Stephens 2025

All rights reserved. No part of this book may be reproduced or transmitted in any form or by any means, electronic or mechanical, including photocopying, recording or by any information storage and retrieval system, without prior permission in writing from the publisher. The Australian *Copyright Act 1968* (the Act) allows a maximum of one chapter or 10 per cent of this book, whichever is the greater, to be photocopied by any educational institution for its educational purposes provided that the educational institution (or body that administers it) has given a remuneration notice to the Copyright Agency (Australia) under the Act.

Atlantic Books Australia
Cammeraygal Country
83 Alexander Street
Crows Nest NSW 2065
Australia
Phone: (61 2) 8425 0100
Email: info@allenandunwin.com
Web: www.allenandunwin.com

Allen & Unwin acknowledges the Traditional Owners of the Country on which we live and work. We pay our respects to all Aboriginal and Torres Strait Islander Elders, past and present.

EU Authorised Representative: Easy Access System Europe, Mustamäe tee 50, 10621 Tallinn, Estonia, gpsr.requests@easproject.com

A catalogue record for this book is available from the National Library of Australia

ISBN 978 1 92292 803 0

Set in 13.2/19.5 pt Adobe Jenson Pro by Bookhouse, Sydney
Printed and bound in Australia by the Opus Group

10 9 8 7 6 5 4 3 2 1

MIX
Paper | Supporting responsible forestry
FSC® C001695

The paper in this book is FSC® certified. FSC® promotes environmentally responsible, socially beneficial and economically viable management of the world's forests.

To Mum and Julieann, for the gift of time

And to Jessie, for showing me I could

effigy (*noun*) /ˈɛfɪdʒi/   Latin. 16th century.
A representation or sculpture of a person, often created for public ridicule, protest, or symbolic destruction.

scapegoat (*noun*) /ˈskeɪpˌɡoʊt/   Hebrew. 16th century.
A goat symbolically burdened with the sins of the community and sent away into the wilderness.

renrou sousuo (人肉搜索)   Chinese. 21st century.
Roughly translates to 'human flesh search'. The practice of crowdsourcing information about an individual, often with the goal of publicly exposing or punishing them, typically through social media and online platforms.

Prologue

For two weeks during a humid, suffocating summer, one where a teenage boy went viral for frying an egg on the pavement and tenants in century-old Art Deco apartments slept with damp towels draped across their foreheads, I was the most hated woman in the country.

My name, once so Caucasian and boring that it afforded me an anonymity I had previously taken for granted, became a trending search term. It appeared in print and online and in comments and captions, and in the mouths of people I'd never met.

My face, with my slightly overlapping front teeth and the faded, silver scar on my chin from when a girl in primary school had stabbed me with a pencil, was plastered across news sites. Photos from overseas holidays and drunken lunches were taken from my social media to accompany stories about me, sitting on homepages between articles about foreign wars and interest rates and celebrity divorces. The journalists always chose the happy photos. The ones where my eyes creased at the corners and my lips thinned around my gums, because then it looked like I was laughing at the people who were angry, and that made them angrier.

When the internet is feasting on you, tearing the flesh from your bones like vultures descending on a corpse, you're not meant to scream. You can, people assure you, simply turn off your phone. You can block it and ignore it and touch some grass or sniff a baby or leave the country. You can throw yourself into the warm, turquoise ocean that hugs the edges of your city, humbled by waves that toss you like a rag doll. Further out, you can dive beneath the surface into the light-pierced, glassy emptiness, cradled by the endless weight of something far bigger and far older than you can possibly comprehend. You can tell yourself, with wet sand between your toes and the taste of salt on your tongue, that the stories filling the phone screens of strangers aren't real, that their outrage is thin and artificial and fleeting. That it's all an illusion, magnified by your own inflated ego.

But then you walk down the bustling main street on your way home, past the people sprawled outside overpriced cafes, and you're certain a woman looks at you for longer than she should. There is a moment of recognition, a flicker of contempt that quickly turns to pity, and it is as real as the sting of the sun on your freckled arms. Because she knows just as well as you do that the internet and the pulsating reality inside it is not an illusion. It is the heartbeat of modern life.

And yet still you are not meant to scream.

Even a whimper will send the feasting vultures into a frenzy. Their violence, you must understand, is so warranted, so justified, that for you to consider yourself a victim of it is a crime in itself. How dare you cry out in pain when you are simply being confronted with the consequences of your own actions? After all, how else can we hold people accountable for their behaviour if we do not destroy them on the internet?

To me, those two weeks felt like a lifetime. In some ways, perhaps it was. A person with my name and my face but who, I assured myself, was *not me* had been born; the product of a zeitgeist that needed a woman to loathe.

Looking back now, I can pinpoint exactly how things went so wrong. How decisions that seemed inconsequential were in fact propelling me towards my own destruction—towards the very specific set of circumstances that made the nightmare inevitable. And so, against the advice of everyone around me, I want to tell you what happened. I want to tell you my story, so that when you search my name and read about me, you know I'm not the monster they say I am.

For a long time, I was obsessed with the idea that, with the help of some perfectly crafted sentences, I could change everyone's minds. My words would be read by people scrolling on their morning commute or procrastinating in soulless offices or distracting themselves on the toilet, and in unison they'd gasp, my humanity thumping them hard in the chest. They would see that Ruby Williams was never a demon, she was not a one-dimensional ideologue deserving of a kind of social death, but a person, with all the complexity and vulnerability that entails. They'd realise that the individuals advocating for justice had used it as an excuse for casual cruelty, and the rest of them, the ones who liked and commented and shared and messaged and laughed and mocked and spread the hate further and further so it burned through cyberspace like wildfire, had been casualties of mass hysteria. They'd feel ashamed of how they'd let a handful of dubious transgressions turn an ordinary woman into the bad guy, when the real bad guy was up there, lording over us all, pulling our strings as if we were puppets. I was certain, so certain, that eventually the rubble I'd been buried under would be lifted and that finally I would be understood.

But, of course, that never happened. There's no use continuing to defend yourself in front of a jury that has already found you guilty.

No. After everything, I know I can't be redeemed in their eyes. But I want to tell you this story in the hopes that maybe, just maybe, I can be redeemed in yours.

PART ONE

Chapter 1

During

At first, I was sure it was someone else's phone. The familiar vibration had been incessant and irritating, sinking into the timber surface of the long table until it seemed to be all around us, disturbing the air like a freight train. It was only when Sarah twisted her phone out of the pocket of her tailored pants, looked vacantly at her screen and tucked it away again that I thought to check my own.

My rose-gold block of metal was sitting facedown beside my laptop, a gesture that had somehow become acceptable in recent years. In our social lives and in the workplace we laid our phones in front of us like weapons, as if to say: *I will put the source of my distraction in front of me so you know I am genuinely listening.*

I had just tapped my screen to life when Ian turned to me and spoke. He always addressed me with an upward inflection, as though my name itself was a question. It had the effect of making him sound insincere, like he was role-playing his job as publisher, performing a character he didn't quite believe in. With the room's attention on me, I ignored the blur of messages and notifications and calendar reminders that had lit up beneath my thumb, and discreetly lowered my phone to my seat. I slid it beneath my thigh, feeling the throb of it against my skin. The bursts were short, like a pulse, not from a phone call but from something else: an email thread or a reinvigorated group chat or an app I regularly thought about deleting.

Bared's reach, Ian was saying, was the highest it had been since we launched. His gaze shifted from me to the slide that now glowed against the white-brick wall at the front of the room, and he explained it in detail, as though none of us were capable of reading a graph. A series of tiny black dots were joined together by a single, volatile line—one that dipped the month there'd been an unexpected algorithm change, and spiked the month a local influencer had been exposed for abusing her toddler. Since I—as editor-in-chief—had been given the resources to hire more people in the content team, the line had climbed rapidly, buoyed by a royal scandal and the cursed press tour for a Hollywood blockbuster and an anonymous story from a woman who sent nudes to a guy who turned out to be her dad. Most recently, a new interview series about hidden abuse in intimate relationships had gone viral. The series struck the rare, sought-after balance of driving traffic *and* serving a greater purpose—persuading our audience to pay attention, just for a moment, to something that actually mattered.

'It's been an exceptional quarter for site traffic and social engagement,' Ian said, leaning back in his chair with his arms folded. He was tall, well over six foot five, and I'd never seen him look comfortable on a piece of office furniture. It was as though he was moving through a dollhouse, a place made of small things with small, disposable people, all of which he could crush with the sole of his foot or the palm of his hand. I found myself involuntarily desperate for his approval, this even-tempered giant. He didn't need to raise his voice or send strongly worded emails because the fear was already there, looming like a face pressed against a doll-sized window.

Being scared of Ian was partly what motivated me at work, but in truth, my job felt like a reflex. A skill I'd been honing ever since I'd discovered the internet. I had a savant-like ability to predict what an audience would care about, the kinds of headlines they'd click on, the posts they'd like, the videos they'd watch and comment on and share. I knew how to find the angle in a mainstream news story that would hook a person mid-scroll, that would draw them in and keep them there, that would answer the question they didn't even know they were asking. I knew how to read the mood online. To tap into the base instincts of human curiosity. To offer you the content you couldn't resist.

In a recent pitch meeting on a day where we were desperate for traffic, I'd announced that we needed to prioritise one kind of story and one kind of story only: anal sex gone wrong.

'It works every time,' I said, wincing. 'I just think today they want poo on the sheets. An upset tummy. Spicy food and then some badly timed experimentation. That sort of thing.'

Amelia, one of our senior writers whose idealism had been crushed from her time working at a tabloid, nodded. 'Yes! I feel like society is yelling at me to try anal and all I can picture is a nugget on the bed.'

'It has to be happening all the time,' I said. 'You can't have a mass adoption of butt plugs without a few accidents, surely? Also, we need a ghost story. Just noises, a door slamming, maybe a kid with an imaginary friend who ends up being a dead person. No figures or apparitions or anything; that's when it starts to sound like bullshit.'

Over the course of a week, both stories attracted more than a million page views.

Now, Ian waved towards the data and returned his gaze to me. 'So what are the insights? The learnings? What can we take from this to get to our BHAG?'

I cringed every time someone used an acronym at work, but I never felt more embarrassed than when 'Bee-Hag' was said out loud. It stood for Big Hairy Audacious Goal, and I think I avoided ever saying it out loud, but if I did, I deserve to have a shoe lobbed at me. Maybe a BHAG made sense in the context of humans landing on the moon, or civilisation-disrupting companies like SpaceX or Google, but *Bared* was only a year old, had twenty-five employees, and most of them just wanted someone to fix the air conditioning. We were one of many outlets under the umbrella of Simmons Corp, and given that we all knew they could close us down tomorrow with very little impact to their bottom line, it was hard to imagine any goal of ours being particularly audacious.

Still, Ian had asked me for insights, and I couldn't tell him that the team's most significant learnings of late were about poo and ghosts. He wasn't heavily involved in the day-to-day of what we produced, insisting he trusted me with the 'content side' of the business while he prioritised revenue. He'd hired me to set the brand's agenda, to build our audience, to be the external face of it all, because apparently a Rolex-wearing tech entrepreneur with salt-and-pepper hair was not a compelling image for a left-leaning, feminist, youth publication.

While I spoke, explaining how our audience's habits were changing, how we'd been investing more resources in short-form video, how news stories resonated most in the morning and personal stories in the evening, my phone continued to buzz. It was bothering me now, the relentlessness. Sometimes it would slow for a few minutes, and I'd think whatever it was had ended, then it would pick up again and I'd get the desperate urge to escape the people I was sharing a meeting room with and attend to the ones in my phone.

Maybe things would've been different if I'd listened to that instinct. If I'd seen it all right at the beginning, the flood of grey, rectangular boxes housing snippets of phrases I would slowly realise were about me.

But I didn't. Instead, I let the vibrations howl against my flesh, and waited for the meeting to end. I sat through the revenue updates and the plans for the site redesign and the ever-increasing traffic targets for the next quarter.

When the others closed their laptops and picked up their coffee cups and slid their chairs out, leaving behind the slightly chemical smell of overheated technology, I remained in my seat and reached for my phone. Immediately, in the fraction of a second it took to wake my screen, I knew something was not right. Swimming in the stream of alerts that dripped one after the other, like a bottomless waterfall, I saw a name that should not have been there. A name that sent icy shards of adrenaline through my veins and froze the air in my lungs. Why was it staring back at me, over and over again, in a context it did not belong?

Above it and beneath it were other words, other messages.

>   This is fucked, are you okay?
>
>   Call me when you see this
>
>   Dude wtf I just saw what's happening

And then there were the adjectives, fired at me from accounts I didn't recognise.

dumb

embarrassing

hypocrite

manipulative

cum stain of a human

The day around me—the chatter and the targets and the list of urgent tasks—faded into the periphery. There was only the rushing surge in my phone, swelling at a faster rate than I could grasp. A person, a real person, was speaking now, suddenly in the room when she hadn't been before.

'Ruby? Have you seen it? I didn't know if you were looking at your phone.'

Yasmin, the managing editor, was standing beside me, her voice high and shaky, the way it was when she'd had to deal with a legal issue in my absence. There was dried saliva in the corners of her mouth and her arms hung stiffly by her sides, as though they didn't know what to do when they weren't attached to something she could type on. The door, I could see, was closed. Yasmin must've shut it on the way in.

'I don't want you to panic,' she said, trying and failing to wheel out a chair that was trapped behind a table leg, forcing her to contort herself in order to sit down. 'But there's this video. And it's about you.'

Chapter 2

Before

Twenty-one days earlier

The space around my desk smelt musky, like the dampness from outside had been absorbed by the floorboards. Dirty drops of rain pounded against the windows, breaking the humidity that had been blanketing the city for days. We'd all been waiting for the storm. Now that it was here, the sky outside getting darker while the ceiling lights cloaked my desk in a warm glow, I would've happily stayed in the office forever. It reminded me of the evenings I used to spend curled in the reading nooks of my university library, researching and writing in a bubble that felt protected from everything. No one to interrupt. Hours sprawled ahead, full of potential.

It was well after six, and everyone else had left for the day. Several people had taken off a little early, mumbling that they wanted to avoid getting caught in the wild weather. I was used to being the last person here. Most afternoons I would barely notice the gradual emptying of our floor, the tapping of fingers on keyboards getting lighter, clusters of voices disappearing, the ding of the lift becoming more frequent until it stopped completely. It was only when one of the eager-to-impress writers hovered beside me, asking if there was anything else they could do, that I realised we were alone.

Of course, theoretically there was always more to do. But modern labour laws stopped me from asking a junior to stay late to write three hundred words on a sexist radio shock jock because we needed the website traffic. So instead I would tell them to finish up, that I'd be heading out soon, too.

The cleaners gave me a nod when they arrived, not speaking as they weaved in and out of poky meeting rooms, squeaking oily handprints from frameless glass walls. They emptied bins and vacuumed while I toggled between unread emails and unpublished stories, regularly glancing up at the screen on the wall opposite me that displayed *Bared*'s real-time analytics. Traffic was strong because of a tragic news story about a murder-suicide, and I had an article about a cheating reality star ready to go live. I knew the numbers would spike and hold steady into the night, hopefully giving the morning team a head start. On socials, we'd just published a video for a travel client, and I deleted a comment from a user complaining that no one could afford to travel during the current cost of living crisis. It wasn't true, and it would unnerve the client. *Yeah, there's a cost of living crisis*, I thought. *And how do you think a media company pays its staff a liveable wage? With advertising like this, you fucking moron.*

I went back to my inbox and attempted to sort through what were mostly bland offers from overly optimistic PRs. Too many capital letters. Dull press releases. Useless gift guides. I opened an email offering an interview with an ambassador no one had ever heard of for a launch no one cared about.

A heaviness crept into my gut. Although I loved the frenetic pace of work, the thrill of capturing people's attention, sometimes it all felt rather hollow. On the walls around me, the televisions buzzed with stories no one would remember tomorrow; the kinds of stories I'd assigned my team to write today so that people mindlessly scrolling their phones would spend an average of forty-seven seconds reading them. Running a brand like *Bared*, I had learnt, was like building a sandcastle that got washed away by the tide every night, needing to be reconstructed from scratch the next day. There was no time, no resources and no incentive to invest in something bigger and better, because the twenty-four-hour news cycle never offered a reprieve. You had no choice but to build the same deformed sandcastle over and over again, and hope for the sake of your job that it continued to produce a viable revenue stream. On an existential level, you hoped that these little things you were building, when taken together, amounted to something more.

Of course, I hadn't known all this when I started in digital media. I wanted to work as a journalist, to write the first draft of history. I imagined myself like Mark Ruffalo in *Spotlight*, dishevelled but passionate, refusing to give up until I spoke truth to power. But then I graduated and searched for a job for almost a year, pulling beer behind a bar and being followed home by regulars for just above minimum wage. When I was eventually hired as a junior writer at one of the country's biggest mastheads, my first assignment was to call a socialite whom everyone hated and ask her to describe, in detail, exactly what she fed her three-year-old. It was the most-read story of the month.

I left my role at *The Daily* to launch *Bared* because I wanted to do work that truly mattered. The whole ethos of the company, Ian explained, was to speak to progressive young people who were seeking candidness in a media landscape that had left them behind. Our tagline was *lay it all bare*, and while the others joked that it gave off the vibe of a porn site, I felt it in my bones. *Bared*'s content was raw, unfiltered and honest. We weren't pretentious about the news—we didn't assume any knowledge that the ordinary person wouldn't have. We covered entertainment and beauty and culture and women's stories with an understanding of what was light and silly and what carried real weight. It was a platform that was feminist because it cared about highlighting the complexities of young women's lives—acknowledging the kinds of experiences that had traditionally been ignored. I thought the openness of *Bared* was radical, that it had the power to challenge our internalised shame. I'm not sure I believe that anymore.

But even then, when I pressed publish on the story about the cheating reality star, when I fed it to the hungry beast of the internet, where it would be clawed at and devoured by hundreds of thousands of people in the finite seconds of their lives, a part of me wondered what it was all for. Was this serving some greater purpose? Or was I just addicted to a game I had become very good at?

That probably explains why I did what I did. Why I needed a project that played into my idealism—my narcissism, really—of believing there was some moral quality to how I'd chosen to spend my days.

It stood out when I clicked back to my inbox. The shaded line of an email I'd missed earlier, directed squarely at me.

ATTN: RUBY WILLIAMS. Katy's story.

I opened it, scanned it, and then read it again, more carefully this time. The woman was writing, she said, because Katy Fenwick, the doe-eyed nurse who was all over the news, her pretty face occupying the banner of our homepage, had been her friend. The story of Katy's murder at the hands of her ex-boyfriend, who then took his own life, was the one our audience had been clicking on for days. The one that hovered at the top of the screen above my desk, dipping briefly below the article about the cheating reality star. We'd published multiple updates as police released more information to the public, our readers poring over the riddle of how a young, educated, adored daughter and sister and colleague could have been involved with the kind of man who was capable of killing her.

Now, blinking behind my cursor, were words from a woman whose grief was coursing through every sentence, every paragraph. *Everyone's talking about the fact that he had never hurt her before*, she wrote. *That's what it says in the headlines: that he didn't beat her. That he never laid a hand on her until the day he killed her.*

She was right. The family's shock, their insistence that there were no signs of violence, added a layer of tension to the story. It triggered people's impulse to comb through the details, to read article after article, trying to spot the smoking gun. To identify something about the whole tragedy that set it at a distance; that proved it could never happen to them. But the emphasis on there being *no signs*, this emailer said, was blatantly dangerous. And it wasn't true.

> He was cruel to Katy in the worst way, because he humiliated her and confused her and controlled her. It was only when she finally decided to leave that he made sure she couldn't. It was more insidious, more manipulative than the kind of domestic violence everyone sees in movies. She told me things, horrible, horrible things, but she thought she was overreacting or that they were her fault. I just think people

should know the details, because maybe if she had been aware that these were signs of a fucking abuser, she might still be here. People need to know what her life looked like *before* he did this.

As I read, my mind was pulling together the loose threads of an idea that had been gently tugging at me for months. I looked up as the older of the cleaners, a man with dark, thinning hair and a face creased with exhaustion, reached towards one of the wall-mounted screens to wipe off a layer of dust.

'Want me to turn these off?' he asked, gesturing towards the half-dozen TVs scattered throughout the office.

'Yes, please,' I said. 'Thank you. I won't be long.'

I opened a blank document and started to type: messy sentences, unfinished dot points, the energy of emerging thoughts captured without hesitation. It was November, and more women had died as a result of domestic violence than in any other year on record. At *Bared*, we reported the familiar stories over and over again, using the same helplines and the same legal caveats and the same detached language. The alleged perpetrator. Known to the victim. The promise of a coronial inquest into systemic failures. Quotes from police about horrific and senseless acts, and witnesses calling said acts cowardly, callous, harrowing. Mothers and fathers grieving daughters, and children grieving mothers, and local communities left shattered, and women and girls quietly confronting their own innate vulnerability.

Surely there was an opportunity to do something of consequence. That was the media's job, wasn't it? To provoke change. To shape the national conversation.

I kept returning to the email.

These were signs of a fucking abuser.

People need to know what her life looked like.

The anguished friend of Katy Fenwick had reached out not to a lawyer, not to a social worker, not to a counsellor, but to me—the editor-in-chief of a publication she believed had at least some kind of power.

I only realised how late it was when I heard the flick of a switch and the entire floor was plunged into darkness. The cleaners had finished, and they'd instinctively turned off the main light. I turned to call out, to remind them that there was still someone here, hunched over in a too-big chair, but the lift doors had already shut, and I was alone.

I returned my gaze to the blue light of my screen and sent a distilled version of my idea to Ian. He was always encouraging us to be bold, to take risks. To capitalise on the agility made possible by publishing online. So here it was: an engaging concept for an editorial campaign, delivered to his inbox out-of-hours. There was never a question of whether he would approve it. A man can't exactly tell a young woman not to run a content series about domestic violence.

I think back to that night often, the cooler air seeping through the worn-down window seals, the world outside turned into a grey smudge by the heavy rain. I can see myself at my desk, pressing send with a sense of achievement. That image—of my face lit up by the glare of my screen, like a spotlight I hadn't meant to stand beneath—haunts me. Because that's the person they destroyed. A person who was impulsive and driven by a constant need for attention, but who underneath it all, I still believe, was trying to do a good thing.

Chapter 3

During

I watched the video with Yasmin beside me, holding my breath for what seemed like all two minutes and sixteen seconds of it. I kept waiting for it to stop, for the worst of it to be over, but then there'd be another blow that made my chest pound, tightened the glands in my throat.

My first instinct was to contact Felicity Cartwright—the familiar face who was clearly so enraged that she needed a crowd of strangers to know about it. To urgently type a message to her and explain the context, that this was all a terrible mistake, a misunderstanding. *Oh no, we're on the same side!* I wanted to write. *How funny! You must've assumed I meant something I didn't! Now that it's all cleared up, you can delete this unnecessarily angry video and we can laugh about this one day over a glass of wine. Your shout!*

I reflexively tapped until I was staring at the blank space where I could write to her, a blue vertical line flashing in anticipation. But sitting in the empty boardroom, Yasmin now back at her desk, I froze. I thought about explaining some of the details that hadn't fit into the 1200-word confines of my published story, or rewording parts of it to make my intention clearer. Then I searched for articles I'd previously published on *Bared*, ones that would prove I had the values that Felicity insisted I didn't. I knew there were people in the office looking at me, seeing a frozen figure beyond the glass. A short, brassy chime echoed through the space, an alert signalling that there was another meeting scheduled to start in a few minutes. Still, I couldn't move. My limbs were made of concrete. My phone turned to stone in my hand.

Every sentence I strung together felt hollow. I could imagine exactly how it would be read from the perspective of a person who hated me, who thought I was manipulative and calculating and self-interested. I imagined Felicity sharing a screenshot of anything I wrote and dissecting it line by line until its meaning became distorted. What was left would be evidence that I was not only malicious but also incapable of taking responsibility. That's the way these things always went. There was no room for explaining; the only permitted response was an apology. But how were you meant to accept responsibility when you didn't believe you'd done anything wrong?

So I sent nothing. I went back to my desk and listened to Amelia call Felicity a sociopath.

'And who are these randoms just scrolling at 2 pm on a Tuesday, ready to call someone they've never met a "fucking crumbmaiden of the patriarchy"?' Amelia asked, reading from the comments.

I wished she wouldn't. Every time I heard a sniff, a yawn, a snigger, I held my breath, certain it was because another vicious insult about me had been posted under that video.

Omg I've always hated her, one of the first comments read. *Ever since she wrote for* The Daily. *I was like . . . wait, how did someone that dumb get a job as a professional writer lol.*

I didn't make a conscious decision not to tell Ian about it. He'd gone offsite for the afternoon, and I naively thought he might not see it. He wasn't Felicity's audience—a straight man in his mid-forties whose social media served him half-naked women and golf. Technically, it was my role to build and protect the brand, so I usually decided how we would respond to public criticism. However, I'd never been in the position of managing a rapidly growing piece of criticism that was unequivocally aimed at me.

As the hours went by, I tried to read and edit and publish and curate the homepage, but my fingers kept finding their way back to my phone. I seethed in silence watching the views on Felicity's video climb higher, the comments turn crueller, the direct messages become more and more brazen. Felicity had to have known that there was a direct line between publicly chastising a woman and people feeling entitled to call that woman a cunt. I repeated the word in my head, the disgusting sound of it, and hated that my visceral reaction to it was fear. I pictured Mum's face, how she bristled so distinctively whenever the word was said in her presence. I wanted to be more evolved than her, to have a thicker skin, an armoured exterior that took the sting out of the words that were meant to humiliate me. But I didn't. When I saw those four letters, my mind went only to the fragility between my legs.

My anger at Jamie was the only thing distracting me from what was happening online. I'd sent him the video straight-away, explaining that I'd written an article and now a person with a social media following larger than the entire population of Iceland was calling me harmful and problematic. He'd responded with two sentences an hour later.

> What a weirdo. Just ignore it, normal people aren't watching that shit.

He knew this wasn't something I could ignore. It didn't matter if Felicity was a 'weirdo'; my reputation mattered. When you're building a brand, when you *are* the brand, you can't have hundreds of people turn against you. Your likeability is crucial. If it's damaged, an entire business is at stake.

And yet he didn't seem to understand the emotional weight of what was unfolding, of what it might mean. The patch of the internet I existed in was inherently foreign to Jamie. It had a hierarchy and a politics he'd never absorbed. Still, after three years together I wanted him to know what to say. To know that the appropriate response was obviously: *I love you, you're not a cum stain, sorry you're being attacked by someone I've never heard of, can I get you a Coke Zero on the way home?*

Liv sensed the gravity of the video straightaway. She'd seen it before I had, calling me repeatedly before sending a stream of frantic texts. I imagined her stiff-haired boss noticing her distress and asking what was wrong, and Liv replying, without a hint of irony, 'Sorry, John, but it's an emergency. My sister is being cancelled by Felicity Cartwright.'

In an attempt to lighten the mood, she sent a screenshot of one of the comments.

> Just looked Ruby Williams up. She looks like she's got an IQ of 0 and an iron deficiency.

Okay, in her defence she's half right, Liv wrote. *But also isn't it ableist to tease someone for having an IQ of 0? You should reply that it's not very nice to bully someone for having an intellectual disability.*

So true, I typed back. *I think I'd get a very rational response if I pointed that out.*

• • •

After work, I walked to the bus stop without looking up. I was like a lab rat trained to press a lever for access to heroin, running my finger down my screen over and over again, refreshing it until there were new bursts of red notifications. Each time, my heart raced with adrenaline, and the field of vision on either side of my phone fell out of focus. Sometimes, someone left a comment mildly defending me. Questioning the tone of the video. Questioning the gravity of what it was insinuating. Then five more comments popped up below it, arguing, name-calling, chastising, and most of the time the original comment disappeared.

I should acknowledge here that a lot of people reached out to check whether I was okay. People I knew and people I didn't, saying this was all absurd, my article had been portrayed as something it wasn't, Felicity wasn't being fair.

But you don't remember the supportive messages. You don't screenshot them and study them. The truth was, the messages of solidarity were almost more humiliating. They reminded me how many people were watching, like my ridicule was being played out live on prime-time television. For every person who reached out to say they felt for me, that they were sorry, there were probably hundreds more quietly enjoying my destruction. Peers or acquaintances sharing their harshest opinions among themselves—opinions even more brutal than those I was receiving directly.

When I got home, the apartment was like a furnace. Jamie had just stepped out of the shower and I forced him, still with a towel wrapped around his waist, to sit on our lumpy couch and watch the entire video with me. Liv rang a few seconds in, and so I put her on speaker, the three of us listening to the brittle tone of Felicity's voice blaring through my phone. I paused it to explain the parts that were factually incorrect, or the lines where she'd blatantly misinterpreted my story. Towards the end, I ranted about the irony of a woman publicly shaming another woman in order to make a point about feminism. My screen angled towards Jamie, trapping him between my body and the arm of the lounge, and he reached for Felicity's face to turn her off.

'I genuinely can't watch it,' he groaned. 'Who has the time to do this? And I'm still confused about who she thinks you've "harmed"?'

'I swear feminism is broken,' Liv shouted into her phone, over the sound of a train pulling up at the station. I could picture her at Central, packed into the crowd of commuters whose days started early and finished late, who struggled to explain their jobs at dinner parties. Liv would be weighed down on one side by a handbag too small for her work laptop, wearing an outfit that was vaguely corporate but not quite right. She'd been told by her boss at the bank that she lacked 'executive presence', and when she pressed him for details, the only example he could give was her shoes.

'Ruby, I get it,' she said in a hushed voice; clearly she was now on the train and conscious of being the person who speaks too loudly in a packed carriage. 'I'm so angry it's killing me not to message her and tell her she has no idea who she's talking about. But DO NOT respond to her. That's what she wants you to do.'

When Liv hung up, Jamie prised my phone from my clawed grasp and stuffed it between the seat cushions, before turning to face me.

'You have to stop engaging with it. None of these people know who you are. They wouldn't say any of these things to you in person.'

There were beads of sweat on his forehead, the water from the shower turning to perspiration before it had the chance to dry. I knew he wanted to relax, to stretch out on the lounge with his feet on the coffee table, scrolling through YouTube clips about JFK's assassination or the most shocking images from World War Two. He was always aching to wind down once he finished work, the energy of classes full of rowdy, hormone-fuelled teenage boys leaving him empty.

'But how can people just say stuff about me that isn't true?' I snapped. 'If I sit back and let them talk more and more shit, everyone assumes the reason I'm not replying is because I either don't care or it all actually has some basis in reality. And it doesn't!' I pointed to the spot where he'd hidden my phone, as though a tiny version of Felicity was inside it. 'All these assumptions and these judgements on my character have been invented, Jamie. Did you even hear what she said?'

Jamie stood up and padded towards the hallway, his feet leaving prints of moisture on the tiled floor.

'A few days from now, no one will remember this,' he called out. 'It might feel urgent and important, but it's seriously not.'

It was only once he'd left the room that I rummaged through the crumb-filled gap between the cushions and retrieved my phone. I needed to think. There had to be a way to respond, to explain myself, to pour a bucket of water over the fire that was tearing through everything I'd built.

Chapter 4

Before

Twenty days earlier

Ian had approved the idea by the time I arrived at the office the next morning. It was overcast but the thick heat was back, covering almost everyone in a layer of shine, turning blow-dried hair into a fluffy mess. Only on Amelia did the warmth make her look even more dewy and fresh. The plumpness of her skin and the natural pinkness of her cheeks reminded me of what I'd seen earlier in the harsh light of my bathroom mirror. I'd studied the thin, veiny skin under my eyes, the colour of bruises. Two sunken semicircles I'd had since I was five, which made me look sick in every school photo. Now, ahead of the morning pitch meeting, I hoped my concealer had disguised them. That enough makeup had left nothing particularly noticeable about my appearance, just a narrow, mousy face that blended in with the others.

Out of the corner of my eye, I saw Yasmin making a beeline for my desk. I'd sent her the email with my idea, too, because I needed her help to execute it. As the managing editor she was aware of everyone's workload, knew who had the time to focus on an additional project. Now, her thick, dark hair was slicked back off her face, and she clutched a takeaway coffee, her overflowing neoprene bag still on her shoulder.

'I'm obsessed,' she said. 'Obsessed. Like, it's brand-defining.'

She glanced around our pod of desks, checking who was in earshot.

'I know you're going to kill me for suggesting it, but I think Beth needs to spearhead this,' she whispered. 'She has the most experience interviewing victim-survivors. She knows all the legal stuff, and she'll do a good job. Even if . . .'

Yasmin must've noticed my limbs stiffening, my shoulders creeping closer to my ears. Beth was our senior features writer, hired at the same time as me. She was well-trained and knew how to negotiate the delicate process of preparing a person's most sensitive story for publication. Her interview skills and her writing were flawless. She also had the most challenging attitude of anyone I'd ever worked with. Whenever Yasmin or I attempted to manage her, to set her priorities or give her feedback, a stoniness settled on her face. She would refuse to take on certain assignments, saying she was 'at capacity'—a phrase that seemed to be used exclusively by people who were not, by any measure, at capacity.

I finished Yasmin's sentence. 'Even if she'll complain about it and make our lives hell? Even if it'll take hours and hours of rearranging and placating to get it to happen?'

Once, on a particularly overwhelming day when I hadn't moved from my desk for nine hours, I'd asked Beth to help me fix an urgent error on the site. She'd snapped that I should do it myself, that's what I got paid for. It was bizarre, more than anything, because it seemed to come out of nowhere. When my voice returned after the initial shock, I asked her to please not speak to me like that, and she stood up and left the office, not returning until the following morning.

She was stressed, she said later. When I asked Simmons Corp's HR department what to do—explaining that she was taking all day to file a single story (every other writer filed a minimum of three), that she'd used all her sick leave, that she was blatantly defiant, they sent me on a course about mental health in the workplace. At no point in the two-day course did I receive any advice about what to do with all the work left behind by a person who was unable to complete it. About how it was meant to get done without impacting other people's mental health. Or how the course itself had allowed for a fresh clump of tasks to grow and fester, while I watched a convenor explain 'stress' to a group of overwhelmed managers.

'Yes,' Yasmin said, sliding her bag off her shoulder and perching on the edge of my desk. 'We can't keep loading everyone else up and letting her get away with working at the slowest pace. It's not fair. Everyone else in the team notices it. We need to set a standard and keep reinforcing it. This is the perfect project to have her on because she doesn't have the option of dropping the ball. And she will actually do a good job, even if she's scowling while she's doing it.'

I knew she was right, but there seemed to be something deeply personal about Beth's anger. After she'd snapped at me, I'd felt the burn of several sets of eyes studying my face. It had taken all my strength to blink back the tears, to take shallow breath after shallow breath while my heart pounded and my throat stung.

Yasmin and I made our way to the far corner of the office, where some of the writers were already spread out over two navy-blue couches and a handful of swivel chairs wheeled over from nearby desks. I stood, leaning my back against the oversized concrete pylon that connected two exposed-brick walls. Yasmin took a seat at the other end of the group, her laptop now open. Beside her, Meg was frowning at her phone, probably trying to come up with a last-minute pitch. While I waited for the rest of the team to join us, I studied the metal-framed windows and the high ceilings with their white-painted timber beams. The space still gave me butterflies. Like there were ideas floating around in the woody air, just waiting to be retrieved by an eager set of hands.

'Before we pitch,' I began, 'I wanted to share the details of a campaign we're planning to roll out over the next few weeks.'

There were eight faces turned towards me, and yet my gaze was instinctively drawn to a twitch in Beth's expression.

'Ian's on board, and I think it's a really powerful way to raise awareness about the deaths from domestic violence that have been dominating the news cycle lately. We've been covering these stories, but I want us to feel like we're actually *doing* something rather than just reporting the gruesome details.

'We had an email yesterday from a close friend of Katy Fenwick. Her name is Alison, and she's distressed by the fact that Katy's partner was manipulative and controlling, but because he never hurt her physically, Katy herself thought she was overreacting. We all know from reporting story after story about this that when a woman is killed by a current or former partner, it almost always follows a clear pattern of coercive control. And a lot of the time, it's not actually physical at first. It's sexual or it's emotional or it's financial, all things that are way harder to seek help for and to explain to other people. So a lot of the time, the victim convinces herself it's her fault, or that she deserved it.'

Amelia nodded earnestly. A couple of seats down, Beth was still. Her arms, I noticed, were crossed tightly against her body.

'I mean, we hold our keys between our fingers and we avoid walking down sketchy streets at night, but women are most likely to be killed in their own homes, by people they love. In our campaign, I want us to tell women's stories of coercive control, in a series called *What No One Saw*. For one month, we publish an interview every day. We build a detailed, diverse, vivid picture of the reality of these relationships for our audience, and we point out how useless it is that the media only reports on these stories once a woman is dead. There are countless Katy Fenwicks, and we have the power to help them recognise the signs of abuse and realise that they're not alone. Those first red flags, they're the beginning of a narrative that I want us at *Bared* to rewrite.'

As I spoke, an image started to form, like a piece of film developing in a darkroom. I continued, building on what I'd pitched to Ian.

'Then, at the end, I think we turn it into an interactive part of the website. Maybe we create a video moving through a dark, suburban house, and when you click on different parts, the stories emerge. We can use all sorts of multimedia, like voice recordings and screenshots of text messages, to turn it into this haunting representation . . . this depiction of an epidemic that's hiding in homes all over the country.'

I saw Meg's eyes light up. She was an expert in code and knew how to build immersive, bespoke content. She was always suggesting we do more digital storytelling, and I was always telling her we didn't have the time.

'This could become something we're known for. Something that really has an impact.'

I scanned the faces in front of me. Heads cocked, brows knitted in thought.

'I think it's really exciting,' Amelia said. She almost exclusively wrote lifestyle and entertainment content, so it wasn't a project she'd be directly involved in. Still, I appreciated her enthusiasm. 'Maybe we could do a photo shoot with the women we speak to? To show that they could be your friend or your sister. Like, really humanise them.'

This was the thing about trying to lead a team in a democratic way, inviting buy-in from every person about every decision. We absolutely could not do a photo shoot, because an essential part of telling these stories would be ensuring the women remained anonymous. Naming them opened up a legal and ethical can of worms. Current or former partners could sue for defamation, or worse. These were dangerous men, and we needed to protect the people brave enough to talk about their experiences.

But the pitch meetings, according to my own rule, were a 'yes, and' environment. You didn't cut anyone down; you either built on their ideas, or you kept your mouth shut. I nodded at Amelia, trying to maintain a neutral expression.

'Yep. Humanising, exactly. But we couldn't do a photo shoot, because—'

'Yeah, wait. I'm confused.' Beth's voice was flat, and she looked at the other writers, the other editors, everyone other than me as she spoke. 'How are we meant to source these stories? These are interviews, right? We can't include any identifying details if they are, because that puts the people we're interviewing at risk of being sued for defamation, not to mention the risk from abusive partners. We have to be really careful and intentional. We can't just throw a whole lot of content out there for the sake of it.'

I saw a woman from a nearby desk poke her head above her monitor. We shared an office with two other small publications, and while we mostly kept to ourselves, I could sometimes sense them trying to read the dynamic of our team. I didn't let myself consider what they thought of me, a twenty-seven-year-old who'd been handed the reins of a media brand.

With her eyebrows raised, Beth finally rested her gaze on me.

'And, sorry, when are we meant to do this? Everyone's workload is at capacity already.'

Behind what she'd said there was a coarseness, a sharpness like the serrated blade of a knife. Somewhere in my gut, I had predicted this reaction. My ideas appeared to grate at her. She pierced holes in them, purposely misrepresenting what I meant, which was made more frustrating by the fact that she rarely suggested any of her own.

I opened my mouth to respond, but Yasmin's voice came out first.

'Actually, Beth, we'd like you to take the lead in managing these interviews. You're right that we have to be careful, and we know how much experience you have in this area. This will be your priority for the next month—we can chat about what needs to come off your plate in order for that to happen.'

It wasn't a question. Yasmin's directness always surprised me, because I was so incapable of it. It didn't come naturally to her, either, the pace of her speech exposing her nerves. But Beth didn't argue. She stared blankly at Yasmin, then, once the team started pitching, she looked down at her phone and started typing. If I'd pulled her up on it, I'm sure she would've claimed she was taking notes, or responding to something urgent, but I knew exactly what she was doing. She'd be bitching to someone about her problematic workplace where she was surrounded by idiots, embellishing details the same way I did when I recounted the annoyances of my day to Liv. I genuinely didn't care what Beth said inside that vortex—what picture of me she painted to the people in her phone. She didn't respect me, but I knew she respected her own by-line, her own writing, and she'd never compromise it.

...

A week later, Beth filed an exclusive interview with Katy Fenwick's friend, Alison. I published it, proofreading passages that bled with the grief of watching your childhood friend slowly disappear in plain sight. Katy was twenty-three, and a man almost twice her age had made her feel like the most beautiful woman in the world, before tearing away at her from the inside out. *What No One Saw* was live, and I'd never seen so much traffic to *Bared* in a single day.

Chapter 5

During

The bathroom was the only place where I could lock the door and be alone with my phone, safe from Jamie's attempts to hide it from me. The Himalayan salts I'd poured into the bath hadn't dissolved, so as I sank into the tub the crystals were hard against my spine. I tried to take deep breaths, to take my mind off the screen sitting on the tub's porcelain rim. To inhale the floral, spicy scent of the obnoxiously expensive candle on the windowsill—the one I never wanted to light because it made me feel like I was burning money. The room was dark apart from the warm flicker, and the shadows hid the black mould embedded deep in the grout. It might've looked quite pretty in a photograph—soft, maybe even romantic. But the air was thick and my scalp was itchy with sweat and even in the silence there was a deafening noise in my head.

I opened the video again and studied the familiar face frozen in the rectangle in my palm. Felicity's auburn hair was parted neatly in the middle, and a light sprinkling of freckles was scattered across her nose as though they'd been painted on. Her teeth were big and straight and white, the result of half-a-dozen veneers she'd been gifted in exchange for promoting an orthodontist.

There was something profoundly unnatural about seeing her lips make the shape of my name. I'd worked alongside her for years at *The Daily*, passing her in the kitchen or standing beside her as I waited for my coffee at the cafe downstairs. She never spoke to me. She was a senior political journalist, lauded for her tenacity when it came to holding elected representatives to account. I'd admired her initially, but up close, I found myself conflicted by her approach. Her own ideological position was strikingly transparent, and it felt as though there was a growing self-righteousness to how she challenged particular members of parliament. I hadn't been at *The Daily* for long when she unearthed photos of a minister's teenage son snorting white powder at a high-school party. It was front-page news, and it drew engagement to the site in numbers I'd never seen before. On her personal social media, she had a growing reputation as a crusader against privilege, railing against the private-school culture so prevalent in the halls of Parliament House. But the kid was seventeen, with his name now permanently associated with an impulsive decision he'd made before his frontal lobe was fully formed. I always wondered whether Felicity saw the story about his admission to a psychiatric ward three months later. I wondered if she cared.

Over the last few years, she'd built a platform that rivalled *The Daily*'s. She had a podcast and a newsletter, and she posted frequent videos weighing in on whatever conversations were dominating the news. Sometimes she wrote polarising op-eds for major publications, and they instantly gained traction, her devoted followers worshipping her words like she was their god. While we'd technically been colleagues, I felt like I 'knew' her in the same way I 'knew' lots of people: because I saw her face more often than my own mother's. Every time I was served one of her videos, I became entirely absorbed in her outrage— the intensity of it, the moral superiority, the air of contempt. It was thrilling. So the algorithm learnt to feed me everything she created, to let me gorge on it, knowing that the more I consumed, the more my appetite would grow. That hunger had built her a following of over half-a-million people, desperate to feast on whatever carcass she deemed worthy of tearing apart. Now, I was the carcass.

I pressed play.

She looked away from the camera as she spoke. It gave the impression of an expert addressing a highly technical question, searching for the most accurate way to express the nuances of her discipline.

'Okay. I just read this article on Bared, and I needed to come on here to talk about how fucked up it is,' she said.

Her hands were flat against each other, with her index fingers pressed against her lips. She bowed her head slightly, as though processing the weight of what she was about to say.

'Some of you may have seen it; to those of you who have, I'm sorry, because I can imagine it was really distressing. To those who haven't, let me explain. Bared *claims* to be a progressive publication, and Ruby Williams herself *claims* to be a feminist. But she isn't. She's a feminist when it suits her. When it helps her.'

She clapped her hands to the beat of her words, saying them slowly, rhythmically.

When. It. Suits. Her.

When. It. Helps. Her.

It felt oddly patronising, like a kindergarten teacher imparting a lesson to a group of five-year-olds.

'Then she publishes a story like this, and either her politics are really obvious, or she's pandering to men in quite a creepy way.'

Behind her was a built-in bookshelf, the spines of the books colour-coded, and an oversized pastel artwork was just visible to one side of it. Her skin texture suggested she had a ring light set up just inches from her face, and her head and shoulders were squarely in the centre of the frame. I pictured her attaching her phone to a stand she'd bought off Amazon, clipping it in, straightening it, checking that the angle was right. I wondered if she'd done more than one take; if she'd shot the video and then noticed a hair was out of place, or she had lipstick on her teeth.

'I don't think I even need to explain why publishing this interview is so dangerous. But look: I think the saddest part is that it doesn't surprise me. Women like Ruby Williams are everywhere, and they're all the same. These women who don't think about anyone other than themselves. Who don't think about how their actions might hurt other people—other women—because they're too busy climbing a capitalist ladder.'

The video ended with Felicity's pursed lips, her eyes wide.

'Honestly, Ruby Williams, I'm sorry, but there's something really fucking wrong with you if you think this is okay.'

Every time I heard that last sentence, I thought I was going to be sick. I felt sweat prick my palms and a mixture of fury and frustration and fear pool in the pit of my stomach.

I sat up to hug my shins, resting my chin in the shallow gap where my knees met. I stared at the bathwater, cloudy from soap and the salts, and longed to be small again. To be a flat-chested child in the stained bath in the home I grew up in, patting a beard made out of bubbles onto Liv's face. I pictured Mum crouching on the floor beside us, trying to wash our fine, dark hair while we splashed and squealed and squirmed away from her grasp.

I hadn't been aware of anything then. Not the shape of myself, or how I looked to other people or how I rubbed against them. No one had told me I was annoying or too sensitive or embarrassing or ugly or wrong. I hadn't known that once you noticed those things about yourself, there was no going back. You lived with the shame buried in your bones, so deep in the fibres that you almost forgot it was there. It was only when it all came at you again, long, grubby fingers poking against your skin, that you realised they were pressing on a bruise.

I stood up and stepped out of the bath, wiping my phone with a towel before I dried my body. I sensed the furriness of my teeth and the crusty remnants of make-up around my eyes. That was the thing about baths. You never truly felt clean afterwards, just as though you'd soaked in your own boiling filth.

It was the silliest part of it all that tipped me over the edge. That made me do something I shouldn't have done. To anyone else, it would've seemed like an inane insult, one of the tamest of hundreds that had been directed at me in the last several hours. But for some reason, one particular comment, ten words posted by a complete stranger, struck me in a way the others hadn't.

hannaroland: She's just a mean girl. She's not a nice person.

And so, feeling like a child with their bloodied nose against the pavement, being kicked and kicked while a crowd of blurry faces watched on, I replied.

Chapter 6

Before

Three days earlier

I should've predicted that Beth was due for a sick day. I was getting ready for work when she called, applying mascara in front of the brass-framed, oversized floor mirror slumped against my bedroom wall. Behind me, the unmade bed was covered in clothes—a white t-shirt with yellow stains under the arms, a coral shirt in desperate need of an iron, light-wash jeans that were unwearable in this weather. I'd worn the same lilac top so many times recently that it had become a running joke, Amelia asking me, deadpan, if it was new, where I'd got it from, if I had seven of them hanging in my wardrobe.

Jamie came into the bedroom while I was on the phone. We'd been for a swim that morning, the sun already so high at 7 am that the ocean outside our windows seemed to be beckoning us towards it. We'd stood in line at the coffee shop afterwards and I'd looked up at him and thought, not for the first time, that I'd never expected love to feel this playful. When I was growing up, I didn't picture the laughter or the fun or the friendship that would come from building a life with someone. Love, to me, was tinged with drama. It was heavy and ominous and demanded to be taken seriously. But from the moment I met him, Jamie had the energy of a little boy in awe of absolutely everything, a face that flickered with warmth whenever he looked at me.

Now, he raised his eyebrows, wordlessly asking whom I was speaking to. I pointed to the phone and mouthed Beth's name, and a corner of his mouth lifted. I'd told him all about Beth—about the day she stormed out of the office, the time she accused me of bullying her when she was rostered on to work a public holiday, the rumours that she'd almost quit when she learnt I was going to be her boss, because she couldn't stand the indignity of being managed by someone who was three years younger than her.

Jamie smiled and shook his head as he rummaged around for a pair of socks. His navy shirt was unbuttoned, revealing his lean, golden stomach and a dusting of dark hair that became thicker as it crawled towards his groin. I was envious of how disciplined he was about exercise, and how definitively he wore that discipline. He had no neuroses about his body, no guilt or shame or overthinking about what he put into it. He'd just always adored sport—that's why he taught it. For a moment I considered the softness of my own belly, the way my underwear cut into the flesh around my hips. I knew if I lingered on that sensation, if I stood in front of the mirror and studied my dimpled thighs and my flat bum and my bloated waist, it would consume me for weeks.

So I was distracted when Beth said there was no one available to interview the woman she was meant to be meeting at 9 am.

'I've looked at the roster,' she croaked. 'We only have Meg, but she's the primary news writer today, so I would assume you can't have her out of the office. I can cancel the interview, but it means we won't have a *What No One Saw* piece for tomorrow.'

I pictured her lying in her dark bedroom, where she claimed to be unable to move because of a crippling migraine. Perhaps she truly was unwell, and it really had come on suddenly, forcing her to miss an unmissable interview with only a couple of hours' notice. But there was an unnatural quality to her voice, an over-egged hoarseness that pulled at me.

The *What No One Saw* series was driving an unprecedented level of traffic to the site. Major news outlets with far larger readerships than ours had written around *Bared*'s interview with Katy Fenwick's friend Alison, and it had been picked up on talk shows and radio. The coverage had the effect of both directing attention towards the campaign, and introducing a whole new audience to the *Bared* brand. We'd then published some of Alison's most compelling quotes in a series of tiles on social media, and that post had been shared tens of thousands of times, including by a former prime minister, a well-known television personality and the host of one of the country's most listened-to podcasts. Our follower count was growing by the day, almost doubling since we'd launched the campaign. We'd received hundreds of submissions from readers wanting to share their own experiences, which made the task of sourcing stories significantly easier for Beth. Still, she showed no enthusiasm, and her attitude towards her work didn't change. She swore under her breath if I asked her when I could expect one of her articles to be filed. She told me to stop micromanaging when I suggested an editorial assistant could help load her copy into the back end. She had stopped pitching altogether in the morning meetings, because she was 'overwhelmed' by *What No One Saw*.

One afternoon, she sent me a message about the 'inappropriate' headline I'd chosen for one of her interviews. She insisted it was exploitative, that I was 'clickbaiting' a woman's suffering. I was mortified. I never understood why Beth spoke to me like she was expecting conflict; like she was confident I'd dismiss her or refute her concerns. I almost always took her suggestions on board, because, as I'd told her again and again, I thought her content instincts were exceptional. I thanked her for the feedback and changed the headline, asking her to please be open with me if she ever thought I was angling a story in a way that was tone-deaf or insensitive. She didn't reply.

On the phone, I asked her for the details of the morning's interview. We couldn't reschedule it—we needed it to run first thing tomorrow. There was a dedicated space on the homepage for the *What No One Saw* series, and the audience, Ian, the executives at Simmons Corp who had picked up on the buzz of the campaign, would notice if it was stagnant for a day. It would also make me appear lazy and disorganised, like I couldn't effectively manage my own team.

'Her name's Jo and she reached out via email,' Beth said, relief creeping into her voice. She knew this meant I would reassign the interview, that her load would be a little lighter when she returned to work. I was only half-listening, anxiously piecing together how I might be able to rearrange the workloads of several already swamped writers in order to cover the overpaid one who technically had no sick leave left.

'She's shared very basic details but she was pretty young when this guy started taking control of her money. She says he sabotaged her career as an actress. She mentioned something about a pregnancy, too, but I don't know what happened with that, if he pressured her to keep it or if she terminated it and he was angry. Might be an interesting angle.'

The words tumbled out like a reflex. I didn't even realise I'd made the decision until I said it out loud. But sitting on my dusty floor, the day coming at me through the window, it seemed like the only option.

'Forward the email to me. It's fine, I'll take the interview.'

Beth took a moment to respond. I could almost hear the flash of confusion across her face.

'Oh, um, okay. Are you sure? I'll send it now. Thank you. Thanks. I appreciate it.'

I've analysed that moment since, trying to figure out exactly why I offered to add an interview and a tight deadline to my already overflowing list of priorities. I didn't have to. I could've called a writer who was rostered off and asked them to come in. I could've contacted a freelancer, or assigned it to Meg and had a junior step in to cover the daily news.

Part of me thought it might help me win Beth over. Ever since primary school, my approach to anyone who didn't like me was to shower them with compliments and over-the-top generosity—to offer them my lunch or my answers to the homework or my turn on the netball court. It always worked. If I helped Beth when she needed it, she might feel indebted to me in a way that mellowed her hatred.

But there was another part of it that wasn't about Beth at all, that's more shameful to admit.

I wanted my name on the campaign. When I'd agreed to launch *Bared* as editor-in-chief, I'd been told the role was 'front-facing'. I'd be hosting events and making guest appearances on TV and radio, and, most importantly, my by-line would be all over *Bared*'s homepage. Initially, I wrote almost every day. Most weeks, one of my stories sat at the top of the leaderboard, and my profile continued to grow with every op-ed or personal essay I published. But then we hired more writers, a social media strategist and a video producer, and my job started to change. Instead of seeing my name beneath the headline of a story, I was seeing it beside meeting requests, or at the top of paragraphs-long email complaints. I heard it at the beginning of out-of-hours phone calls and in mid-morning 'can I steal you for a moment?' interruptions that added to my pile of invisible, monotonous problems to solve. Anything creative had to be done on top of all that, so it was rushed and malformed.

There was nothing like the thrill of knowing your words were being read and shared, that your thoughts were the sole object of a person's attention. It had rankled me that while *What No One Saw* was my idea, it was Beth's name that appeared on every piece in the series.

I wanted to write the interview that would launch the campaign into the stratosphere. It was nearing the end of the month, and this was my chance to get the external credit for my own work. To be the author of the story everyone would be talking about.

Chapter 7

During

Of course, I was well aware that you should never engage with personal attacks online, because it only ever made things worse. I'd seen it over and over again in my years of watching conflict play out on social media. If a person was poking at you, baiting you with claims that weren't true or were entirely devoid of context or struck at the core of your character, the part you guarded most fiercely, they wanted you to react. It was like a prosecutor interrogating a murder suspect in court, waiting to see if they snapped. Once they did, the lawyer could simply smirk at the jury—*See? That's the kind of person who's guilty*—before quietly taking their seat.

I knew this. And yet I stood in my damp bathroom, the steam fogging up the mirror and the small, casement window that looked straight out onto the main road, and typed.

A woman with the handle 'hannaroland' had left the comment. A stranger. Someone I'd never met, who, surely, had no reliable insight into who I was. I clicked on the small image of her—she couldn't have been older than twenty-five—and landed on an unassuming private account. On this page, the photo was slightly enlarged, and now I could make out the shape of her nose and the arches of her eyebrows over the top of her tortoiseshell sunglasses. This person called Hanna smiled with her face squashed beside someone who looked a lot like her—her sister, perhaps, or just a friend who happened to have the same colouring and gummy smile. I wondered how Hanna would react if someone she loved was being attacked on the internet. If they were being labelled a 'mean girl' and 'not a nice person'. How absurd it would seem, how uncalled for. She'd look at the people around her and they'd shake their heads, lamenting the fact that the world had gone mad. That everyone was so unnecessarily cruel these days, so full of hate.

The other photos of Hanna were locked. I could only see the few words at the top of her profile: *Artist. Empath. Humanist.* 'An EMPATH?' I wanted to type. 'What kind of shitty empath fails to consider how attacking a stranger online might make them feel?'

I couldn't let her words stand unchallenged. I read over my reply and almost deleted it. Then I glanced at the stagnant bathwater beside me and felt the pinch of my damp, tangled hair. Unable to stand in the heat any longer, and with my muscles stiff from indecision, I pressed send.

> **hannaroland**: She's just a mean girl. She's not a nice person.
>
> > **rubymwilliams**: I have never met you. How can you make a statement like this? There's a whole lot of context to the story I wrote that isn't being shared here. But I don't know what about me would ever make someone think I'm mean.

It wasn't expressed perfectly, but it was true. For a moment, I felt vindicated. Maybe people scrolling through the comments would see it and remember that I was an actual person who was reading every insult and every snide joke. Who could see that I was like an awkward teenager stuck in a toilet cubicle while a group of girls stood by the basins and bitched about her.

That's what was so shocking to me about the tone of people online: that it was so similar to the viciousness of high school. It was considered appropriate to mock and to bully and to alienate and to name-call. In fact, that behaviour was applauded and seen to be an expression of morality somehow, a sign of just how much you cared about ensuring *people do the right thing*.

I picked up my oversized pyjama shirt and undies from the floor and peeled them on. When I checked my phone again, an untamed river of comments had flooded in.

lol imagine responding to a comment about you being 'mean' and not responding to, like, the harm you've caused. wild.

tell me you don't get it without telling me you don't get it.

She . . . she doesn't get it.

@felicitycartwright has done the work of explaining how hurtful and frankly fucked up your behaviour has been, and instead of thanking her and apologising, you're getting petty in the comments? girl, what?

GUYS DON'T SAY I'M MEAN I ONLY EVER WANTED TO WRITE A MISGUIDED, PROBLEMATIC ARTICLE WITH ABSOLUTELY NO CONSEQUENCES.

They kept coming. I'd injected more energy, more intensity, into the mess, and there weren't enough words to explain why I'd responded to that particular comment, or why I hadn't apologised. It was bizarre, I thought, that if a person took offence to something you said, you owed them both an apology and a thank you. What if their offence wasn't sincere? What if their offence was informed by their own biases, which themselves were offensive? What if *you* were offended, because people were now calling you a cunt and a moll and a dumb, manipulative mean girl when you didn't feel you deserved it?

I walked down the hallway, the steam from the bathroom following me and thinning out as it hit the cooler air. I attached my phone to its charger on the floor beside my bed, watching the screen fill and fill with more responses, more reactions, more strangers dissecting both my words and my silence, demanding remorse. Telling me to delete the article. To publicly apologise. To remove my comment. To do my research. To listen. To learn. To do better. Simply being near my phone now was intimidating, like I could hear the angry voices yelling at me behind the glass.

I sat on the edge of my bed and flopped forward, my head between my knees, the way I was told to sit when I was a kid and thought I was about to faint. Anything I did now would make it worse. The closer I was to my phone while the outrage was still pulsating, the more damage I'd do. So I unplugged the charger and moved it to the power point behind the bedroom door. For the rest of the night it would be banished, out of my reach. But you can never really detach yourself from the internet. Not when your avatar remains there; a shadow-self moulded out of everything you've ever posted, ready to take on a life of its own.

Chapter 8

Before

Three days earlier

I planned to meet Jo at a cafe a few blocks from the office, one known for its 'deconstructed' avocado toast. It hummed at a volume loud enough that it was easy to feel anonymous; that you wouldn't be overheard or noticed. I'd found a table in the back corner where Jo could sit facing the wall, giving our conversation the illusion of privacy. When I'd emailed saying I'd be interviewing her today instead of Beth, she'd responded immediately.

> omg I follow you haha looking forward to meeting you. I'll be able to spot you from a mile away xx

I was flattered, but lately I'd noticed a slight twinge of dread when someone said they were familiar with my work. I wondered whether the real-life version of me—uncomfortable and shy with foundation that had probably worn off—would be disappointing to people who only knew me online. I wasn't as articulate in person as I was in writing, and the videos I posted were filmed in the most flattering light I could find, usually after an emotionally exhausting session perfecting my hair and make-up. Even my voice had a different tone when I was speaking into a camera; more energetic, less shrill.

But I hoped Jo's familiarity with me might be a short cut to establishing trust. If she already saw me as a friend, she might be more open than she would've been with Beth.

She arrived a few minutes late, scanning the cafe until her eyes met mine. Jo had the haircut I had tried once, only to find I didn't have the face for it. It sat an inch below her ears, bleached and messy, the volume of it making her neck and shoulders look even tinier than they were. As she took her seat opposite me, I wasn't surprised she'd been an aspiring actress. She had the kind of straight, Roman nose you're taught to hate as a woman, even when it looks like it's been carved by an artist to complement your bone structure perfectly, and deep-set, piercing eyes so light they seemed almost painful to look through.

We ordered coffees and chatted easily until they arrived. Then I pulled out the handwritten notes I'd prepared before

I left home, as well as my phone to record our conversation. She glanced at it before looking up at me.

'So I don't want my name in this, please,' she said. 'No one in my life knows.'

'Of course,' I said. 'We'll use a pseudonym. And I'll change any identifying details. I know it's a big deal to share something like this, and my priority is that you're okay. So if you feel uncomfortable at any time, if you want to stop, just let me know.'

Jo nodded. Around her neck she wore two fine, gold chains of slightly different lengths, and she tugged at the longer one with her forefinger.

As I went to press the voice recorder on my phone, I saw there were already messages from the editorial team back at the office. I'd had to run the morning pitch meeting and then come straight here, leaving Yasmin to assign the day's stories. But there were always questions; people fluttering with uncertainty when there wasn't someone to tell them exactly what to do. *Should I delete this angry comment? Do you want me to film that video idea from last week? Will a snarky article about these ugly pants piss off our fashion client?* I could feel their impatience through the screen.

It was irritating to feel like I couldn't be fully present when my attention required it. Working online seemed to be a never-ending exercise in fracturing yourself, trying to be in infinite places at once. I was never just at a cafe, noticing the squeal of boiling milk or the scrape of metal on metal or the buttery smell of freshly baked pastries. My consciousness was like bits of shrapnel, some of it here, right now, attached to the current moment, some of it trapped in *Bared*'s messaging software, some of it caught in the stories that made up the homepage. But a lot of it was scattered throughout the ether of the whole internet: memes and viral trends and gossip and backlash and news and tragedy and hacks and celebrity folklore. Sometimes I wondered if I'd ever be able to put it back together again, or if I was doomed to an existence where the bits of shrapnel got smaller and smaller, my awareness spread increasingly thin across an ever-expanding universe.

I turned my phone over so the notifications could drill silently into the oak laminate table, and tried to take a steadying breath. The lined page in front of me was filled with details I'd taken down from Jo's initial email.

'So, how old were you when you met Ben?'

Jo had been twenty-two and working casual shifts at a bar after finishing drama school. Ben was a few years older than her, with dark features and olive skin and a Bon Iver tattoo on the back of his upper arm. It was a fine-line drawing of a log cabin, a tiny window sketched in a way that looked three-dimensional. Sometimes, when Ben was wiping down the bar, Jo would study the careful strokes of the bushy pine trees in the background, imagining the stillness it must've taken to sit through all those perfectly placed punctures to the skin. Later, she found out he'd had it done over three sessions.

The tattoo artist had apparently insisted they do it in stages because of the complexity of the design, but by that point Jo didn't believe anything Ben said. He probably just couldn't withstand the pain.

The Bon Iver tattoo was what started it all. It was how they got talking during slow, mid-week shifts, and what led, after months and months of passive flirting, to their first proper date. They saw Bon Iver together at the Sydney Opera House, and Jo told me it was the best live show she'd ever seen. There was an intimacy that spilt from the lamp-lit horseshoe stage into their magenta seats, a warmth that made the timber shell of the concert hall feel like a womb. And beside her was Ben, his awed gaze framed by the most magnificent eyelashes, with the feeling of all of this magic tattooed on his arm.

'It's as though the guy sitting there that night was honestly a different person,' she said, shifting in her chair. 'Which I know is how a lot of relationships feel. You think you've fallen in love when you've really just invented someone. But Ben just . . . I didn't think he had a bad bone in his body. I couldn't have imagined it. He's this quiet guy who's got two sisters.'

I wanted to interject. To validate what she was saying, to reassure her that you can't know the worst parts of a person at the beginning. But I knew that those basic social instincts can derail an interview. My job was to unravel her story by gently tugging at it with simple, thoughtful questions.

'When was the first time you saw this other side to him?'

Ben lived alone in an exposed-concrete apartment block that looked like it belonged in Soviet Russia. It was ugly and dark but walking distance from the Surry Hills bar where he and Jo worked, so she started spending most weekends there. His pillows were yellowed from sweat and oil, and his bathroom sink was carelessly dusted with short, thick hairs from his electric razor, but she didn't mind. He seemed so grown up, with his sets of keys and the bottle of red wine that sat unopened on his counter.

For a while, she told herself his meanness was just honesty. She needed his help submitting audition tapes—setting up the camera and reading against her and choosing the best take to send to her agent—and she was grateful for his attention. He told her which clothes made her look dumpy and soft. 'You don't go to the gym so you're obviously not going to have an amazing body,' he said, staring at his phone while she sat on the floor surrounded by the contents of her wardrobe. 'Maybe another guy would lie to you . . . do you want me to lie? Like, I can, but I think it's better if we tell the truth.'

Ben said the same thing about Jo's face. He looked up photos of other actors—Margot Robbie and Blake Lively and Emilia Clarke—and explained why her face wasn't as technically beautiful. Her mouth was asymmetrical when she spoke, lifting slightly on one side. He paused her once to notice out loud that her bone structure was harsh, almost masculine. 'It's nothing you can change without surgery,' he said matter-of-factly. 'I guess it's just something to be aware of.'

She stopped auditioning.

She was working full-time hours at the bar, and every night she went back to Ben's. It didn't make sense for her to keep paying rent at her share house, so she moved out, lugging a suitcase containing everything she owned up the stairs to Ben's cramped studio. He suggested that now they were living together, it would be simpler if they just combined their money. With a dual income they could start investing, open a high-interest savings account, eventually buy a place. Jo liked the idea of getting out of the brutalist hellhole on Foveaux Street, so she agreed.

It wasn't long before she realised there was no point setting up a savings account, and there would be no investing. Because there was no money.

On the nights she was working and Ben wasn't, he went out drinking with a group of old schoolfriends. She didn't think she wanted to know what he was doing, but more than once she woke up the next morning to dozens of notifications from her banking app, hundreds of dollars withdrawn and transferred and tapped away. She suspected some of it was cocaine—they'd done coke together at the beginning, before it stopped being fun—and hoped it wasn't meth or heroin, or some other drug too terrifying to name.

Still, no one could make her laugh like Ben. She'd be convinced she needed to leave, that she didn't love him anymore, and then he'd say something so self-deprecating that she realised she adored every imperfect inch of him. Even though she hadn't auditioned in months, Ben told everyone she was going to be a famous actress. 'Let's hope she stays with her loser boyfriend when she makes it in Hollywood,' he'd say with a laugh. 'I'll be a househusband. I'm happy to cook and clean while she rakes in the millions. My dream has always been to be thanked in an Oscars speech.'

Jo had been looking down at the coffee-stained paper napkin in her hands, tearing it into little pieces while she spoke. Now, she rolled the shreds into balls, rubbing them absent-mindedly with her fingers.

'I think I knew something was very wrong. But the financial stuff . . . obviously I've learnt since that it was financial abuse, whereas back then I just thought it was unfair. But that's not actually why I reached out to *Bared*. You can put it in the story if you want, but now it's like, he can have the money. I don't care about the money.'

She must've sensed my interest in Ben's reckless spending, my curiosity about what he did on those nights out. My mind had gone straight to sex workers, because Jamie had told me once that he was surprised by how many guys on his soccer team regularly paid for sex. But whatever Jo wanted to talk about seemed worse than cheating.

It wasn't until she spoke again that I realised she was crying.

'Gah, I told myself I wouldn't cry,' she said, feigning a laugh as she pressed her palms to her cheeks. For the first time I noticed the pink blotches that had crept up her neck, like an uneven sunburn from the places you missed with sunscreen. She inhaled a jagged breath.

'But I can't . . .'

Her voice was shaking now, her hands still wiping tears from her face.

'I'll never forgive him for the baby.'

She said it so faintly that it took me a moment to piece her words together. The baby. There had been a baby. The email had mentioned a pregnancy, but nothing about a baby.

I nodded, trying to meet Jo's gaze. For a brief moment, we locked eyes.

'How old?'

At this, Jo's face crumpled. Her lips were pressed together, her eyes clamped shut. Her features were different now, bent out of shape by this buried pain finding its way to the surface.

But I was confused. She'd said no one in her life knew about this, but how could she have hidden a baby? And if Ben had done something to the baby, wouldn't he be in prison? It didn't make sense.

'I'm so sorry for your loss,' I said, the words coming out too flat. 'Was it a boy or a girl?'

'It was a girl,' Jo said. 'She'd be five now. Starting school.'

The image sent a coldness down my body. A tiny version of Jo, blonde and pale with knobbly knees and a schoolbag too big for her body. I couldn't tell what the past tense meant— whether the child was growing up without her mother, or never got to grow up at all.

'What was her name?' I asked, lowering my voice.

Something unreadable passed over Jo's face. Perhaps it was the wrong question. I thought I must've misread the intimacy of the conversation, or what Jo had meant.

'She didn't have a name.'

She spoke quickly, rubbing her eyes and avoiding my gaze.

'I never got to meet her. Because she was never born.'

Chapter 9

During

I really was planning on speaking to Ian. Especially after I'd replied to the comment on Felicity's video, attracting a fresh surge of attention to the article, to me, to *Bared*. But that morning, the day after the video was posted, I wasn't thinking clearly.

I'd hardly slept, the brutal words I'd read about myself echoing in my head, weaving themselves into strange half-dreams. At some point I must've fallen asleep, because I missed my alarm, not even having a chance to dread the day before I faced it.

I arrived at the office eight minutes late, running straight into the morning meeting with my hair still wet from the shower. The team's pitches felt dull. A sex worker who slept with two thousand men in one day. A woman claiming to be Madeleine McCann. A post-baby body that made everyone feel like shit. Hadn't we written these stories already? Was there nothing else worth reporting on? But I hadn't had any time to get across the day's news, so I had no alternatives to offer.

I'd barely taken a breath when Ian leant over my desk and asked if I had a minute. I didn't, of course. There were stories from the pitch meeting to be assigned and a video waiting to be approved and our editorial assistant wanted to speak to me about an influx of unmoderated comments she hadn't let through yet. I knew what they were about. They'd be flooding my article about Jo, demanding for it to be taken down, quoting Felicity's criticisms.

Still, I stood and followed him past rows of busy screens, to the far end of the floor. His office was bathed, warehouse-style, in natural light, looking out over a two-way road and buildings just like ours across the street. It smelt like coffee and aftershave, and today it made me nauseous.

Sarah arrived moments after I did, with a freshly made tea that suggested she'd had at least a few minutes' notice that she was needed. She was the head of strategy across a patch of Simmons Corp's publications, including *Bared*. We were, according to one of her more patronising analogies, the innocent newborn in her little tribe of media brands. Young and exciting and full of potential, but it would take clients a while to trust us. In order to grow we needed to distinguish ourselves from our siblings, to fight for attention from our parents, to develop a personality that was instantly recognisable. I flinched at the image of my team and everything we created as a wrinkly, naive infant. There was nothing helpful about it, nothing empowering. It just reinforced that she didn't seem to take me seriously, that so long as I was in my twenties and didn't wear a suit and heels to work, I was just a cute little girl playing on the internet.

Sarah's two most profitable brands were an auto website and an online destination for aspirational home owners, and she shared their 'learnings' with us via a condescending Friday email. Every Friday afternoon, once we'd opened the first bottle of office-supplied wine at 3 pm, we dissected Sarah's insights in our editorial-lols chat.

> **Yasmin**: Guys, AutoGuide just won a $2 million campaign with Tesla. I think what we can learn is we should write more about cars xxx
>
> **Amelia**: Ah yes I've heard the youth are desperate for more car content. It reminds them of their mouldy Toyota Camry that they can't afford to fill up with petrol.
>
> **Meg**: Idea for an article. '5 reasons your car is shit.' 1. You're poor.
>
> **Ruby**: Wow yes approved. We'll have car brands gagging for ad space.

> **Yasmin**: I personally love that we're meant to get insights about how to grow Bared from a website about renovations. Like, babes, our audience aren't allowed to put a hook on the wall of their rental.

Now, Sarah—the source of all this wisdom—stood squarely in the middle of Ian's stuffy office, wondering out loud where she should sit. She joked about wanting to be under the air-conditioning vent, even though there didn't seem to be any air coming out, and then she moved a stack of business books from one side of Ian's stiff charcoal couch to make room for herself. I could tell from the feigned casualness in the room that this would not be a casual conversation.

Opposite Sarah, I sat on a solitary lounge chair that suddenly felt like it belonged in a psychologist's office. I glanced at the oversized TV screen to the right of Sarah's head, the one mounted on the wall just beyond Ian's glass door. My story was at the top of the display, thousands of people currently reading it. Seeing it above every other headline filled me with both pride and terror, because it was obvious that Felicity's commentary had directed them there. Each reader, I knew, had the potential to add a gust of wind to the wildfire, spreading the outrage further. But I also hoped that fresh eyes might douse the flames. Perhaps by reading the story for themselves, actually absorbing the nuances of Jo's experience, people would see that the article didn't do what Felicity claimed it did. There had to be a rational portion of the audience out there, even just one loud voice to challenge the vitriol that was still rapidly filling my phone.

Ian wheeled his chair out from behind his desk and parked it so that the three of us formed a semicircle. He could've fit beside Sarah, but he'd probably learnt that the configurations in a meeting matter: if they were together, facing me, it would feel like an interrogation. But Ian didn't subscribe to that form of management. He was a proponent of radical honesty, embracing disagreements, letting nothing go unspoken. In one of our early one-on-ones, when he was mentoring me about leadership, he explained that he would never say anything *about* someone that he wouldn't say *to* them. I imagined it was meant to be comforting, but it made every muscle in my body tense up. I was sure he was going to tell me I had bad breath or that I looked chronically unwell, and even though he was yet to say anything broadly offensive, I'd been on edge ever since.

'I've just been on the phone to Sue from Simmons Corp,' he said, his head angled towards his impossibly long, polished shoes. 'You know Sue? She's one of the directors. She was asking what we're planning to do about this Felicity Cartwright situation. So here I am, madly looking up who this Felicity person is while Sue is saying we need to act before we have clients pull their ads, and I see she's made a viral video about an article you've written.'

He looked up at me, resting his elbows on his thighs, his thumbs under his chin.

'So I'm thinking, maybe Ruby didn't know about it? Maybe she didn't see it? Seems unlikely but I'll always give you the benefit of the doubt.'

I wanted to vomit. Why on earth hadn't I sent a two-sentence email? Or picked up the phone like an adult? The impact was coming, and I just wanted it to be over.

'But then I'm scrolling through the comments—bloody brutal by the way, a nightmare for any brand—and I see that you've responded.'

Sarah was studying me, nodding. I wondered what she'd been told. What role she was meant to be playing.

'I have a lot of questions,' Ian said, his voice even. 'And we'll get to the fact that you didn't alert anyone that this was happening, which is really quite odd to me. But let's start at the beginning—tell me what happened with this interview.'

Chapter 10

Before

Three days earlier

I hadn't expected this to be a story about abortion. But as Jo spoke, her tidy eyebrows furrowed in concentration and her jaw tight, it became clear that's what it was. Here, in a noisy cafe a few streets behind the office, I was sitting opposite a woman pouring out the details of what she termed reproductive coercion. She'd had an abortion, and it had not been her choice.

Jo had been on the pill. When her prescription ran out, it had taken her a week to get a bulk-billed doctor's appointment to get a new one. She'd never understood why they made you keep going back to the doctor once you'd been taking the pill for years. They never seemed to run any tests or check in about your health more broadly, although this time the doctor asked if Jo had considered an IUD. She took home a pamphlet, slipping it into her messy handbag, and when she saw it months later, it only made her feel more stupid.

She'd heard friends say you had to be off the pill for months and months before you fell pregnant, so she hadn't thought too much about the week when she wasn't taking it. To be honest, she'd always worried she'd struggle to fall pregnant, so maybe part of her was aware she was playing Russian roulette, putting a small possibility of fertility into a revolver and seeing if it fired. She didn't tell Ben about the pill or the doctor because she could predict what he'd say. He'd take her by the shoulders and lecture her about the 'chaos' of her life, how she never thought ahead or planned properly, how she was the most disorganised person he'd ever known. They must've had sex during that week, because a month later, she was pregnant.

She just knew. Jo didn't throw up into a bin like they do in the movies, or have a sudden, clichéd realisation that she couldn't remember her last period. But she felt different. Her breasts were painful and she bled, but only a little bit, and then it stopped. There was no way she could buy a pregnancy test on the card she shared with Ben, because the notification would instantly come through on his phone and she didn't have the energy to navigate his response. So after a Thursday night shift at the bar, she went to the chemist on the main road and brushed a pregnancy test off the shelf and into her handbag.

When she walked out, she half-expected to be followed. Maybe a pharmacist would chase her, yelling that he'd seen what she'd stolen and was going to call the police. She didn't care. Nothing, and no one, was as scary as Ben.

Almost immediately, there were two lines. They were pink and clear and she sat on the seat of a shit-stained public toilet holding the test like it was a spark in a room full of flammable gas. She realised that this was one of those few moments in life when the foundations around you were going to collapse, and you were powerless to stop it. No matter what she did, the pin on the grenade had already been pulled.

She would have to tell Ben. They had spoken about kids as though they were an inevitability, but he had made it clear that he didn't think they were financially ready. Having a baby was a hypothetical step for the future; a future in which they had better jobs and presumably Ben didn't snort her wages up his nose.

'It was always about how *I* wasn't ready,' she told me now, bunching her short hair together with one hand and then letting it go, 'when *he* was the one who didn't feel like his life had properly started yet. I was ready. I was always ready.'

Jo didn't tell anyone at first. She wanted to figure out a plan, work out exactly what she was going to do, before she said it out loud and made it real. For a month she thought of nothing else. In the shower and on the train and while counting the till at work and when Ben was inside her—especially when Ben was inside her—she thought of the baby. As she drifted off to sleep, she studied the space between her edge of the bed and the wall and wondered whether a cot would fit there. She imagined being woken by hungry cries, and it made her smile.

She started keeping a list of baby names in her phone. Almost all of them were names for baby girls, because she was certain that's what she was having. Several times, on the phone to her mum, she almost told her. Jo's mum lived on the other side of the country, in a small town a few hours north of Perth. Jo had moved to Sydney when she finished school to attend a prestigious performing arts college, but even if she hadn't got into the acting course, she still would've left. She'd felt claustrophobic in that house. Her parents were reclusive, and spent almost all their time in front of the television, bickering about politics and annoying in-laws and the things her dad promised to fix and then never did. Jo's mum loved babies—she'd had four of her own. But once they were old enough, they'd all got as far away from that house as they could, and none of them had any intention of coming back. Something sad festered there, living in the walls and under the carpet and threatening to pull you in the longer you stayed.

'I should never have told Ben,' Jo said. 'That's my regret. That I didn't just disappear and do it on my own. But I wanted her to have a dad, even if he wasn't perfect.'

The morning rush in the cafe had slowed, and for the first time since we'd sat down there was no one lining up at the counter. A lanky waiter with shoulder-length curly hair was wiping down the table behind Jo, carefully stacking plates and coffee cups that he was never going to be able to carry in one load. He bumped the back of Jo's chair as he attempted to straighten the table, and it seemed to jolt her back into the moment.

'Sorry, please let me know if you need to get back,' she said, glancing at my phone on the edge of the table. 'I start talking about the Ben stuff and I can't stop.' She smiled self-consciously, and picked at a short, unpainted fingernail on her left hand.

I was worried to check the time. I'd expected the interview to go for forty-five minutes, and it had been well over an hour. The team would be filing their morning stories and there were several of them I had assigned myself to publish. Ones that needed a legal check or a stronger headline; ones I didn't want to leave to any of the other editors.

But I couldn't rush this. I had never considered the fraught reality of having an abortion that wasn't your choice. The prevailing narrative—and rightly so—was about how systems and institutions had the potential to restrict women's reproductive freedom, denying them the right to healthy and safe abortions. But what about cases where a partner used power and control to interfere in a wanted pregnancy? Jo's story was one that spoke to the impossible complexities of women's lives. It was a story about how the same decision can mean freedom to one person and oppression to another.

'No, please don't worry about my time,' I said. 'Let me just send a message to the team so we don't have to rush.'

I quickly opened *Bared*'s messaging system. There were dozens of notifications in there—mentions of my name and question marks and alerts for tasks that were overdue. I clicked on the editors' chat.

> **Ruby**: Sorry guys, I'm doing a sensitive interview and it's going overtime. Don't want to rush her. I'll be back as soon as I can. Please defer to @Yasmin for anything urgent.

I checked that the audio was still recording, and then turned my phone facedown.

'So,' I said, scrambling to remember where we'd left off. 'What happened when you told Ben?'

Chapter 11

During

Ian listened without interrupting, still bent forward in his chair, his legs spread wider than the seat. I spoke quickly, gathering from his corded neck and squinting eyes that he was far more interested in dealing with the situation than getting bogged down in all the details of it. But this was one of his management tactics—inviting you to share what led to a certain decision, so you might identify your own errors, your own misjudgements. Then the criticism became easier to deliver, more readily absorbed.

But Sarah seemed to have realised that I wouldn't be admitting any fault.

This was making her nostrils flare, and from the way her lips were clamped together, it was taking all her self-control not to interject.

'It was a complex story but I reported it sensitively and referenced three research studies documenting this specific kind of reproductive coercion. It's exactly the kind of thing we wanted to talk about when we launched *What No One Saw*.'

I explained that I'd sent the article to Jo (whom I'd pseudonymised as 'Michelle') before it was published, and asked her if there was anything she felt was misrepresented. She'd called straightaway to say it had been a healing experience for her, and she hoped it might help other women feel less alone.

'Felicity Cartwright clearly has an issue with me and with *Bared*, but we haven't done anything wrong. If you read the interview, it's a gut-wrenching story about intimate partner abuse. It's about how men can manipulate and control women and force them to do things they don't want to do. Felicity Cartwright has just taken the abortion element of it and made it sound like we think everyone regrets their abortion. Which we never said. And we obviously don't believe.'

Their silence was upsetting me now. I wanted Ian and Sarah to tell me how grateful they were that I'd covered Beth's interview in the first place. How impressed they were that I was able to pull off a heavy piece of reporting and manage an entire team at the same time. They should've been telling me how unfair this was, how unhinged the Felicitys of the world were. But they said nothing.

'I mean, there are literally comments saying I'm some conservative stooge who made up the story to push my agenda,' I said. 'I've got the entire audio recording if either of you would like to listen to it.'

Sarah dipped her tea bag in and out of her ceramic mug, stopping only when she noticed she was splashing golden brown droplets onto her linen pants.

'I don't doubt it's really this "Michelle's" story,' she said, turning to Ian as if to acknowledge their shared understanding of the situation. 'The question for me is whether it was appropriate to publish it in the current climate, when we know abortion is such a hot-button issue that has the potential to be triggering to women in all sorts of ways. And if we were going to run a piece that was so sensitive, I would imagine it should've been run past several sets of eyes, to ensure we didn't end up in this situation.'

Her eyes bored into mine as she took a sip from her mug. She was so far removed from the editorial team that her input made me irrationally angry. She didn't know the first thing about 'sensitive' topics or the publishing process. How many 'sets of eyes' did she think I had access to? Why weren't mine enough?

My agitation must've been obvious, because Ian lifted his shoulders in a half shrug and angled his body towards me.

'Look, often these things can't be foreseen,' he said. 'And I know you're juggling a million jobs at once. But in this case, the story should've been escalated. Maybe if we had known we were about to publish something controversial, we could've planned a response, mitigated some of the risk.'

'The story itself wasn't controversial, though.' My voice was higher than I'd intended. 'It's only that one person on the internet read it a certain way and decided it was saying something it wasn't. That's the entire reason this has blown up.'

Sarah raised her chin and opened her mouth to speak, but I kept going.

'And we never escalate stories beyond me. Not for legals, not for brand sensitivities, never. So I'm not sure who I should've gone to about this one and when I would've had the time.'

It was a terrible argument, and as the words came out of my mouth, I knew I was only making things worse. If I just nodded and agreed, it would all be over more quickly, and the outcome would inevitably be the same.

But my heart was pounding and heat was rushing through my body. The demand for stronger traffic was relentless, a constant push from every direction to produce more content, to spread it more widely, to grow the *Bared* audience. Maybe if anyone had taken me seriously when I raised how Beth's sick leave was impacting the team, I wouldn't have had to write the story at all. Then it would be Beth's name coming out of Felicity's mouth and in the stream of comments below her video.

'We obviously need to take the story down,' Sarah said, directing the statement not to me but to Ian. 'We can mitigate some of the damage if we just remove it now, issue an apology, and move on.'

'I think that's in everyone's best interests,' Ian said. 'This woman you've interviewed will understand that it hasn't been received in the way anyone intended, and it's invited brand-damaging comments about *Bared* and about you, too, Ruby—and, of course, we want to protect you from that. One story isn't worth this kind of negative attention.'

No.

The word echoed in my head, so loudly there was room for nothing else, as though it was being shouted in my ear. This was always the instinct when something was criticised online. Delete and apologise and capitulate to the loudest voices, even when those voices were wrong.

'If we remove the story,' I said slowly, desperate to come across as experienced and considered instead of petulant, 'it strips away all the context. Felicity's version of the article becomes fact. It also looks like we're admitting fault, like we were acting maliciously in telling this story, which makes people feel their anger is justified.'

Sarah raised her eyebrows and looked down at the floor, as though being forced to listen to me was an exhaustive exercise in restraint.

'At this point, it's confirmation bias,' she said, shaking her head in frustration. 'Everyone's reading the interview having already decided what they think. They're pulling out the references to abortion and they're feeling like it's a value judgement on them. That's not what any of us want. Unfortunately, we can't undo that. If we take the article down, we've taken their concerns seriously, and by next week everyone will be talking about something else.'

Ian took my brief silence as a sign of agreement.

'So it's decided,' he said. 'The article is coming down. I'll consult with Simmons' publicity team to draft a brief apology that we'll put on socials. No mention of you, Ruby. Just that *Bared* published a story we've now removed because we recognise it was insensitive and—'

'It wasn't insensitive,' I protested. 'It's not insensitive to tell a person's story of coercive—'

But both Ian and Sarah were already on their feet, Sarah hurrying towards the door with her mug in one hand and her laptop in the other.

Through the glass of Ian's office, I watched rows of headlines jump around like player rankings in a video game, dropping and climbing moment to moment. Each title sat in line with columns of associated numbers—real-time readers, dwell time, total page views. My story remained locked at the top.

Thirteen words. Ninety-three characters. The ideal length for reader engagement: *I've never told anyone this before.'* One *woman's harrowing account of reproductive coercion.*

Chapter 12

Before

Three days earlier

'He found out by accident, before I'd worked out how I wanted to tell him,' Jo said. She spoke more quietly now the cafe was clearing out, no longer fighting to be heard over a symphony of nearby conversations. She often whispered at the end of sentences, becoming barely audible, as though she was conscious of taking up too much air.

'That's another regret. If I had been more organised, if I had eased him into it, maybe it wouldn't have ended the way it did. Maybe I'd still have my baby.'

A month after the positive test, Jo booked an ultrasound. She filled out the forms so quickly that she wasn't sure her handwriting was legible, but for the first time she'd put the truth on paper. She was Jodie Ryan. And she was—according to her very approximate calculations—nine weeks pregnant.

She was also in trouble from the receptionist for not drinking the required one litre of water an hour before her scan. The woman took the forms and rolled her eyes, muttering about how Jo would have received all the relevant information in an email, including a very simple set of instructions to follow before she saw the sonographer.

'Why the fuck would you be unnecessarily rude to someone who's about to get an ultrasound?' Jo said, shaking her head. 'Like, you have no idea why I'm here or what I'm going through. Anyway, the clinic had a feedback form on their website and I ripped poor Sharon to shreds.'

I laughed. In another context, I thought, Jo and I might've been friends. She was about my age, and in her moments of lightness, she was funny. I almost wished we were sharing a bottle of wine rather than the clinical boundaries of an interview. I wanted to know more about Ben, the parts Jo wouldn't tell a journalist. Was he sexy? Was that part of the appeal? Could I see a photo? What school did he go to and where did he grow up? Maybe he was a friend of a friend, maybe I'd been at the same party as him once, maybe I'd seen his face on one of Liv's dating apps.

But Jo was guarded. She looked at me like I was a teacher or a boss, like she was wary of saying the wrong thing. Like

I might hear her story and decide it wasn't worth telling, that this had all been a waste of time.

The baby looked like a tadpole. According to the internet it was the size of a bean, or an olive, or a strawberry, which made no sense to Jo because, in her mind, all those things were different sizes. When she saw the black-and-white video on the screen, she didn't immediately see her child. She saw a grainy blur in a black hole, and if her stomach hadn't been covered in cold, sticky goo, she could've easily been convinced it was an image of her hip joint or breast tissue. Still, when the woman holding the doppler asked if she wanted a printed copy to stick on her fridge, she said yes. On her way out, she folded it into the pocket of her handbag. She liked knowing it was there—the piece of thin, glossy paper that captured the most common and most extraordinary thing in the world.

Jo was cooking dinner when Ben discovered it. She was standing over the stove, having just poured fat tubes of pasta into a pan of bubbling sauce that had come entirely from a jar. Her phone was lying on the edge of the chipped benchtop, softly playing a song that reminded her of high school, and Ben was at the other end of the narrow kitchen, reaching for the bowls on the shelf above the sink. The evening had been light and peaceful, like the nights at the beginning of their relationship, when Ben would make her laugh so much her face got sore from straining the muscles around her mouth. Now, he was joking about how every piece of crockery they owned had been stealthily borrowed from his mum's house, which was obvious because they were all hideous. He pulled out a blue-and-white baking dish and insisted that every single household in Australia had one of them, and Jo giggled. It was true. She was fairly certain her grandmother had three.

As he went to put the bowls down on their two-seater dining table, she heard the metal buckle of her handbag hit the ground. He must've knocked it off the edge—he was always bumping things in their cramped apartment, rather than simply moving them to create more space. He'd break a glass or up-end the washing basket, reacting with contempt as though it was the fault of the inanimate object, like it had purposely got in his way.

In the time it took for her to whip her head around, Jo knew what she was about to see. The contents of her unzipped bag were everywhere—tissues and lipsticks and pens and tampons. But as she instinctively moved towards the pile of her belongings, she spotted the folded, shiny ultrasound photo looking up at them, as though it had crawled from its pocket to take a comfortable seat between its parents.

Ben didn't know what it was initially. He was viscerally irritated by the mess, in the same way he was quick to anger when a gust of wind caused the bedroom door to slam. He swore under his breath and leant down, reaching for the pens before turning his gaze to the blurry image of a baby he didn't know was his. He started to ask, 'Why do you have . . . ?' but he knew the answer before he finished the question.

Jo remembered that night as the worst one of her life. They never ate the pasta, and by the time she cleaned the pan, the sauce had hardened and burnt itself into the steel, leaving a thick brown stain that nothing could remove. She hated the way he'd found out. It gave him the excuse of having been lied to, of being entitled to his anger, of being the victim when he wasn't. He had designed a relationship in which she needed to keep secrets, in which she had to hold the things that mattered most out of his reach, to stop him from prising them from her hands.

'I still have the ultrasound photo,' Jo said, shaking her head and letting out a small laugh, as if to check whether that was ridiculous. I stiffened, hoping she wouldn't pull it out. I didn't trust myself to react appropriately to an image of a foetus; to say the right thing in the right tone about an indistinguishable ball of cells. But from what I could gather, Jo kept the photo tucked away at home, somewhere she'd only come across it when she wanted to. But she'd thought about it a lot in the years since that fight in the kitchen. Now, she told me, the image reminded her of one of those ink-blot cards, the ones that are intentionally ambiguous. The ones where you're shown a black-and-white splotch and you see what you want to see.

Chapter 13

During

The apology on *Bared*'s social media had gone down just as badly as I'd predicted. People assumed I was behind the brief, emotionless statement that sounded like it had been generated by AI. Every word of it was being dissected, first in the comments section below the apology, and then, when that was closed off, in threads belonging to other accounts. It was screenshotted, reposted, shared with people's own annotations—arrows and underlines and question marks and clown emojis.

Then, as I was walking back to the office after a lunch break in which I'd consumed nothing but online venom, I got an email from Ian. The subject line was 'FYI'. I stopped outside the panelled wooden door at the back of the building, hoping no one familiar would come out. I was exhausted from pretending to Yasmin, to Amelia, to the rest of the content team that everything was fine. All day I'd known they were watching me, trying to discern how broken I was. I wondered if there was a part of them that agreed with the comments, agreed with Felicity. If they'd decided that, come to think of it, I was a bit of a dumb bitch.

Ian's email contained only a link to *The Daily*—no greeting, no sign-off.

I saw the feature image first. It was one of my headshots, taken in the *Bared* office earlier that year, when my hair was shorter and a little darker. The five letters of our logo, joined together in a cursive font, beamed on a fluorescent sign behind me. I remembered the day it was taken, the photographer asking me to cross my arms and then to let them hang by my sides, sighing as he discovered there was no way of positioning me so that I looked natural. He showed me one of the shots on his screen and all I saw was my shiny forehead, my oily roots, my crooked smile, teeth yellowing from coffee and wine. I said I loved it, before leaving the office and walking around the block until I stopped panicking. When I came back, Beth was having her photo taken, and I studied her heavy foundation, her fake eyelashes, the tape of her hair extensions poking through when she turned her head. I wished I'd tried harder.

Now, I didn't mind the photo. I saw someone young and creative, someone who wore a boxy denim shirt to work.

It's probably a reflection of how shattered I was, how warped my mind had already become, that I pored over the photo for some time. I supposed it was good that they'd used my headshot for the feature image and not a photo of me holding a glass of champagne next to an inflatable penis at a hens' night.

But my relief was short-lived, because then I read what was below it. A column by Felicity Cartwright, who only wrote for *The Daily* sporadically. Her by-line attracted significant traffic, I knew from my time working there, but I thought perhaps they might have some shred of loyalty to me. It wasn't so long ago that I had been the person writing and editing and commissioning for them. Here I was, just a few hundred metres away from their office, reading an opinion they'd published about my incompetency.

WHY BARED MEDIA JUST DELETED A STORY ABOUT COERCIVE CONTROL the headline read. The standfirst—the brief summary of the article that sat at the top of the page—explicitly named me.

> The article, written by their editor-in-chief Ruby Williams, isn't only problematic—it's dangerous.

Parts of the copy hit me like a sharp slap to the face, leaving a hot sting. Felicity wrote that there had been 'growing online criticism from advocacy groups and those with lived experience', as though that criticism had been organic and not pointedly fuelled by her. And what about Jo's lived experience? Why did that count for nothing?

> Michelle (not her real name) claimed that during the course of an abusive relationship she was forced by her partner to undergo an abortion she now regrets. Michelle also shared her certainty that the child was a girl, despite not being far enough along in her pregnancy for the sex to be medically determined. Ruby Williams invited Michelle to paint a picture of how she imagines her child now, as though this is somehow meaningful and not an entirely hypothetical exercise that serves only to give ammunition to those who wish to restrict women's access to abortion.

I was shaking. Jo's 'certainty' that her baby was a girl had no basis in logic, it wasn't a medical fact—it was a feeling. And I hadn't 'invited' her to imagine her child as some sort of ideological weapon; I had simply listened as she revealed a part of herself that she had been reluctant to share, precisely because it felt drenched in wrongness. *There's a difference,* I wanted to yell, *between what we know intellectually and what we know emotionally. The great tension of life is that those two things can clash, and we then have to confront the mess that's left behind.*

My mouth fell open as I read on. Felicity's tone was so bitter, so full of contempt, that I couldn't believe her words had been published.

Bared printed quotes about Michelle's 'guilt' and 'shame', promulgating the false notion that those who choose to terminate a pregnancy are plagued by such emotions. The myth that 'abortion regret' is real and common has been used historically to manipulate women into carrying unwanted pregnancies to term. It is also an argument adopted by pro-life policymakers.

Women do not regret abortions. And in the context of reproductive coercion, women are overwhelmingly coerced to *keep* an unwanted pregnancy, not to terminate a wanted one.

That was a reality I had acknowledged in my article. An article that was now gone, wiped from the internet. All that remained were Felicity's claims, her wilful misinterpretation of what I'd written. Here, in the most-read publication in the country, she was scolding me for saying something I had not said.

How, I wondered, could she argue that one woman's lived experience was a myth? That Jo's suffering wasn't real? That an authentic emotional reality existed to serve some ideological purpose, and therefore deserved to be dismissed, erased, eradicated?

Towards the end, she interrogated *Bared*'s apology.

At the time of reporting, *Bared* has removed the article and released a statement apologising to their readers. It reads: *An article was published earlier this week that has caused distress to a number of our readers. It was an editorial misjudgement for which we apologise unreservedly. We have now removed it, and are deeply sorry to those who found the article triggering.*

Felicity continued:

For many of us, the issue at hand is not that the article was 'triggering'. It's that it contains blatant bias and threatens women's rights. *Bared*'s apology does not address why this particular experience of reproductive coercion was represented, how future 'misjudgements' will be avoided, or what consequences this editorial misjudgement will have on Ruby Williams' employment.

Consequences for my employment.
Was Felicity suggesting that I should be fired? Had she honestly written a column for my former employer, arguing that I didn't deserve my current job?
The piece ended with a reference to my 'silence'.

Williams, apart from a comment asking a distressed reader not to call her 'mean,' has remained silent.

I stood there, the world beyond the glow of my phone screen no longer real. I had fallen into the black hole that was effectively glued to my palm, this portal that housed another dimension, another universe. Inside it, I was a version of myself I didn't recognise. The face staring back at me was mine, yes, and Felicity Cartwright had published my name and my job title and referenced the headline of the article I wrote, but none of it was me.

I was Ruby Williams, my heartbeat pounding in my ears, my stomach turned to clay, my breathing quick and shallow, like my body thought it was being chased by a predator.

I was Ruby Williams, sweating into a too-tight crimson top I hated.

I was Ruby Williams, who had once been loved simply because I was born, who had been so small I had fit comfortably in my grandmother's cupped hand. I had been a baby then a toddler then a child then a teenager then a woman, this woman, the one so worthy of contempt that it was now front-page news.

I was Ruby Williams, standing alone outside my office building in the pounding summer heat, trying with every muscle, trying with every remaining shred of energy, not to cry.

Chapter 14

Before

Three days earlier

What I couldn't tell anyone—not people at work or people on the internet—was that something happened that day in the cafe with Jo.

I can still picture her sitting opposite me, how haunted she looked. The way she sat as if every bone in her body was on the verge of collapse. I have the transcript of what she said, certain parts highlighted because I knew I wanted to quote them in the article, but neither her words, nor my words, were ever going to be able to tell the whole story.

I had never had an abortion. At that time, I had never fallen pregnant, but I believed unequivocally in a woman's right to safely access reproductive health care. Several of my friends had chosen to terminate pregnancies, and had shared their stories, trading details about pain and bleeding and the man who never had to see it or feel it. The man who sometimes didn't know about it at all.

When we were in our early twenties, I'd gone to the doctor with Liv to get a prescription for the abortion pill, which wasn't actually one pill but several. The guy who got her pregnant was someone she'd just started dating, and they both knew they weren't having a baby. He lived three hours away, and she asked me to stay at her place while it happened, and I did. Those few days, spent under a scratchy blanket on her IKEA couch, challenged what I thought I knew about abortion. What I saw was a person who expected to be immune to the machinations of her body and what they meant. Who would frame it as a heavy period, because in essence that's what it was: blood and tissue being expelled from a uterus that would not be carrying a baby.

But as her womb cramped and this thing that she did not want seeped out of her, she went quiet. We watched hours of bad reality TV, and between episodes she said only, 'I need this to be over.'

She didn't have to tell me. I could feel it. I knew then that for some women—for Liv, at least—an abortion isn't something they want like a fruity cocktail on a sunny afternoon. Liv wanted an abortion, as the saying goes, like a person in a burning building wants to smash a window. Like they want to break down the door. Like they need to, because they would asphyxiate or be consumed by the flames otherwise. I knew then that anyone who advocated for restricted access to abortion, anyone who suggested women should be punished for it, didn't consider the person in that burning building to be fully human. Men, in particular, were ignoring the limits of their own empathy—the reality that they'd never find themselves inside that building. That they'd never have to make the choice about whether to burn or be free.

That belief, that conviction of mine, was somehow deepened as I listened to Jo. It was the complexity of her emotional reality, the way she talked about imagining her baby's cry, picturing the child she might have become. She felt pressured into her termination by Ben. She'd been pushed out that window; she hadn't broken the window willingly. And that had nothing to do with anyone else's abortion rights.

'He was furious when he first found out, calling me a liar and saying I was trying to ruin his life,' she told me. 'He accused me of intentionally falling pregnant because I was bored and desperate. Then his mood seemed to change, and the manipulation started.'

Her fingers were wrapped around her half-empty water glass, and she stared at it blankly.

'He didn't take me to the doctor with a gun to my head, or force the pills down my throat. He never outright said, "You have no choice but to get an abortion," because he didn't need to say it.'

For the entirety of their relationship, he had chipped away at her, turning her instincts and her own sense of judgement into dust. He'd convinced her, with a strategically positioned chisel and hammer, that she was irresponsible, disorganised, chaotic, silly, naive and incapable of looking after herself. How did she think she could look after someone else?

He let his opinion on the pregnancy settle into the atmosphere, like tiny, almost imperceptible fragments. The only thing he said directly after that night was a question about 'when' she was having an abortion, and Jo was so taken aback that she instinctively muttered something about a doctor's appointment. Two days later, as she was getting ready for work, he looked up from his laptop and rested his eyes on her stomach. She was wearing high-waisted black pants and fishing in the wardrobe for a shirt.

'You should probably hurry up and book it because your belly is already sticking out. And I can't have my family or people at work seeing you like that.'

Jo's lips quivered as she recalled how cold he'd sounded.

'I was only, like, ten weeks at that point, so there was no bump,' she told me. 'And the way he talked about it, like it was a cancerous growth, something festering, he seemed disgusted by me.'

She went to the doctor later that week, got a prescription for the pills, had it filled at the pharmacy. It was only once she had them, once they were in her possession, once it seemed inescapable what was going to happen, that she spoke honestly with Ben.

I watched the tears run down Jo's face. They left silver stains in their tracks, the pale skin underneath her foundation tinted with diffused mascara. She pressed her palms against her damp cheeks, her chin wobbling through ragged breaths.

'I sat him down and told him I wanted this baby, that I felt like she was already mine, that I had a name for her and could feel her with my soul. I said I was prepared to do it on my own, he didn't have to be involved, he didn't owe me anything. People have babies all the time and they make it work. *I* could make it work. I'd always wanted to be a mum and I was ready. I was ready for her.'

She was gasping now, almost hyperventilating. She briefly squeezed her eyes shut, like she was trying to force out the remaining tears.

'He looked at me like I was insane. He said, "You've already made your decision—and it was *your* decision. You went to the doctor and you bought the pills." Then he told me I was trying to blame him for a situation I had created by stuffing up my birth control in the first place. But when I got upset and I begged . . . that made him really, really angry.'

Ben had stood up and pushed his face up to Jo's, his fingernails digging into the flesh on her thighs. He was stepping on her bare toes with the thick rubber soles of his work boots, but he didn't move back when she tried to push him away. Her hands were flat against his chest as he squashed his nose into hers, hissing that she needed to grow up, to take responsibility, to act like a fucking adult. He dug his nails in harder and asked her if she wanted a baby whose father hated it, whose father knew it only existed because its mother was a fucking moron. Then he released her and stormed into the bedroom, shouting that he didn't care what she did, that she could raise it on the street.

'I get that it was his baby, too,' she said quietly. She wrapped her arms across her body, her hands clutching her elbows. 'But I'm the one who has to live with it. I'm the one who felt like a monster.'

She paused and looked up at me. Her eyes were direct and severe.

'But I need you to know that's not how I feel about abortion,' she said. 'That's how I feel about *my* abortion.'

She wasn't really thinking when she took the first pill. It hit her hours later, while she was getting ready for bed. Suddenly Jo felt a wave of panic set in, like Ben's work boot was resting on her chest, and she googled whether she could reverse it. If she could just not take the second set of pills and keep the baby. The results were definitive: no, it was too late.

A couple of days later, she let the remaining four pills dissolve in her mouth. She didn't take any pain relief, because she believed she deserved to feel it all.

In the cafe, her voice was soft. There was something in her eyes I recognised.

'I can't explain the feeling of watching something that you wanted disappear and knowing . . . knowing that it's your fault,' she said. 'You did it. You're grieving but you did it to yourself.'

In that moment, she had no reason to know that she'd just pressed on something I'd felt for most of my life. Something I did not talk about, something I tried not to think about, even when I woke in the middle of the night drenched in the memory of it.

But still, there was a flicker across her face. I am certain that in the space between us, a hidden part of me came forward and met a hidden part of her. It wasn't a phenomenon that could be seen or heard or articulated, an experience that could fit in a headline or be expressed in paragraphs of copy on a two-dimensional website, between ads for a fast-fashion brand and a new action film. It could only be felt. A faint pull, like gravity. And like gravity, these broken parts of us, the ones that emerged from the darkness and hung in the air, seemed like they were at the centre of everything.

It was strange, really. To be sitting under a rattling ceiling fan in the heat, surrounded by strangers, and suddenly be struck by the sense that all of it—all of us—were profoundly interconnected. That Jo and I were linked in some grand cosmic tapestry. I'd had that feeling once before, on the worst day of my life, when a single scream had ripped the universe open. In that moment, I'd realised that an unspoken truth drifted among us, and that most people spent their lives trying to avoid it.

But when Jo looked at me, the grief sewn into every layer of her skin, I *knew* her.

...

Perhaps that's why the criticism of the story I wrote was so difficult for me to process. Because it was like they were denying the contradictions of reality, the messiness of human life, the web of vibrating strings that binds us together.

Now, years later, I know it's impossible to reflect all that complexity in a 1200-word article. The medium flattens it. Simplifies it. I know that the piece I wrote—the story I was telling when I returned to the office and pounded away on my keyboard, determined to fit the weight of Jo's experience within the crowded chamber of a website—was not what people read.

Where I described Jo's sense of connection to the baby inside her, they saw a pointed attempt to humanise a foetus.

Where I described Jo's grief, they saw the perpetuation of an age-old narrative: that women often regret their terminations. That women are haunted by their decisions. They saw fear-mongering, a shameless attempt to manufacture moral panic.

Where I described how Jo felt coerced, how she felt the abortion wasn't her choice, they saw the most dangerous suggestion of all: that taking the pills had been too easy. That it should be harder to terminate a pregnancy—that the healthcare system should confront women more forcefully with the consequences of their decision.

None of that, none of it, was what I meant.

But on the internet, that didn't matter. To condemn me was to fight for women's reproductive rights. To be an advocate, a social-justice warrior, without having to actually do anything tangible.

I wonder if they saw what I felt then but didn't have the words to articulate: that in the online battle to make the world a fairer, safer, more equitable place for women, it seemed to be overwhelmingly women who were the casualties.

PART TWO

Chapter 15

Three days after Felicity had published her article about me, it was still in the 'trending' section on *The Daily*'s homepage. According to Rachel, an old colleague of mine who still worked there, it was currently the most-read story on the site.

I read her message while I was out with Liv on Sunday morning, almost tripping on an uneven patch of pavement as I looked down at my phone.

> **Rachel**: It's because you're pretty! Everyone wants to hate pretty people. Take it as a compliment. And you've got so many followers since this whole thing happened, you'll be able to monetise that shit once it all dies down.

Rachel was right about the new followers. Thousands of them were flooding my notifications, clearly curious about the woman whose name was everywhere. It must've been helpful for them to connect a face to it—to scroll through the intimate moments I'd chronicled on my page and build a more comprehensive picture of who I was. Here was Ruby Williams on a narrow, cobblestoned street in the south of France, surrounded by old terracotta houses with brightly painted shutters. That must be her boyfriend, with kind eyes and a full head of dark, curly hair, his skin golden from the European sun. Here she was onstage perched on a stool, wearing an oversized blazer, looking not at the camera but at the three well-known personalities she was interviewing for International Women's Day. Here was a meme she'd shared about a local woman taking a brief break from feminism by watching an episode of *Married At First Sight*. A two-word caption below the image: *it me.*

I'd considered making my account private so that when nosy strangers searched for me they would find nothing, but I hoped the fragments of myself I'd posted over the last decade might save me. That in one of my photos or videos someone would see a brief glimpse of themselves, and it might dilute their anger.

The reason I'd reached out to Rachel was because I was certain she'd tell me there had been an uproar about Felicity's op-ed at *The Daily*. Surely someone who knew me, who'd been out for Friday afternoon drinks with me, who'd sat in meetings beside me and seen what kind of person I was, would've challenged the decision to publish it. But Rachel clearly thought I was fine. She must've assumed that years of working online had given me a skin so thick it was virtually impenetrable.

I imagined the weekly editorial meeting at *The Daily*, where they presented the audience data for the previous seven days. This week, would they talk about me? Would they discuss whether I was deserving of the criticism they'd published? I could almost hear the inevitable conversation about where to take the story next. The editors there were always talking about making 'data-driven decisions', capitalising on what they knew was likely to drive traffic. If my fuck-up had attracted half-a-million page views, what did that mean? Where else was there to go?

I couldn't let myself think about it.

Liv and I were doing the coastal walk, along with what felt like every other person in Sydney. It was the first time I'd left the apartment since Friday. A slow crowd snaked ahead of us, making their way down the narrow path between overhanging rocks and the translucent ocean. I'd left my hat at home and could feel the unforgiving sun beating down on my forehead, threatening to burn me, to fry permanent lines into my skin. With one hand shading my face and one hand gripping my phone, I asked Liv if she wanted to stop for a juice in Bronte.

'Obviously,' she said. 'Or a Diet Coke. Jesus, I forgot that I never feel uglier than when I'm in the eastern suburbs. I swear we've passed a dozen models. I don't get how you live here; I'd find it exhausting.'

When I'd first moved to Bondi, I'd noticed it, too. The smooth, glowing complexions and the athletic bodies. It was like everyone had come off a movie set, and you were the only one with creased clothing and scuffed shoes. Then one day I realised the beautiful people had become invisible, the same way you simply stop seeing the painting you've hung in your hallway. What I didn't tell Liv was that there was something aspirational about living here. I hoped I'd absorb it all—the energy, the striving. That I'd wake up and suddenly discover I'd blossomed into one of *them*, purely by osmosis.

Liv had clearly been trying to avoid the topic of Felicity, but she could tell it was all I wanted to talk about. When the crowd started to thin, she slowed down and indulged me.

'So what did Mum say about the Felicity stuff?' she asked. 'Had she seen it?'

'Holy shit, I didn't tell you,' I said, weaving around an exhausted dog who had decided to take a nap on the path. 'So she asked me to send her the video, which I did ONLY so she would say, "Oh my God, that's awful, you poor thing, what is wrong with people," blah blah, but she fucking messaged Felicity. She messaged her! Wrote some incomprehensible rant about how there's nothing to be gained from tearing apart other women. Luckily Felicity didn't put together that it was Mum, because she would've had a field day, but she wrote back the bitchiest reply—I have to read it to you.'

I scrolled through my photo gallery, now full of screenshots of comments and messages. The one from Mum still shocked me, although I knew it would make Liv laugh. I needed to be reminded of the absurdity, of the fact that this was all ridiculous.

'Okay found it. Ahem. "Donna. Ruby Williams is a big, grown-up girl, with a big, grown-up job. I think she can handle her work being interrogated. I suggest you look more closely at this person you're so determined to defend, and I'm certain you'll find that she is not who you think she is. She is the type of woman who cannot see beyond her own interests, and in truth, she doesn't deserve the position she currently has if she is too weak to listen to the voices of the people she has harmed. Felicity."'

I looked at Liv's horrified expression and grinned. *This would make a great story one day*, I thought. How an angry person on the internet believed she knew me better than my own mother.

'When Mum sent me the screenshot, I was like "you need to never, ever reply, and if you engage with anything else related to this I will end your social media privileges". I made her give me her login so I could change her username and her photo. Like Mum, no. We don't just go around messaging Felicity.'

'I'm dying,' Liv said. 'What the actual fuck? Why is this woman so bent on destroying you? Surely that's, like, slander? I get that she was angry about the article, but now she's literally bitching about you to . . . Mum.'

The drama with Mum had been a welcome reprieve. It had only happened that morning, and I'd felt a brief rush of satisfaction from taking control of a situation that could've become so much worse.

I was curious, though, about what Felicity might've said if she'd figured out the message was from Ruby Williams' mother. Would she have softened when she was confronted with that biological, instinctive desire to protect someone you loved? Would she have seen me—just for a moment—as someone's daughter? Did she have a technologically illiterate but fiercely passionate mother who would do the same for her?

'I was thinking . . . this is probably a good time for you to recalibrate a bit,' Liv said. She had sped up again, now able to see Bronte and the string of shops behind the beach.

'Like, set some goals for what you actually want. Sometimes you get caught up in trivial stuff and it distracts you. You're the best version of yourself when you stop caring what other people think. What do *you* think? What do you *want*? Because the world is way bigger than a few people on the internet and one shitty website—no offence.'

We had an ongoing joke that Liv was more evolved than me. She didn't have the same craving for validation, the same jealousies and competitiveness, the same struggles with self-discipline. She knew who she was, she meant what she said, and she followed through on what she promised. But I had no idea what I wanted, and it left me chasing the nearest shiny thing. That's what my media career was, really. A series of impulsive decisions based on whatever exciting opportunity was within reach.

'I want people not to hate me for something I didn't even do,' I said, my tone drier than I'd intended.

Liv was quiet; she wasn't going to indulge my wallowing. We walked side by side in silence, and I watched as a glassy wave crashed and swallowed a group of swimmers. I wished I'd worn my bathers. That was the sign that, despite how much I was pretending, I'd never really be a beach person. Beach people were always wearing a bikini under their clothes. They started their days three hours before me and didn't squeal the moment a wave broke above their waist. They probably also weren't filled with a pathological fear of a shark emerging from beneath them and ripping them in half.

'I want to write a book,' I said.

Now, Liv looked at me.

'What about?'

'I don't know yet.'

'Wow. Inspiring. What else?'

'I guess I want to do something more permanent.'

From here I could just make out the headstones of Waverley Cemetery. Tens of thousands of graves dotted along the cliff, the white marble crucifixes strikingly still against the swaying swell beneath them. The coastal walk took you straight past the cemetery, and whenever Jamie and I did it together, he lamented the waste of prime, waterfront real estate. But I liked the unspoken acknowledgement that death wasn't moving aside. That it was an enduring feature in a breathtaking landscape.

'Like, I think I hate this thing?' I said, waving the hand that was clutching my phone. 'I don't enjoy constantly being on it. I'm pretty sure I'm wasting my life away, and when that thought hits me at 2 am I have to scroll to distract myself from it.'

Liv laughed.

'And when I'm gone, no one's going to go back through the witty one-liners I posted or the niche opinions I had about stories that have lost all their context. I want to write or create something that lasts beyond the day or two of attention I might get from strangers on the internet. I want to be able to explore complexity and nuance and not have to dumb everything down so it fits into a ninety-character headline.'

I waited for Liv to challenge me, to tell me the work I was doing now had meaning. But she wasn't going to. She was asking me to tap into a compass buried so deep within me that I could hardly feel it was there.

'If that's the goal,' Liv said at last, 'then all the bullshit happening online truly doesn't matter. Because being universally liked isn't even something you want. And trying to convince the Felicity Cartwrights of the world that you're not who they think you are is a massive waste of time.'

The cemetery disappeared from view as we climbed down the stairs to the beach.

'That's lovely in theory,' I said. 'But if everyone hates you it's kind of difficult to "create" for a living. And I think it's fair to acknowledge the disproportionate amount of shit you get as a woman who puts things out into the world.'

'Then get a job in corporate communications or marketing or consulting!' Liv said, puffed from the stairs and also exhausted by this conversation. 'I don't know, make some money and go on nice holidays. But don't choose to do something that makes you miserable. If you don't want people talking about you on the internet, don't have a job that requires you to live on it. It's not that hard.'

I didn't have the resolve to argue. I hadn't invented a world where choosing to be a journalist, choosing to share ideas, meant choosing to chain myself to a never-ending online performance. I hadn't asked to *become* the news. Had I?

'Or I could just make decisions I regret and complain about them like a normal person.'

Liv groaned, and we instinctively made our way across the road to an air-conditioned cafe. We sat at an unsteady silver table and ordered two Diet Cokes. When they arrived, Liv looked at me seriously and said, 'I bet Felicity doesn't drink Diet Coke because it's a tool of the patriarchy.'

'It's my favourite tool of the patriarchy,' I said, taking a sip. 'Mmm. Tastes like chemicals.'

'Mmm. Tastes like participating in my own oppression.'

I was glad to joke about the person whose name still made my blood rush with anger. It gave me hope that her power over me might wane, until what she'd done no longer hurt at all.

Chapter 16

It wasn't until Jamie came across Felicity's op-ed in his own newsfeed, unprompted, that the impact truly seemed to dawn on him. For the first time, he was livid. That Sunday night he sat in bed, propped up against his pillow, staring at several open articles on his laptop. The sheets underneath us were covered in crumbs from toast and chips—the remnants of my mostly bed-bound weekend, spent consuming exclusively golden-brown food—and I loved him for pretending not to notice.

On Saturday I'd stayed in bed watching a TV show set in Paris that was equal parts glorious and terrible, and Jamie came in every few hours to check on me. 'Repeat after me,' he'd say, glistening from his mid-morning swim. He'd be panting from his run back up the hill from the beach, from the three flights of stairs up to our apartment. Standing beside me, his hands on his hips like an athlete after a race, he filled the dim room with the smell of salt and sunscreen.

'Felicity probably has a personality disorder, and it is sad for her.'

'Or: Felicity has a weird vendetta against me, which is embarrassing because it's completely one-sided.'

'Or: I am grateful that I look hot in the photo *The Daily* has used on their website, even if it is in the context of trying to ruin my career.'

I didn't repeat his absurd affirmations, but they made me giggle. He kissed the top of my head and let me continue to rot in the dim bedroom, the curtains drawn to keep out any cracks of light.

But when he saw Felicity's story on the homepage of a website that wasn't *The Daily*, he was shocked.

I, of course, wasn't surprised. Several of the major news sites had syndication rights with each other, all being owned by the same parent company, so my face and name was passed around from editor to editor with a silent acknowledgement that yes, people would click on this story because it had the ingredients of the very best ones: a hot-button issue, and a woman to direct your fury towards.

'I just don't get it,' he said, flicking between multiple tabs. 'No one thought, hold on, let's fact-check this, let's maybe see whether this is personal and vindictive and not actually remotely newsworthy?'

'Felicity's a respected journalist,' I said, resting my head on his shoulder. I was drained, defeated. 'If she writes something, it gets published.'

'Yeah, but isn't she a political journalist? You're not a politician.'

'I guess abortion is a political issue.'

'But you deleted the article!' he said. 'The story she's written is *about* you deleting it! Isn't that what she wanted? She was mad when it was on the website, and now she's still mad—even though the interview she's mad about doesn't exist anymore. She's lost the plot.'

It all seemed so obvious to me after years of watching outrage play out online. When you made a mistake on the internet, it was never about an apology, or retracting what you said, or making amends. It was about 'holding you to account', except no one could actually define what that meant. It was about using your perceived misstep to make a sweeping statement about exactly who you were and who you always would be.

I'd felt calmer after my walk with Liv, zapped by the sun and ready to shift my focus beyond the words that had been published about me online. They didn't exist if I wasn't looking at them. But seeing Jamie's disbelief, his fresh indignation, stirred something new in me. I read the comments on one of the articles open on his screen.

Bared is garbage journalism. Who knew?

Bared and Ruby Williams ought to be ashamed.

Speaking as a psychologist, I cannot imagine how hurtful this article must've been for readers who have had an abortion. Sickening. Shame on you Ruby Williams.

I've had an abortion, and it was the best decision I've ever made for myself and my life. People like Ruby Williams are trash.

Every unchallenged comment was like a fleck of boiling water burning my flesh.

According to these people—and I may have never met them, but they were real, living, breathing people—I had become synonymous with women being denied abortion rights. Not the men who for centuries had crafted ethical arguments against it, who had stigmatised it, who had drafted legislation preventing women from accessing it. No. Me.

The heat was everywhere now, on my skin and inside my veins, bubbling and spitting and spilling over. I hated the culture that allowed the Felicitys of the world to thrive—these personalities who made a living by policing the voices of other women. There was such an arrogance to it. This narcissistic assumption that you deserved to be the sole moral arbiter of how everyone should behave.

'It's fucked,' Jamie said. 'Like, it's one thing to have a random woman make a video about you; it's another thing to have your face front and centre on a homepage that people like me check every day. What are you meant to do? Get a PR crisis manager or something?'

I stopped myself from challenging his reference to Felicity as a 'random woman'. I'd tried to explain multiple times that she had far more power than he gave her credit for. Hundreds of thousands of people were tuned in to what she posted, trusting that their shared values meant Felicity's opinion probably aligned with theirs.

'Ian sent an email yesterday about a crisis manager ... apparently Simmons Corp have someone internally who deals with this stuff. The current advice is that under no circumstances am I to engage with or respond to any of it. Which I wouldn't anyway, because I'm not a moron.'

I cringed at the thought of the comment I had replied to, and considered going back and deleting it. But that would probably make it more embarrassing, like I was trying to pretend I'd never written it. It might also constitute 'engaging' with the outrage, which I was banned from doing.

'It's really unfair,' Jamie said. 'People will forget, though.'

He closed his laptop and stared straight ahead, sinking further into his pillow.

'There's a kid in my year nine class who shat himself in term one. Said he was feeling sick, I told him to go to sick bay, he shits himself before he could even stand up. Whole gym smells of shit, he's got it running down the back of his shorts, mortifying. Now, term four? No one talks about it. They've moved on. It's one of the upsides of everyone's attention span being broken. They honestly don't remember.'

I wordlessly turned to him, my mouth open in horror, until we both started laughing.

'I guarantee no one has forgotten about that,' I said. 'I, personally, will never forget.'

But I did think about that boy, the humiliation that must've burnt for days. And the relief when there was something else, something more outrageous, for everyone to talk about.

Chapter 17

By Monday morning, it was obvious we were going to have to pull down the entire *What No One Saw* series.

We'd published four more stories in the days after Jo's interview went live, and every single one was inundated by people finding them problematic in some way. It was as though the decision to interview individual women was itself a trap, because none of the pieces were capable of reflecting every possible version of lived experience all at once.

Beth had spoken to a woman whose husband's emotional abuse had started in the birthing suite while she was in labour, and the comments were infuriating.

Bared—stop. Just stop. You have lost all credibility. Stop co-opting trauma for clicks.

Ah yes, I forgot, we can only care about abuse when it happens to mothers. Or women who regret their abortions. Ignore those women who have an abortion in order to escape domestic violence, or who have one to save their lives! They're not important at all.

Not everyone who experiences abuse is a heterosexual woman.

How about pregnancy? Did you know femicide is the leading cause of death among pregnant women? Although that wouldn't be convenient for Bared's pro-life agenda.

Can't believe you expect us to take you seriously after what you've done.

In the morning pitch meeting, Amelia was enraged. 'It's like, these people care so much about raising awareness about domestic violence that they want us to stop publishing stories about domestic violence?'

'Correct.'

I was mostly trying to remain impartial in front of the team, to avoid sharing my pulsating hatred for Felicity, or my fury with the people relentlessly criticising *Bared*. But sometimes I couldn't repress the cynicism hiding just under the surface.

Still, I needed to be careful. For all I knew, there were staff here who thought I'd been in the wrong. Who'd had cocktails with friends over the weekend and exchanged gossip about how I didn't seem to 'get it', how I showed no sign of remorse. In an email to the team that morning I'd apologised unreservedly, saying I was taking Felicity's feedback seriously and was committed to learning and growing and trying to do better—whatever that meant.

Most of the editorial team had been outwardly supportive, arguing that it was absurd for *The Daily* to publish a piece questioning my employment when there were rumours one of their sales executives had recently been charged with domestic violence. Some of them wanted to reply to the comments, but they'd been specifically instructed to refrain from posting anything online. Any response would just fuel the story, doing even more damage to the *Bared* brand.

It was only Beth who seemed conspicuously silent. I was surprised she hadn't spoken to me, given that everything started with me covering for her when she was sick. Yasmin said she was probably just frustrated that she'd been working on the *What No One Saw* series and now it was being pulled. She'd have to face the awkward task of telling her remaining leads that she wouldn't be interviewing them, that the stories they'd so bravely offered to share weren't going to be published.

The rest of the pitch meeting passed uneventfully, and afterwards, I assigned a day's worth of work to the writers. Intermittently, cruel phrases intruded into my thoughts, but I pushed them out, turning my attention to the next article

I had to edit, the next headline, the next email about Meg's holiday leave.

By mid-afternoon, website traffic was strong and the mood had lifted. One of the marketing co-ordinators at the other end of the office had started playing music, and while we usually responded by pointedly wearing our headphones, because unlike them we actually had to *concentrate*, today we let it float towards us. The sun pounded against the nearby windows, dancing along the weathered floorboards and across our pod of desks. It promised an afternoon that would be light for hours yet, one of those rare evenings when you could go to the beach after work.

Even Beth appeared to have cheered up, laughing at Yasmin's description of the time she was invited onto the set of *Survivor* and was traumatised by the smell.

'They don't use deodorant!' Yasmin said. She was editing a story about two former contestants who had announced their divorce.

'They're all sweaty because they're doing weird activities all day, and they stink like BO. Up close there's no way they're using shampoo. Their roots are saturated. And the waft of oil and dead skin is everywhere. Everywhere! I swear I could smell it from way behind the crew.'

'It just feels unnecessary,' Amelia said, leaning back in the chair she'd wheeled away from her desk in order to hear the conversation better. I was pretty sure she'd decided to stop work for the day, distracting the other writers and editors with inquiries for gossip. 'They all look hot on TV. I reckon I'd do *Survivor*. I'd love all the mind games.'

Yasmin shook her head, her eyes still fixed on her monitor.

'Hell no, you couldn't pay me fifty dollars to appear on national television with grown-out eyebrows and visible blackheads and trench foot.'

It was Beth who saw the Christmas ad first. It had just started trending, gaining traction in a forum only people in media seemed to use.

'Um, guys, look at the link I just put in the window,' she said, loudly enough that we could all hear. 'HomeMart has just released a Christmas campaign and it's the worst thing I've ever seen.'

When I opened the link, it took me a few seconds to identify the problem. The image appeared to be from a catalogue, the distinctive glossy finish of the page reflecting the flash of a smartphone camera. It was a scene that could've fallen straight out of a movie about the night before Christmas, all cherry red and pine green and neutral chocolate tones, a dash of sandy beige ribbons wrapped around the gifts. A little boy and a little girl, too, sitting in front of the tree. Except they looked terrified, these fictional siblings, their eyes wide open and their limbs stiff, forcibly restrained while surrounded by tinsel and fairy lights and wrapping paper. They were bound and gagged by rope, flanked by bold, white text that read: *Shut Them Up This Christmas.*

'Oh God,' I said, running my eyes over the comments. 'Was it meant to be a joke? Did they think it was funny?'

Several people online believed the ad trivialised the torture of children and was reminiscent of child pornography. They were furious. I could see how this would be pushed to the surface of the outrage machine, how group chats would light up and spouses would shake their heads over dinner, glad to have found something they could agree on. *What on earth were they thinking?*

'Should I jump on this?' Meg asked from two desks down, craning her neck to meet my gaze. 'It's about to be everywhere.'

I hesitated. There was someone, some team, behind this campaign. A person who thought they had an edgy idea, whose vision got mixed up with a photographer and a copywriter and an editor who butchered the execution. But nowhere online was anyone identifying the individual responsible for the ad. There wasn't a name to pillory, a human being to tear apart, to hold accountable for the broad social ill of child abuse and sexualisation.

HomeMart was a big enough brand that no single person's reputation was going to be damaged over this. A quick Google revealed their CEO was a generic white guy, and it wouldn't be particularly interesting for anyone to drag him into the controversy. He obviously hadn't been behind the camera, or ideating the ad copy.

I knew the story would drive enormous traffic. Articles hooked on controversial images always did. It was a cheap way to get clicks, tempting the reader with what they'd find if they looked just a little more closely at this seemingly benign picture. A big red arrow or circle to identify the offending element usually helped. No one had the time to figure it out themselves.

'Yep,' I said. 'Just report it super straight. No tone. And only include a couple of comments, ones that point out why it's problematic but aren't overly snarky.'

Conversation stalled while Meg typed furiously, Amelia letting her know that she'd resized the image for the site, Yasmin sending across a headline.

Once it was published, we watched it float to the top of the leaderboard. The traffic grew with each minute, readers unable to resist their instinctive curiosity. It was only now that we giggled, imagining the thought process that had led a marketing team so far astray.

'As they were tying the ropes around the kids, did it not occur to anyone that maybe this didn't quite capture the spirit of Christmas?' Amelia said, squinting in mock confusion.

Once we started laughing, we couldn't stop.

'When the photographer asked the seven-year-old girl to pretend to choke on her gag, did anyone consider how it might land?' Yasmin asked. 'Any *one*, single fucking person?'

'What I would give to have been in the room where they made that decision,' Amelia said. 'To overhear the conversation. Huge campaign. Big budget. You know what people love? Violence against children. Because as a family-friendly retailer, we should acknowledge that kids' excitement around Christmas can be really annoying. Should we put guns to their heads? Hmm, perhaps not, Steven—that might be going a bit too far.'

There were tears streaming down Yasmin's face, and I felt a pang of fondness for her. I knew that part of the reason we were laughing, pulling apart the mechanics of a tone-deaf Christmas ad, was because we were relieved that, this time, the villain wasn't us.

Chapter 18

I had been working at *The Daily* for two years when I first realised there were people who hated me.

In the morning pitch meetings with the digital team, I felt a sense of belonging I'd never known before. It was like a second chance of what school was meant to be, an environment where you became so familiar with the people you sat alongside every day that you could make each other double over in laughter with a reference no one outside the room would understand. There were friendships so strong that co-workers had become roommates, and hook-ups played out so openly that updates were shared like daily news bulletins. Group chats were created and nicknamed and filled with the details of overheard conversations, of rumours and dramas and grievances. Even when people left, the group chats remained, so the whispers of who did what to whom extended across the whole industry, an incestuous pit in which everyone was connected via a toxic co-worker or a cruelly timed redundancy that forced them to write for the one publication they'd sworn they'd never touch.

I loved the people and the pace and the ideas. It all suited me—my impulsivity and my impatience and my bursts of creative energy. I could come up with an idea in the morning and have it published by noon, knowing instantly whether it had worked. But in hindsight, I did change at *The Daily*. It's probably time for me to be honest about how.

• • •

When you get a job writing online, essentially being paid to be 'good at internet', you really do feel like you've hit the jackpot. Yes, you might've graduated with a media and communications degree from a sandstone university. You might know the principles of journalism and how to tell stories with data and the basic tenets of media law. But that's only a tiny part of what you're employed to do. The way you thrive as a young person in a digital newsroom is to spend a sickening amount of time on social media. That's where the news is, but it's also where the mood is. You scour it—convincing yourself that you're lucky, because if you weren't 'working' you'd probably just be on social media anyway—and you begin to specialise in the kinds of stories that will get the most traction.

Quite quickly, you learn that people will always want to read about murders and billionaires, about sports scandals and celebrity weddings. But as you're writing about the pop star who cried on her wedding day because the flowers were the wrong colour, you notice something. What you're doing isn't straight, objective reporting. There is a tone to your article, and that tone is sarcastic, irreverent, because wealth is gross and capitalism is broken and famous people are heinously out of touch. That's why people are clicking. They don't want to know what happened—they want to know how to feel about it.

On slow news days, you still need to reach your story count. And by now you've discovered that the easiest way to jolt an increasingly desensitised audience to attention is to have a hot take, to be provocative. It's tempting to just invent unpopular opinions you don't believe in for the sake of driving traffic, but you resist. Instead, you write an article slamming a health guru who spouts pseudoscientific nonsense in his new book. You recap a reality show in which strangers date each other and you mock their desperation for fame. You gush over a feminist speech at the Emmys and point out the seventeen things that don't make sense in the Netflix show everyone's watching. You weigh in on the musician who's gone public with his bipolar diagnosis, you spit out eight hundred words about the annoying model who's whingeing about 'skinny shaming'. And with every piece, you build a following of your own.

You barely notice at first. A few hundred followers turns into a few thousand. Sometimes you pitch stories about the need for more women in STEM or the human toll of the famine in Yemen, but your editors either reject them or you write them and no one clicks. The truth is, they're also not as fun or freeing as the pieces where you exercise your voice, strengthening it like a muscle.

You think you're being scammed when you receive the email from the TV network. They're inviting you to be a guest on their Wednesday evening panel show, *One Big Question*, to give a young person's perspective on the trending topic of the week. You say yes before even consulting your boss at *The Daily*, but thankfully she's supportive. Anything that boosts your profile is to your employer's advantage, too.

The studio is far smaller than it appears onscreen. There's a live audience, but only two dozen of them, and there's a man employed to make sure they laugh and applaud in the right places. Your hair and make-up takes less than thirty minutes. A chatty woman who has a daughter your age liberally applies a foundation you can't afford. She contours your nose and your forehead and your cheeks and attaches individual fake eyelashes with the precision of a surgeon, before using what seems like half a can of hairspray to secure your loose waves. You look in the mirror and don't recognise yourself, which feels wonderful.

You sweat profusely in the green room. The wardrobe department has given you special pads to put under your arms so you don't stain the dress. You brought a striped silk shirt to wear, but stripes don't work on camera apparently, so they've dressed you in a dusty pink structured mini-dress with bishop sleeves. You hope pink doesn't make you look dumb.

This week's Big Question is about whether public beaches should ban revealing swimwear, and you wonder if that really is the most pressing issue of the week, the one that urgently needs to be debated on prime-time TV. But it's too late. You research and prepare and you're excited to argue with the ageing, conservative commentator who will be sitting beside you.

You're terrified as a guy slips a tiny microphone down the front of your dress, asking you to secure the battery pack to the waistband of your underwear. But once the studio light is on and you're live nationwide, you feel like you're flying. There's a weightlessness, a complete detachment from all the normal worries that plague you. You can't afford to focus on anything other than the present: the sound of your voice speaking thoughts that seem to emerge from thin air, the nod of another panellist when you articulate an argument, the laughter from the audience when you pose the question of whether police resources should really be used to prosecute the thickness of a G-string.

The producers beam at you afterwards, and when you check your phone, you see the new followers, the messages, the reposts. A few days later, a clip from the show goes viral, one where you're in a heated exchange with the grey-haired old guy. Overwhelmingly, the comments adore you.

You become a guest panellist on a few different shows, and every time a snippet on social media gets traction, your following grows. Sometimes you post videos of your own, when you get the time. Piece-to-camera commentary about red-carpet fashion. Angry rants about gender inequality. Straightforward arguments about vaccines, dangerous wellness crazes, the appalling rental market.

It's your growing profile that eventually—after four years at *The Daily*—attracts the attention of Ian. He invites you to have a coffee with him around the corner from your office, and he tells you he's starting a feminist media brand for young people and wants you to be at the helm. Your voice, your vision, your persona. The money is good, much better than your current salary. You'd be the editor-in-chief, and Simmons Corp would put you forward for more panel shows, live events, podcasts, speaking gigs.

You say yes, because you're ambitious, and you're hungry to work and to build and to create. By now, you know how to exploit people's attention. You know what they care about and what they don't, you know which words make them click, you know how to write a headline that feels more like a riddle. That's how your time at *The Daily* changed you: you got too good at a game you never consciously decided to play.

But on this one particular morning, you haven't met Ian yet. You're two years into your stint at *The Daily*, and you're about to learn that if you're going to put something out there, you need to be tough enough to withstand what might come back.

• • •

I pitched a story about a royal wedding. Not one of the major ones—just the marriage of some distant cousin with a forgettable name—but significant enough that all the interesting members of the royal family were there, wearing fitted midi dresses and silly hats. I wanted to write a fictional account of the event from the perspective of one of the royal children. The littlest one, a toddler, who probably couldn't speak yet.

'I just reckon he'd be thinking, "Why am I dressed as a little ghost?"' I explained in the pitch meeting.

Jen smacked her hands on the oak table we were all sitting around and yelled, 'OH MY FUCKING GOD, SO TRUE,' as I continued, '"And why does everyone hate that lady and shouldn't that man over there be in prison?"'

So I'd done it. Nine hundred words with images and speech bubbles and a headline that—I hoped—made it clear that this was an entirely fabricated day in the life of a tiny royal. For reasons I couldn't quite understand, the royal family drove more traffic to *The Daily* than any other individual or family I'd written about. A made-up story about them attracted more eyeballs than a true story about the country's most influential politicians. Even the biggest celebrities in Hollywood couldn't compete with the man on a colonialist throne and all his feuding relatives.

I walked to the bus stop that night with a sense of accomplishment. My article had been the top performing piece of the day, getting even more traffic than an anonymous column from a mum who confessed she loved one of her kids more than the other. From a high seat up the back of the bus, beside a middle-aged man in a too-big suit who was responding to emails and looked like he wanted to die, I refreshed the numbers dashboard. I knew I would easily hit my monthly traffic target at this rate, and a track record of sharp content instincts was what I needed to get promoted. I wondered what it must be like to be the weathered, greasy guy beside me, working some job in finance or law that made him money but chipped away at his soul, so that he walked through the world like a zombie, devoid of the joys that made life worth living.

Then I'd got a comment on a photo. It was one of me and Jamie after a hike in Byron Bay, our limbs glistening with sweat as the sun set behind us.

> wow you're really fkn ugly

The mortification slapped me, silencing the loud conversation of the two uni students standing in the aisle. The words danced on my phone, not quite making sense, and I slid my thumb to the left and deleted them.

Within seconds, the same person commented on another photo: one from Dad's sixtieth, of our family in the dim function space of an inner-city pub, our eyes red from the flash of Aunt Faye's camera. I recalled how hard I'd tried to be present that night, soaking in the smell of spilt beer on the wooden bar top and the Simon & Garfunkel song that floated from the speaker.

> Ahh they're all hideous. Looks like the sloth gene runs strong.

The account belonged to an 'anthonypalmer.art' and I went to his profile, full of sketches and political cartoons, and blocked him.

Suddenly, I had a sinking feeling. This wasn't a coincidence.

I flicked back to *The Daily*'s real-time analytics and clicked on my royal story for more data. The platform would show me exactly where the traffic was coming from, whether users were accessing it from Google or the homepage or if someone had shared the link elsewhere.

There it was.

A post. On a social media site I only looked at late at night when I wanted to feel angry. It came from the account of another journalist, the lifestyle editor at a prestigious masthead. I had applied for a job there multiple times and never received a response.

> **erinmcconnell**: Is this really what journalism has become? It's just embarrassing. Surely there are more important things this poor girl can write about.

It had been up for hours, and probably explained the influx of traffic to the story. People had been hate-reading it, and dissecting the *poor girl* who wrote it. In one of the comments, someone had shared my social media profile, and anthonypalmer.art had replied simply: *thank u kind sir.*

Now, the post had more than three thousand likes and hundreds of responses unfurling beneath.

> i hate it
>
> i think she's probably really dumb. But why is a dumb person writing all your stories @TheDaily?
>
> and that, kids, is why we stay in school
>
> imagine this child growing up and reading what some weird lady on the internet wrote about him on a random wednesday. He'll be like . . . chill, hun, get a life
>
> omg i've seen her stories popping up and i cringe literally every time. my best friend and i now send them to each other because we can't cope

I recognised one of the names—it was a girl I'd known as a kid. Mum had been friends with her mum, and they'd lived a couple of streets away. We'd swum in their pool on Saturday afternoons one summer while our parents drank wine and pretended to watch our out-of-time synchronised swimming routines.

> **sophiekramer:** I knew this girl in primary school and this checks out. Massive loser lol. She thought she was funny but was just a weirdo. Clearly nothing has changed.

I wasn't sure if it was the motion of the bus combined with having my eyes fixed on my phone, or the humiliation of what I'd just read, but a queasiness bubbled in my stomach and overflowed to my limbs, leaving my hands clammy on my screen and my feet prickling inside my socks. I'd been nine when I played with Sophie. Of course I wasn't funny. My idea of humour was quoting *The Simpsons* and burping after sculling an entire bottle of Coke.

I glanced at the man beside me, to check he hadn't been watching my suffering unfold over my shoulder, and was relieved to find he was still replying to emails. His phone was closer to me now, his arms pressed to his sides because of the overcrowded aisle, and I could see his email signature. Shane. That was his name.

And he wasn't in finance or consulting or law. His automated sign-off read:

> Shane Gallagher
> Chief Executive Officer, Disability Advocacy Australia

He was a CEO. Getting the bus home from work instead of driving a fancy car because he had dedicated his life to making the world a better place. Here I was, smug about writing a made-up story about a royal toddler, while he was still replying to emails at 6 pm—emails that actually did something real.

A wave of heaviness washed over me, and I rested my head against the cool glass of the window to shock myself out of it. Of course, all the words I was reading about myself—*embarrassing, poor girl, dumb, weird, cringe, not funny*—hurt so much because they were true. There were more important things I could be writing about. Some journalists were reporting on violent regimes in war-torn countries, and I was sitting at my ergonomically designed desk in a temperature-controlled, converted warehouse in Surry Hills pitching pure fiction.

But that didn't make the name-calling any easier to digest.

The bus had emptied out by the time it reached my stop. Shane had got off on a wide, leafy street dotted with near-identical Victorian terraces, and I pictured him opening his front door to the cosiness of an open fire warming the charming living space of his small but tasteful home.

I didn't live in a terrace. Back then, I lived in a damp studio apartment above a grocer, and I walked there with my shoulders hunched under the weight of my backpack. My gaze remained fixed on my screen the whole way home, reading and re-reading the criticism of a story I wished I'd never written. Part of me was desperate to respond. To type, *hey, I'm the person you're talking about and it was just meant to be a funny story and you're all being really cruel right now.* But there were no words to express what I truly wanted to say. That a thread by another journalist—one whose career I admired—had broken my heart. That I hated myself enough without the weight of thousands of words from strangers. That I already thought I was stupid and embarrassing and not funny, so there was really no need for anyone to reinforce it.

When I'd walked in the door that night, to the mustiness of a flat so cramped we could barely fit a bar fridge, I collapsed into Jamie. I slowly and flatly explained what had happened, and he held me, calling them all cunts and asking whether *The Daily* had any power to ask the journalist to delete what she'd written.

'What is wrong with people?' he said, once I'd explained that *The Daily* reaching out would only make the whole thing more mortifying. His voice was muffled as he buried his face in my hair. 'What kind of losers spend a weeknight bullying someone they've never met on the internet?'

But after we'd ordered Thai for dinner and climbed into bed, he'd whispered that everyone would forget about it by tomorrow, and slipped effortlessly into sleep. I closed my eyes, and the words came to me again.

This poor girl.

It's just embarrassing.

I quietly made my way to the lounge room, and six hours into a mindless reality show later, I messaged my boss and said I'd been up with food poisoning all night. I wouldn't be coming into work.

I had always wondered if the rest of the digital team knew why I'd called in sick that day. They'd never brought it up, and when I returned to work, I'd pitched a straight news story about the causes of famine in the Horn of Africa.

For weeks, I wrote only news or celebrity stories with no tone. I didn't pitch anything personal or anything that reflected my opinion. I didn't try to write anything funny. Every time I saw a story of mine fail to reach its traffic targets, I was quietly relieved. If no one was reading my words, no one could mock them.

Slowly, though, the burn for attention, for success, for people to *know* me, returned. And I resolved to ignore the comments as much as I could. To focus only on the readers who seemed to get it.

Looking back, it's entirely predictable that I was going to be challenged and criticised. I was screaming for attention. Deep down, I wanted something like fame.

But I think people assume that in order to put yourself out there, you must like yourself. You must have a level of confidence and self-assurance that's inaccessible to them.

I need you to know that it's the opposite.

The reason I craved attention was not out of pride or self-worth but out of shame. There was a black hole inside me that I thought only external validation could fill. I felt so fundamentally unworthy that I'd built a career out of begging strangers to convince me otherwise. And perhaps I always knew it would backfire spectacularly. So when the witch-hunt really, truly began, the pain was unbearable. But it also felt familiar. Like I deserved it.

Chapter 19

It turns out that when you stop responding, when you refuse to give the outrage any oxygen, it really does start to die down. A week after Felicity had first posted her video, I could feel the tide receding, and somehow I was still intact.

But I was now ideologically attached to a broader social cancer. And it hadn't occurred to me that it was the kind of disease that might lie dormant for a moment, but not for long.

Another woman was dead. Killed by her ex-husband, who had been waiting for her with a knife in the driveway of her friend's house. The woman had tried to leave, to start over, to get as far away from this man as she could while still being able to live the life she'd built. But he'd taken it, and now the story was everywhere.

At this point, you might be wondering how on earth the senseless murder of a thirty-one-year-old woman had anything to do with me. And you probably think it's wildly narcissistic of me to think that her death could be part of my story. You're right. Of course you are. But the internet has turned us all into narcissists, seeing our own reflections in the puddles of other people's pain.

Her name was Lucy Wong. She was beautiful, which shouldn't matter, but once you've worked in digital media for long enough, watching what people click on and what they ignore, you know that it does. On the news, photos of a smiling Lucy at her university graduation sat on one half of the screen, while on the other half a journalist described in harrowing detail exactly what her ex-husband did to her body. He stabbed her, but the weapon was a hunting knife, so the attack was probably better described as an execution. He stabbed her in the stomach, then the chest, and then he slit her throat. That's what killed her.

I say this not to give you nightmares. But broadcasting tragedy has become second nature in a world where big corporations make money by keeping you watching and sharing content that shocks you. Graphic images and horrifying videos are everywhere, and there's no shut-off valve. A photo of a dead baby might come up directly after an easy dinner recipe or an online clothing sale, especially if you happen to be a new parent, for whom that exact image represents your single greatest fear.

I don't know how it happened, but footage of Lucy's attack made it onto the internet. Someone filmed it from nearby, capturing her spine-chilling scream and the blood spurting from her neck, and thought it was their duty, or their one chance at notoriety, to post it. Or maybe they sent it to a friend, and the friend sent it to another friend, and that person shared it. It doesn't really matter.

The question I've always wanted to ask is: if you were close enough to film, were you close enough to do something? Was the person thinking that they were being helpful, that the video might be used as evidence, might prove what happened to Lucy so that at least she'd receive justice after her death? Sure. But when the police got there, she was lying in the driveway, dead, and the man standing over her was holding a knife and covered in blood. It wasn't exactly fodder for an eight-part true-crime documentary.

I'm fairly certain that if you look hard enough, the video still exists somewhere on the internet. We all have that one friend who could find it, who's in the right forum, familiar enough with the cold, dark corners of the web that they can reach for it without any trouble, if anyone wants to watch something fucked up on their Saturday afternoon. The video and the stills from it were taken down from social media platforms eventually. Not fast enough. Not as fast as a photo of a woman daring to expose her nipple.

When you become a news story, I've learnt, you cease to be a person. You're a body or a victim or a Sydney woman or a student or a girlfriend; a sack of flesh that, in Lucy's case, bled out so profusely that the blood ran down the driveway, into the gutter. I can't imagine Lucy's family enjoyed hearing the gruesome details of their daughter's final moments played over the airwaves or aired on prime-time television or presented as neat, informative tiles on newsfeeds or served as video after video after video on the phones of strangers.

Again, I'm not trying to disturb you. I'm sharing all this—about the knife and the video and the throat and the blood—because I think when you're scrolling on a platform that shows you images of a dead woman, and then footage of an air strike on the other side of the world, and then an interest rate hike that makes it even more unlikely you'll ever own a home, you don't react normally when you see something that annoys you. You conflate it all. And the irritating, tone-deaf, pointy-nosed person whose face *you keep seeing*—probably because the algorithm is clever and knows how to grab your attention faster than you can resist it—becomes the oppressor. The terrorist. The murderer.

So that's why I'm telling you this. Because that's what I became.

Chapter 20

The news broke while I was in Ian's office, arguing with Sarah about botox.

A cosmetics client wanted to advertise with *Bared*, offering a six-figure sum in exchange for a series of branded content about their new app. It sounded harmless at first, until Sarah explained that its purpose was to scan a woman's face to identify her 'cosmetic age' and suggest what products she could use to lower it.

She sat opposite me with her closed laptop beside her, while Ian stood behind his desk. He was reading over the brief from the client, and he couldn't see what the issue was. We weren't exactly in a position to turn down advertising dollars, not unless there was a strong business case for doing so.

'Our audience will see right through it,' I said. 'We can't position ourselves as a feminist publication and then encourage women to download an app that tells them they look older than they are to persuade them to buy stuff they don't need. It doesn't make any sense.'

Ian's gaze was still fixed on his screen. He repeated the figure on offer out loud. To him, there was always a solution to a problem worth that amount of money.

He moved towards Sarah and me with his hands in his pockets.

'Do you know how much the anti-ageing industry is currently valued at?' he asked gently. 'Tens of billions. Maybe hundreds of billions. Are we going to pretend women aren't interested in it? That they don't care about it? That their bathroom cabinets aren't full of these kinds of products? It's a weird hill for us to die on, isn't it?'

I was struggling to disguise my frustration. I took a sharp breath and opened my mouth to argue but Sarah got in first.

'Look around—everyone's getting botox,' she scoffed, glancing briefly at my forehead. I'd never had it, and I wondered if she could tell. 'We're all trying not to age! I just think women are smart enough to absorb the information they need without feeling attacked by it.'

'Not everyone's getting botox,' I said. 'Specifically, men aren't getting botox.'

Out of the corner of my eye I saw Yasmin, down the other end of the floor, stand up from her desk and approach the TV.

She reached behind it, presumably toggling the volume up. We'd lost the remotes months ago, and we only ever switched the sound on when there was a breaking news bulletin. Meg, too, stood up from her chair, crossing her arms as she stared flatly at the screen.

'Are you not curious?' Sarah was saying. 'If this app told you your cosmetic age was forty, forty-five, wouldn't you want to know the truth and have the opportunity to do something about it?'

She said the phrase 'cosmetic age' like it was a scientific concept, and not a buzzword a marketing guy had come up with five minutes before a pitch meeting.

I was distracted by the time Ian made the call for the campaign to go ahead. Part of the reason I was so resistant to the idea was that I knew it would be me—my integrity, my reputation—that would be at stake if our audience had a problem with it. *Bared* and Ruby Williams were synonymous now, like the brand was purely the digitalisation of my brain. I was aware that there were people who thought I personally was behind every decision, every advertising dollar, every published word. But from the way Yasmin was now hovering around the team's workstations, I could tell there was a bigger priority.

Half an hour later, I knew every available detail of the Lucy Wong story.

By early evening the news anchors had changed shifts, so now a round-faced older man sat in front of a green screen of

Sydney at dusk, his hands resting on the polished desk. He crossed to an interview with a bystander, a teenage boy who looked like he should've been at school. He was skittish, too excited to be talking about a woman's death. He stared down the barrel of the camera and said he'd heard an argument between 'the knife guy and his girlfriend'.

'He was calling her names, like calling her a slut. Calling her a cu—'

The reporter cut him off then, and quickly crossed back to the studio. They might be standing just metres from where a woman was brutally bludgeoned to death, but no one needed to hear profanities on the TV while they were preparing to put dinner on.

Since the news broke, *Bared* had published three articles about Lucy Wong's murder. She was identified almost immediately, because her ex-partner had been known to police. He'd threatened her before, once in front of her parents, and she'd gone through the painstaking process of taking out an apprehended violence order against him. The AVO hadn't carried much weight once he'd discovered where she was living and purchased a knife the size of her forearm.

Soon after the articles went live, we had to disable the comments. Readers often had a visceral reaction to seeing the word 'alleged' in a headline about violence against women, arguing that using it was disrespectful or cast doubt on the victim's suffering. I'd published stories before explaining that terms such as 'alleged' were legally necessary until a person was found guilty in court—that without it, the case against the perpetrator could be compromised. But a rational explanation is far less interesting than misplaced outrage. Commenters kept publishing the attacker's name, alongside unverifiable claims of exactly what he'd done.

> Mark Keough. I went to school with him and he was always into weird sex shit. BDSM but like actually dangerous. Heard he made girlfriends do degrading stuff. Really sick guy.

> Clearly he's a psychopath. These men always follow the same pattern. Target and exploit young, impressionable girls, and when they can't control them anymore, they can't handle it. Disgusting. Burn in hell, Mark Keough.

> Hey @baredmedia—headlines matter. He didn't 'allegedly' kill Lucy Wong. He did it. We have eyewitnesses. Sick of media misreporting on domestic and sexual violence. Enough.

>> THIS!! And, she wasn't killed, she was murdered. Tell the TRUTH.

> I just left an abusive relationship and seeing @baredmedia misrepresent this story is heartbreaking. I've also noticed them deleting comments that question them. Probably not surprising given that their editor is completely unable to take feedback.

Comments about the attacker, we knew, could seriously prejudice future legal proceedings. The perpetrator could argue—like many before him—that he'd endured a trial by media that made it completely impossible to secure a fair and impartial jury. He could get away with murder. And *Bared*, meanwhile, would be in court dealing with defamation and contempt charges, because media organisations—as I'd been reminded time and time again—are legally liable for the comments on their sites and social platforms, responsible for every sloppy word typed beneath every single news story. We didn't have the staff to moderate every comment as it appeared, to assign an editor or writer to play an incessant game of whack-a-mole with claims that might plunge the company and all the livelihoods that depended on it into financial ruin. So the comments were turned off and, predictably, the outrage migrated.

Without a comments section, and with the residual anger around Jo's story, our inbox was overflowing with complaints. We were *cowards* and *liars* and how dare we *pretend to care about domestic violence* and then *erase a woman's murder*. First, we *hijacked* a *national emergency* in order to push our *own sick agenda*, and now we'd chosen to *silence victims* who were just sharing their *valid responses* to our *misreporting*. I almost wrote out a detailed response to copy and paste in reply to each email—explaining the context, the risks, the necessity of choosing our language carefully—but then I imagined a group of aggrieved people connecting online and sharing their identical responses, feeling more ignored than if I hadn't engaged at all.

I closed my crowded email tab and examined the homepage. Each of our stories about Lucy Wong used a different photo of her, thanks to the better-resourced national newsrooms that had quickly assigned staff to trawl through her social media accounts and curate the most evocative images. There was the one from her graduation, and then there was Lucy holding a fat, giggling baby. Lucy in a beret, beaming with the Eiffel Tower behind her. Lucy lying on her back in the grass, her gaze on a person out of frame. An ordinary day, the invisible subtext read. A day she'll never get again.

The more candid, the more effortlessly attractive, the better. She had a doll-like face, all big eyes and full lips and meticulously styled hair, and if the site traffic was anything to go by, a face like hers made the tragedy of her murder sadder. I was shocked when I learnt journalists could lift photos from personal social media accounts with absolutely no consequences. Most of us don't imagine that the upload from a drunken birthday lunch or a sun-drenched tropical holiday isn't really ours—that if our name drifted into the public interest, those images would be published to represent who we are. Or who we were.

Beside me, Meg exhaled and leant back in her chair. She arched her back and faced the ceiling, stretching her neck, attempting to counteract some of the stiffness that came with the concave hunching of a workday spent behind a screen.

'Okay. Latest update is done. I've just filed it to Yas.'

Like a vigilant meerkat, Yasmin looked up from behind her monitor and nodded. She'd barely moved from her seat since the news broke, assigning and publishing stories, curating the homepage and scanning for updates. It was now almost 6 pm and we were the only three left in the office. I'd asked Beth to stay back, to take over from Yasmin who had been in the office since 7 am and was the colour of the concrete pipes that ran along the ceiling above her. But Beth didn't work late, she had boundaries, so she left just as the clock struck 5 pm—a clock she must've been watching, because her accuracy was astounding.

Meg picked up her phone, waiting politely for me to send her home. I was contemplating whether to ask her to schedule the stories for our newsfeed overnight or just do it myself when she saw it.

'Ah, fuck.'

Both Yasmin and I turned to her, the violence of the news still pumping through our veins.

'A family member of Lucy Wong has posted about the media using unauthorised photos of her. But they've called us out specifically. Fuck.'

She was still reading it. Her right hand was resting on her forehead and her attention was locked on the wall of text on her screen. She didn't look up.

'She's Lucy Wong's cousin. Same last name. Cara Wong. She's written . . . oh, Jesus. This is so bad.'

She swivelled in my direction, but her gaze didn't lift. She held her phone with both hands now, like it was made of lead, heavy and dense and toxic. Yasmin made her way behind her, leaning on the mesh back of Meg's chair to read over her shoulder.

Meg started to read, her voice flat.

'*While we've been reeling over the loss of our beloved friend, sister, daughter, granddaughter and cousin, photos of Lucy have been splashed around the internet with no concern for her grieving family.*

'*We have not given permission for any images of Lucy to be shared, and I cannot understand how the media can be so callous as to simply take them. I'd expect these sorts of tactics from tabloids, but then there are publications like* Bared *who claim to care about victims and their stories, and then reduce them to a clickbait headline and a private photo.*

'*Please take them down. We beg you. You have created such unnecessary pain on what is already the worst day of our lives.*'

I took the phone from Meg's hands without speaking. I could feel that the clamminess from my palms was leaving a damp residue on the glass of her screen, the oils from my fingers coating her camera lens. It felt too intimate to be holding it, this thing she carried with her all day—when she ran and when she ate and when she pissed. But my eyes caught the raw, growing numbers of likes and comments and shares, and I couldn't let go. We didn't have time, I knew we didn't have time, and yet I was scrolling, reading the words of strangers on the internet because I could not stop. The anger, I realised, had crawled out of my inbox and found its way here, where it was even more laden with emotion.

> @carawong get in contact with Ruby Williams and hold her to account for what Bared has done. She should be ashamed of this disturbing behaviour. I'm so sorry.

> I emailed Ruby Williams with a complaint about their coverage earlier today. No response. I know others have emailed, too. Completely ignored. Bared has also closed comments on all posts about this story, so no way to contact them there. It's like they want to profit off this tragedy without having to engage in any of the discourse about it.

> HEY @rubywilliams you SICK FUCK why don't you LISTEN to ACTUAL VICTIMS and their FAMILIES and RESPECT THEIR WISHES. When Felicity Cartwright called you out, you ignored it like the arrogant, smug bitch that you are. You are a HUMAN SHIT STAIN. I can't believe you still have a job at this point wtf @baredmedia

> I would expect nothing less from Ruby Williams at this point. Appalling track record. Still hasn't apologised for the fucked up story she ran this week, trying to Trojan horse a pro-life message into a story about domestic violence????? And now this.

'Take all the photos of Lucy Wong down,' I said, still clutching Meg's phone. 'Replace them with anything. Just . . .

stock images of a crime scene. Anything. And then delete and repost everything we posted this afternoon. Yasmin, can you update the homepage as soon as those changes come through? I need to call Ian.'

While I'd been holding her phone, Meg had turned back to her desktop and found the post there. She and Yasmin were studying it, side by side, the cold light from the monitor illuminating their panic-stricken faces.

'But that's not fair,' Yasmin said, her voice cracking with exhaustion. She stood back, crossing her arms, her loose-fit, button-up shirt wearing the creases of a day spent bunched against her tense body. 'The photos are everywhere. They're in the public domain now. They were on the news. Why do we have to—'

I cut her off. Every moment those photos remained published on *Bared* was a moment that seemed crueller, more callous.

'Because a grieving woman has asked us to. It doesn't really matter whether it's justified or not.'

I sounded robotic. Not because I didn't believe the words I was saying, but because I was shattered. Fragments of me were smashed like glass across the internet, jagged edges piercing exposed flesh, drawing blood. The truth was—and I couldn't admit it then, I only recognise it now—that through the eyes of the people whose wounds were gaping, whose tissue had been cut by my shards, I hated me, too.

I hated the person whose job it was to plaster a dead woman's face on newsfeeds and in the papers and on the television so that strangers could be titillated by a tragedy that wasn't theirs to grieve. I hated the sound of the 'death knock' on the front door of a mother's home, a mother who was too consumed by loss to have the energy to turn the journalist away. I hated the voice of the person who told her to take her time, to have a sip of icy water, who waited patiently for the quote that would make the perfect headline. I hated the person behind the camera, focusing the lens on that mother's falling features—a moving portrait to air that evening on a TV network so that their ads for yoghurt and gambling and alcohol would be worth something. So that CEOs in air-conditioned boardrooms would get big bonuses that year, while a haunted mother tried, in the lonely quiet of her home, to continue living, when living would never be the same.

I saw myself as a cartoonish devil, a gleeful smile on my face while I looked at page views and time on site and social engagement, like the value of death could be quantified. Like death was just another story, equivalent to a politician's humiliating gaffe or a cockroach spotted in a bag of supermarket lettuce.

• • •

Ian's phone rang out over and over again, ending in a hollow invitation to leave a message on his voicemail. I pictured the phone buried in the pocket of his suit jacket, screaming for attention beside a clump of old tissues. Between calls I paced the length of the bathroom sink, the four empty stalls on one side of me, the damp basins, with paper towels stuck to them like lazy papier-mâché, on the other. It smelt of loose particles of deodorant and dry shampoo, of women who used their brief moments of privacy to disguise their oils and their sweat, to mask the shame that followed them everywhere, even into locked cubicles.

On my screen, there was a series of unanswered messages from my friend Jen. We were meant to be meeting after work for a drink.

> **Jen**: I'm sitting at Rover—no rush. I've ordered a margarita. I also have an agenda of gossip for us to discuss when you get here xxx
>
> **Jen**: Let me know if you want me to get you a drink, it's happy hour
>
> **Jen**: Just realised you're probably stuck in the office because of that horrific story. All good if you can't make it I'm having a lovely time people-watching hehe

I quickly typed a reply.

> **Ruby**: Sorry—crisis. Will be there as soon as I can.

I wanted to be having a drink on a Friday night like everyone else, not paralysed by indecision in this oppressive, unventilated bathroom.

The meeting with Ian and Sarah after Felicity's video had been unequivocal about the need to escalate crises like this one. I apparently had the *responsibility* of managing *Bared*'s digital presence—every story choice, every headline, every quarterly strategy—but not the *right* to decide how to respond when that presence was being vilified; not even when my own identity was tied to it. But *this* exact scenario, of me repeatedly calling a number that didn't answer, of me sending messages that went unseen, was why I so rarely pursued Ian's input. Because Ian didn't live in the hands of a round-the-clock news cycle, where algorithms demanded urgency like human lungs demanded air. Ian could leave the office and be uncontactable, could focus exclusively on whatever corporate dinner he was at.

I intended to use the call as a plea for permission. I needed to respond directly to the post, under my own name, like an actual human being. No layers of bureaucracy. No AI-generated statement. I needed to throw my hands up and accept the online flagellation—no matter how brutal, no matter how frenzied. To acknowledge that I heard the chorus of voices aimed in my direction, that I had done what had been asked of me, that I understood. And I needed to do it urgently— while *Bared* was in the process of deleting the photos of Lucy Wong, not after—so that it didn't seem like I had seen the pain, seen the begging, and capitulated silently, like a coward.

I gave Ian one more opportunity to answer. There were other senior people I could've called, like Sarah, but she wouldn't understand. Only I knew how this criticism of *Bared* would metastasise and harden, attaching to the brand like an inoperable tumour, until it became part of the unerasable mythology of us. Of me. To be fair, I was relatively certain Ian wouldn't understand, either. Perhaps that was why I felt relief when the call rang out yet again, and why I rushed back to my desk, a woman possessed by the need to follow my own instincts.

...

'All the photos have been taken down,' Yasmin said, straightening her tech-bent spine to look at me over her monitor. 'And the homepage has been updated. What did Ian say?'

'Great, thank you. He didn't answer, so I'm just going to respond. We've done exactly as the cousin asked and I want her to know we heard her.'

I opened the homepage and scanned the dull stock photos that now sat above the news headlines about Lucy Wong. In the right-hand corner of my screen, Meg's avatar—a thumbnail from when she'd dyed her hair copper and worn lensless glasses, bearing no resemblance to the person sitting beside me now—appeared with a link.

'I just sent you the cousin's post,' she said. 'It's been getting more traction. A few people with big followings have shared it . . . so if we can get her to take it down, that would be ideal.'

The thread was alive. Throbbing. I was pulled into it, the pain of *WHAT THE FUCK*s and *can we cancel her already*s coming in a series of regular beats. I knew with unshakeable certainty what I needed to do, the words I needed to craft, the truth I needed to share. So I typed. Even as Yasmin stood beside me, her overstuffed handbag on her shoulder, asking quietly if I was sure. If it wouldn't be better to wait for Ian, wait until tomorrow, wait until my name was buried so deep in the mud that there was no way of ever rinsing it off.

I pretended to listen. I nodded, but still I typed, and then I heard her leave, with Meg behind her, the echoes of tired feet against wearied wood.

The response itself flowed out effortlessly, the result of studying apologies for years and watching the surgical dissection of them. It needed to take full responsibility, offering no excuses, voicing an unconditional 'sorry', and promising to learn and do better. It should be a public performance of shame.

I didn't flinch when I published it.

> **Ruby Williams**: Hi Kara. I'm so sorry for your loss, and I cannot imagine what you're going through right now. We have removed all photos of Lucy from our website and our socials. I sincerely apologise for the hurt we have caused you and your family at this time. We are revising our editorial policies to ensure that sensitivity towards grieving families is of primary importance. We are committed to learning from our mistakes and doing better. If you want to speak to me directly, please feel free to contact me. We are all so sorry, and thinking of you and your family.

It took me until someone pointed it out to notice.

The second word. The name of the person I was directing my apology to. The wrong first letter, like I was thoughtless. Glib. Like I hadn't read her post at all. I had a cousin Kara. So when I said the name in my head, her spelling was what came out.

> If you're going to offer a fake apology, at least spell the person's name right.

> Wow. Just shows how much she cares.

I edited it, amending the K to C, but it was too late. Editing was not a skill to be practised in public, in front of an audience. And the internet wasn't exactly forgiving of errors. Every error, the mob insisted, carried meaning. There were no oversights or typos or misunderstandings, no room for the flawed nature of attention and behaviour. Errors were Freudian slips, my wrong letter revealing a truth about myself that even I didn't know. A mistaken K meant I didn't care about Cara or her family or the dead woman on the news, I didn't care about violence or loss or pain. I had plastered photos of Lucy Wong on 'my' website for the simple reason that I was vile.

Even if I'd caught my own mistake, corrected it before my comment was published, the outcome, I knew, would've still been catastrophic. Because I'd forgotten, in my haze of urgency, that the anatomy of an apology is always dismembered, always taken apart piece by piece until there is nothing left.

> Ah. So she's taken this from the 'learning and growing and doing better' playbook. Totally original. So genuine. Almost like she wrote it herself.
>
> @rubywilliams you've only responded because you were called out PUBLICLY. How about owning up to your mistakes and holding yourself accountable in private, where you're not just searching for validation?
>
> When you need to work on an 'editorial policy' to implement BASIC HUMAN EMPATHY.

I've since learnt you should never watch the dismemberment of your own words and their intended meaning. It will make you too angry. It will make you do things (more things) you regret. Because we all have a delicate part of ourselves that will haemorrhage if it's pierced. Of course, you don't even know it's there until the blade strikes it.

> Imagine asking a grieving person to contact you. Like she wants to. Like she has the time.
>
> @rubywilliams you clearly don't know the first fucking thing about grief.

I froze. It didn't seem real, the absurdity of such a claim. The wrongness of it. Almost like this stranger knew where to hurt me, how to make me bleed.

I messaged Jen.

> **Ruby**: Sorry. Everyone on the internet hates me. On my way.

She replied instantly.

> **Jen**: Am ordering you a spicy marg. Step away from the crazy people.

I rummaged through my backpack for my make-up bag and took it with me into the bathroom, staring at my reflection in the cloudy mirror. My hands shook as I took out my eyeliner brush, tracing my upper lash line with the inky tip. I slapped on another layer of liquid foundation, applied some bronzer, coated my lashes in mascara. I looked better. Less tired. But those words still echoed in my head.

The first fucking thing about grief.

Apparently I didn't know. The first fucking thing. About grief.

Chapter 21

I knew grief like I knew the sound of my mother's primal scream. Like an untamed howl that came from her but was nothing like her voice. It's a noise I'm certain is programmed into us at birth, one we're biologically wired to recognise, because it signals the end of everything.

I knew grief like I knew the scent of desperation soaking through my father's skin. Like the whispered prayers that got quieter and quieter until they stopped completely.

I knew grief like I knew the feeling of our house afterwards, like the sadness had seeped into the carpet and the walls, like it had changed the colour of the light bulbs. Like it had stained all the photos of us, covered them in something thick and dark and sticky, so that when you tried to prise them apart, they tore, ripping eyes and smiles and intertwined limbs from the memory.

I knew grief like I knew the dusty brown petals of decaying flowers. Like I knew the rancid smell of food rotting on the kitchen counter. White porcelain dishes dropped at our door by people I didn't recognise to say that there was nothing to say.

I knew grief like I knew why Mum took such long showers. Like the blurry shape of her through the keyhole of the door, slumped on the tiles, her shoulders convulsing under the stream of water that drowned out her cries.

I knew grief like I knew a single day could tear through the fabric of the universe, eviscerating the assumptions any of us dared to have about how life should unfold. Like I knew the gaping hole where logic and fairness and justice would ordinarily be. Like I knew how it felt for the world to break a promise—one, you realise, it never actually made.

Chapter 22

We sat in a booth against the tinted window, sweat pooling from our thighs onto the leather seats. I had almost finished my slightly warm, too-syrupy margarita, making the mistake of drinking it to quench my genuine thirst, downing it like a glass of water after a marathon.

Jen still had her hair and make-up done from her early-afternoon news slot. She'd left *The Daily* before I did to be a producer at a TV network, and was eventually promoted to a job presenting the weather, then the news. Now, she was a well-known face with her own Wikipedia page.

'It's not that bad,' she said when I showed her the comments under Cara Wong's post. 'But you can't give it any more oxygen. They'll tire themselves out. They always do.'

I was frenzied, my nervous system still attached to the relentless updates we'd been publishing all day.

'Everyone thinks I'm a sociopath who went rogue and published private photos of a woman who was murdered,' I whispered. I was paranoid that an internet sleuth might be seated at the table behind us, recording me, ready to share whatever I said with the masses. I kept tapping my phone, too, to check I wasn't unknowingly live-streaming or calling someone. It had never happened, but I figured if I was ever going to be the victim of a freak technical accident, it would be now. 'But those photos were everywhere! Everyone used them. They don't understand how media works. Hundreds of years from now, my descendants could read all this stuff about me and it's not true. History will remember me inaccurately.'

Jen almost spat out her drink.

'Okay, that is the most self-important bullshit I've ever heard. Honey, your descendants won't be googling you. They'll be too busy being burnt alive by an overheated planet or uploading their brains so they become immortal. No one cares about you, and that is both terrifying and liberating.'

'Isn't that all the more reason to stand up for myself then?' I said. 'Because no one really cares anyway? Shouldn't I be refuting the narrative? At least then I'd feel like I had some integrity.'

Jen reached for the laminated menu near the window. She scanned it and then glanced up at me.

'And what would that look like?'

'I respond to everything that's being said about me like a rational, normal person. I explain the interview, and Jo, and how the story was misrepresented. I say that while we're tearing apart women for sharing their complex personal stories about abortion—in the context of an abusive relationship, for fuck's sake!—we're *not* talking about the *actual* men with *actual* power who *actually* want to take away women's reproductive rights.'

Jen nodded. 'Or John Cook, who hosts his own show and rambles about how women should be punished for having abortions.'

'Exactly! Felicity doesn't go after John. Somehow it's far more important to attack a woman who literally shares your values but might express them in a slightly different way. So I'd say that, and then I'd explain why we used the photos of Lucy Wong. I'd say that reporting on domestic violence is important for raising awareness, that we care about telling her story and honouring her life, that all media used those photos, but we took them down once we knew the family was distressed.'

I could hear how it sounded as soon as it came out of my mouth.

'I don't think the family cares about you raising awareness or honouring her life,' Jen said, looking over my shoulder. 'That would come across as really disingenuous.'

She was distracted by a group that had just walked in the door. I turned around and recognised them immediately. They all worked at *The Daily*, some when I had been there and some who started after I left. They had probably been working late covering the Lucy Wong story, hunched over desks that had a view of St Mary's Cathedral or the Sydney Harbour Bridge or the Sydney Opera House, depending on where you sat. On Fridays, an assistant pushed a fully stocked bar cart around the office, delivering wine and champagne and beer and snacks to the staff while they filed the last of their copy. I missed it. I had loved finishing the last hours of my week slightly tipsy, knowing that we'd be drinking well into the night, making each other laugh in the way only co-workers who share a toxic work environment can.

But now I felt embarrassed at the thought of them seeing me. Felicity's article had been on the homepage of the publication they all worked for, and people who worked in media were the ones most invested in these stories. They lived in the muckiness of comments sections and snarky videos, of call-outs and pile-ons and online slinging matches.

Jen turned back to the menu.

'I'm getting a burger. You want food?'

That was one of the reasons I loved her. She was hungry, in every sense of the word.

She had sauce on her chin when we got back to the subject of my online apology.

'So how would you do it?' she asked. 'Like a piece to camera? Clearly reading something out of a notebook, like an absolute wanker?'

'Or just posting something in writing,' I said. I was on my third margarita, and the more I drank, the more certain I was that I had to act. It was absurd for me to stay silent, watching while strangers took handfuls of incomplete information and built a sculpture with it, an effigy of me to burn for a cheering crowd.

'If you do a notes app apology I'll never look you in the eye again,' Jen said. 'You don't need to be out here making statements. You are not a Hollywood celebrity getting a divorce.'

I nodded.

Our conversation moved to the guy Jen had been seeing, who looked like a young Leonardo DiCaprio but kept telling her stories that sounded just a little bit made up. His inconsequential web of lies was funny, but I was distracted.

Jen didn't know that the comment about grief had crawled under my skin, and she wouldn't have understood why. Apart from my family, very few people in my life knew what had happened when I was thirteen. The only person I'd told in recent years was Jamie, and even that was agonising. It had come out one night in the dark, when I couldn't see the look of pity I knew would creep across his face.

Our glasses were empty, and Jen hit both her palms against the table decisively, as she always did before she stood up.

'I'm off,' she said. 'Message me before you post anything acknowledging the social media shit. You know I used to get death threats about the weather, yeah? You know I was personally blamed for rain?'

Once she was gone, I reached for my phone, which was bursting with neglected notifications. The pull of it was overpowering. I allowed myself to scroll through them, hoping that being in a room full of people while I witnessed my own character assassination would make it hurt less.

I was tagged in hundreds more comments from the original post, most of them mocking my apology. There was glee in their responses, like I had given them a shiny new toy to play with—one they could kick and throw in order to bond with each other. There were in-jokes already, something about how women like me were known for how we made everything about ourselves.

> Just waiting for the op-ed: 'How the death of a woman I've never met is actually about me'.
>
> HAHAHA stop I'm dying, I genuinely wouldn't be surprised by that headline at this point.
>
> She probably wishes the family would shut up so she could get some more airtime.

I had never said that. But apparently I had used the word 'I' too many times in my apology and that was pretty much the same. I was centring myself. *But how do you expect me to apologise for something you want me to take sole responsibility for without speaking in first person?* I wanted to ask.

My inbox, too, was marked by a characteristic red bubble, the dopamine-inducing symbol of unread messages. After so many years of associating that signal with the excitement of the great unknown, my brain hadn't yet recalibrated. Of course, it now meant there were insults screaming for my attention. A normal person would run. An indoctrinated person, a sick person, needed to look. I clicked.

> journos are scum ur fkn disgusting
>
> i hope the family sues you for breaching their privacy
>
> how do u sleep at night i hope ur haunted by nightmares of lucy's bloodied body. u didn't even wait until her body was cold to trawl through her photos.

There was something almost violent about being the target of people's outrage just hours after a woman had been murdered in broad daylight. Like their anger had turned in the wrong direction, and the anger that should be aimed at a crazed, knife-wielding man was now directed at me.

One of the messages was a voice note, and I tentatively held the bottom of my phone to my ear to listen to it. I was surprised to find the person wasn't yelling. They were hissing.

'*Hey, bitch, just wondering what is actually wrong with you. I am sickened, genuinely disgusted, a family is grieving and all you care about is exploiting them so people will click on your shitty website. You are a cunt and I can't believe you have no empathy for a young woman who has lost her life—shame on you.'*

I instinctively pulled the phone away, shutting off the eerie callousness of a voice that sounded like it belonged to a woman in her forties. I was stunned by the vitriol injected into every word, so that her message came out as menacing. Threatening. I tried to imagine where she had been when she decided to record herself and send it to me. Was she alone? Was a friend watching? Had they laughed afterwards, proud to have spoken somewhat directly to this person they hated, this person who deserved to be called a bitch and a cunt in order to restore an ambiguous moral order?

Suddenly, the bar seemed very loud and very hot. I was aware that I was by myself and realised how conspicuous that was, sitting in a four-seater booth on my phone while everyone around me, gathered in tight groups, was laughing and shouting and drinking. It reminded me of the sharp, adolescent pain of being conspicuous in your aloneness, wanting more than anything to disappear into the crowd.

Chapter 23

For my first few months of high school, I didn't have a single friend. It's humiliating to admit now, as an adult, because you picture a friendless thirteen-year-old as someone who was fundamentally weird, intrinsically annoying. Maybe I was those things. Maybe I still am.

There was only one other girl from my local primary school who went to my private high school, and her name was Loretta Neilsen. She had honey blonde hair that snaked down her back in a thick plait with a white, silk bow at the end. She was one of the best long-distance runners in the state, and I remember watching her receive a trophy at assembly, her lean, bronzed legs glowing against the pale blue checks of our uniform. We had all seen her in the cereal ad on TV, playing the adorable daughter of a beloved Olympian. The ad was meant to be funny, something about the very accomplished professional swimmer still being a quintessentially dopey dad, but when it came on during an ad break, all I could think about was Loretta's face. Her sea-green eyes sparkling under a row of dark eyelashes, her doll-like lips curving into a warm, endearing smile. Back then we were amazed that the same person could exist both inside our television *and* in the playground.

I didn't have a lot to do with Loretta in primary school. I wasn't sporty, so she had her group of friends and I had mine. But then I started high school, and my friends were gone—all at the local public school together, walking distance from their houses. My nana paid for Liv and me to go to St Margaret's, a few suburbs over, because Mum and my aunties had gone there. My parents had been against it, having hushed arguments with Nana over the phone. It wasn't until the first day that I understood why.

As I walked through the school gates, I noticed everyone's shoes. They were exactly the same: black, leather Colorado boat shoes, with chunky soles. I looked down at my own, bought on sale from a shop that had 'Less' in its name. I hadn't cared when I'd tried them on with Mum, but now I was appalled by how childish they seemed, how ugly. Why did everyone else know what school shoes to wear? And why didn't I have them?

'Because they're a hundred dollars,' Mum told me when I asked her. 'And that's a ridiculous amount of money for shoes you're going to grow out of in a couple of months.'

It felt like the only thing money should ever be used for: to buy whatever it was that might allow you to blend in, to be invisible.

At the swimming carnival a few weeks into the term, I was the only girl in a no-brand swimsuit. My runners, too, were noticeably different, an awkward shape with one extra stripe that loudly announced their wrongness.

Loretta owned the right shoes, the right swimsuit, the right pencil case, the right lunch box. She had the right number of piercings dotted along each ear, the right tiny diamond studs to fill them. It's almost impressive how teenage girls manage to invent so many markers of status in an environment designed to strip them away. I studied those markers like variables in an equation, observing how they interacted with each other, how having fleshy, intact earlobes might be fine if there were highlights in your hair, how a hand-me-down schoolbag might be counterbalanced by a pretty face. But no matter how I did the calculations, my value stayed the same: hovering dangerously close to zero.

Throughout that first term, I felt like I was an insect trapped inside an upside-down glass. I would find myself on the outskirts of conversations about skiing and European summers and holiday houses, and try to scratch my way into them. Sometimes, when girls were talking about a band I knew or a TV show I'd watched, I'd rehearse a story or a comment about it in my head, but when I opened my mouth to say it out loud, it seemed so pointless I closed it again.

I also wasn't smart anymore. In primary school, I'd been at the top of my class. I kept a record of every book I read in a tattered, gold-edged journal, and I read everything from fantasy fiction to science to history. But at St Margaret's, I was suddenly average. I didn't realise that the test we'd taken on open day would determine the class level we were assigned in year seven. They were graded A to F, and I was in C for everything except English, where I was in B. Even in those classes, I was entirely unexceptional. It didn't matter if Loretta wasn't in the top classes, because she had athletics. She had her TV ad, and now she was modelling clothes in a catalogue for a department store. But if I wasn't clever, who was I meant to be?

At lunch, the quad looked like a field of perfectly manicured crop circles. Neat rings of girls sitting in groups of six or eight or ten, spaced out evenly with no gaps. Already, the boundaries of the groups were so rigid. A lot of the girls had been friends from primary school or, in Loretta's case, knew each other through sport. Dotted around them were those of us who had no place to be, who wanted lunchtime to be over so at least we could be assigned a seat in a classroom.

I wanted to be part of a group so desperately. To have people to talk to about my day, to validate my existence. I'd had Liv, then I'd had my friends in primary school, and now I was alone. At home one afternoon, Mum said she'd run into Loretta's mum in Coles and told her I was struggling to find a group of friends. I was mortified. I swore never to tell her anything ever again, because she clearly had no understanding of privacy. The thought of Loretta's family knowing I was a loner made me sick. Her fit, smiley dad. Her hot older brother.

'She said you should just sit with Loretta, she'd love to include you,' Mum said. 'She's really enjoying St Margaret's, says everyone's friends with everyone.'

So that's where the idea came from.

I thought about it for days, rehearsing exactly what I'd say and how I'd say it. I even practised it out loud in my room, trying to make my voice sound relaxed, casual. I spent the whole maths lesson before lunch picturing my life a week from now—walking arm in arm with Loretta down the halls, giggling, wondering why on earth it had taken us so long to discover we were actually destined to be best friends.

When the lunch bell rang, I packed up my books and felt a surge of adrenaline. This was it. School would be different from now on. I'd finally feel like a teenager, having sleepovers with my friends and sharing secrets and trying on each other's clothes.

I walked over to the corner of the quad where Loretta was sitting with half-a-dozen other girls. They didn't look up as I approached, all enthralled in a story Loretta was telling, slowly opening their lunch boxes while she spoke. I hovered just far enough away that my presence might go unnoticed. I didn't know what to do with my arms, hanging heavily on either side of my body. When another girl started speaking, and Loretta's attention was briefly available, I tapped her on the shoulder.

'Hey,' I said. It came out as a whisper, which I hadn't planned. I peeled my bag off my shoulder so this would all look spontaneous, as though I'd just thought of it as I'd been walking past. 'Do you guys mind if I sit with you?'

Loretta gave me a puzzled look, like she had no idea who I was. The girl next to her—Kim—pursed her lips in a smile, and I could've sworn she glanced down at my shoes.

'Ruby?' Loretta said finally.

For a moment I thought she was just surprised. Maybe she had forgotten I was here at St Margaret's, even though we caught the same bus. She was usually so busy with her friends, she might not have noticed me.

'Why on earth would you sit with us?'

Kim's laugh came out like a choke. She covered her mouth to try to stop it, but the other girls were looking now, wondering what was funny.

I was whispering again, my voice quivering. 'I just thought because I don't know anyone, but, like, I know you from school. Before.'

It felt so pathetic. Standing there with my unisex school shoes, my bulky retainer that gave me a lisp, my painful cluster of forehead pimples that got worse when I squeezed them.

'But you don't know me,' Loretta said, frowning. 'You can't just assume we'll be friends because we went to the same primary school. That's so . . .'

'Weird?'

Kim said the word like it was the most shameful thing in the world.

I stood there silently, so overcome with humiliation that I didn't know what I was supposed to do. They all stared at me with blank faces. Maybe I was waiting for someone to stand up for me, or for Loretta to break and admit she was joking.

'Kim was about to tell us something kind of private,' Loretta said, glancing around at the group. 'She can't have just anyone sitting here. So.'

I was still frozen in place, a heavy statue, as though if I waited long enough time would reverse itself. I must've looked strange. Aggressive almost, like I was refusing to move.

'Go,' Loretta said, so sharply that I jumped.

I started walking before I could decide which direction to head in, and so I ended up marching towards the fence, where the quad ended and the harbour began. I had to clumsily change direction, sensing their laughter sinking into my skin, my messy hair, the fibres of my baggy uniform.

That's when I started fantasising about becoming someone else. At night, I invented a different version of myself and dreamt up a life for her. She had a prettier name and she lived in a bigger house. She was a swan-like netball player, a lean, striking blonde who did casual modelling on the weekends. She was smart, too. The teachers all recognised her brilliance, marvelling at how one person could be so talented. She was the type of girl you paid attention to.

That's who I was trying to become when the accident happened. If I'm really honest with myself, that's *why* the accident happened.

One psychologist told me that when you experience trauma in childhood or adolescence, you can become emotionally stuck at the age it occurred. I was an adult then, and I guess he was trying to tell me I had the maturity of a teenager. I wasn't offended. I didn't care about his theories, because I knew he couldn't help. I was only there because my partner at the time had made me promise to go.

In that session, this bearded, middle-aged man with too many certificates on the wall behind him gestured to an empty chair, and encouraged me to picture my year seven self sitting on it. An awkward, blotchy-faced Ruby, a few months older than the one who had that exchange with Loretta. Whose world had been torn apart in an instant.

He wanted me to speak to her. To show her compassion. To accept that she was only a child, and none of it had been her fault.

Eventually, so that the session would end, I self-consciously angled myself towards the empty chair. For a moment I did see myself: a wiry teenager, eyebrows unfamiliar with wax, and deep-set eyes not yet introduced to make-up. I looked back at the psychologist and mumbled that I forgave her.

Both of us knew it was a lie.

Chapter 24

It took all my self-control not to engage with the comment about grief. Not in the Uber taking me home. Not as I unlocked the front door, my eyes magnetically attached to my screen. Not as I studied it under the doona while Jamie snored beside me, becoming angrier and angrier the more times I read it.

> you clearly don't know the first fucking thing about grief

It was so presumptive, so naive, that I wanted to print it out, blow it up and demand that it be stared at. Examined as a sign of how the internet makes us hysterical, how it dehumanises us. How it begs us to mock and maim, to ruin people whose destruction is utterly purposeless.

I didn't engage with it in all the hours I spent scrolling that night. Now that the alcohol had worn off, I was consumed again by my phone. It was a vortex, and once I was sucked in I couldn't escape.

I came across one message that made me stiffen.

> i seen u walking to ur apartment in bondi lol watch ur back

My eyes darted to the window beside me, the curtains drawn, obscuring the street from view. I imagined a man in a trench coat standing in the middle of the road, staring at the apartment he knew was mine. Had I locked the front door? Was there a way for someone to break in, to get through the entrance door downstairs and then climb up to the second floor, jamming something in our keyhole until it sprung open? Could someone reasonably scale the side of our building and get in through the balcony?

I couldn't breathe. For several minutes, every creak was a footstep, every gust of wind was a man disturbing the air, appearing in my doorway and then launching himself at me as I lay still, powerless to stop him.

The only way to get the irrational, spiralling thoughts out of my mind was to read more messages, ones that would ground me in a less disturbing version of reality. Personal insults were a welcome distraction, so I opened my email inbox, which was littered with them, too.

Of course, there were people who were still only just stumbling across Felicity's video, entirely unaware there was a second controversy. Sometimes it took me a moment to understand which one of my public offences they were referring to, and a lot of the time I couldn't tell.

> What a toxic disgrace you are.

> How you still have a job astounds me. Do the decent thing and disappear. You have inflicted so much pain and done so much damage. Listen to the people who are telling you to STOP.

> You are everything that's wrong with feminism. White. Rich. Entitled. Privileged. And completely fucking tone deaf.

Once the terror of a potential intruder passed, and I convinced myself that he was just a sad person sitting in his mother's basement with a stock-standard message he sent to women on the internet, it was the comment on grief I kept circling back to. I couldn't stop fighting in my head with the man who wrote it. A man who was probably sleeping peacefully, ignorant as to how his attempt to advocate for empathy had been entirely devoid of it.

I put my phone down and pleaded for quiet. For the voices inside it to stay trapped behind the glass. For my thoughts, too, to stop.

And yet, just as I was slipping into sleep, my rage would shake me awake. The faceless man was pressing his lips to my ear, taunting me, baiting me. It was so loud, so unrelenting, and yet if I had woken Jamie, he would've only heard the tinny sound of our cheap pedestal fan whirring in the corner.

No one standing in a crowded room with actual people, I argued into the darkness, would be so bold as to approach a complete stranger and tell them they knew nothing about grief. To do so would be absurd. It contravened the very essence of what it meant to be human, what it meant to be part of a species cursed with not only the inevitability of death but also a brain sophisticated enough to comprehend it; the finality of it, the tragedy of it, the injustice of it.

Surely, I thought, it takes only the most basic degree of empathy to understand that all of us—even the people we disagree with or despise—know something of pain. That the breath leaving a set of lungs, the heart pumping its last beat, the brain sending its final signal before going permanently quiet is the great equaliser.

What are you doing? I wanted to yell at this man. *Do you not see what you have lost? That you are unable to fathom the inherent complexity, the innate vulnerability, of another person?*

I was bursting with responses, but the more I argued with the invisible man in my head, the more certain I was that there was no use replying to any of it. To me, it all felt connected, but from the outside it wasn't. I had simply published a terrible, harmful story, and then made another terrible, harmful editorial decision, probably because, as far as common denominators go, I was a terrible, harmful person.

And now, my inexperience with grief would remain unchallenged in that comment thread. Just one of many lies about me that I had to find a way to live with.

• • •

I woke from a nightmare drenched in sweat, my cotton t-shirt clinging to my chest. I hadn't had a nightmare in years. It was very early in the morning, and I could sense the loneliness of stray cars on the road, the quiet of the apartment upstairs, the steady rise and fall of Jamie's breathing. Every inhale sounded like a slow, rattling engine, and yet he remained deaf to it, wrapped in the armour of deep sleep.

I tried to push the images away. The nightmare had let them trickle in, like a stream I couldn't block, rapidly filling the space around me and threatening to pull me under. I thought I had mastered the art of burying them. For a long time they had come uninvited at night—harrowing and vivid and painful—and when they did, they tended to stay until dawn. My phone usually helped. It allowed me to be somewhere other than my own mind while I lay sleepless, and by the time I put it down, I was so exhausted that I sank into sleep, with no room for the past.

But on this night, the night I was haunted by the comment about grief, the night of the bad dream, the images started to appear in my mind's eye.

I saw the coffin. Dark wood, tapered edges.

The white roses. Bunches of them tied to the pews, a wreath on the altar, in front of the pulpit. The stapled booklet. Prayers inside, readings, words that were meant to make sense of a thing that would never make sense. I remember wondering who had organised the casket and the flowers and the service. I knew my parents, gaunt, haunted, had not been capable of it.

I saw the school uniforms, freshly ironed, worn by kids who stood with their heads down, too scared to look up at their red-eyed mothers and fathers.

I tried to replace the images with blackness. Nothingness. To pour a pot of thick ink over them, to drown them. But then I watched the ink coagulate and now it was blood, pooling around our feet.

That moment. That scene. The one I never wanted to return to. The split second in which it had struck me that something was deeply, irreparably wrong.

I knew that once the memories returned, I wouldn't be able to stop them. That's why I worked so hard to stay busy, to immerse myself in layers and layers of distraction.

But the hate, the shame, had struck the precise spot of my wound. While they were telling me I was Wrong, I was Bad, that I had done A Terrible Thing, The Worst Thing, I knew what they didn't.

That the worst thing I'd ever done happened when I was thirteen, and it wasn't defined by the anger of strangers, but by a single, sickening scream.

Chapter 25

I had completely forgotten about Mum's birthday. Liv called on Saturday morning, asking if I wanted to go halves in a pair of statement earrings as a gift. Real gold, embellished with multicoloured crystals, tassels on the bottom. 'Hideous,' she said. 'She'll love them.'

I was still in bed and couldn't imagine summoning the energy to drive over the bridge. The lunch at Mum and Dad's place had been organised in one of the too-many family group chats, and now I regretted ever agreeing to it.

'I'm a mess,' I told her. I had her on speaker while I refreshed my apps, the red bubble inevitably appearing with every swipe. More comments, more messages, more people discovering Cara Wong's post and responding to it. There was a sick part of me that was almost curious about how much I could withstand. How many people had to call you a cunt before you fell entirely to pieces? Before you threw up your hands, walked away from it all and joined a commune?

Ian had responded to my calls late last night, texting to say that while it was the right call to take down the photos immediately, my apology was inappropriate.

> I thought I made it clear that you cannot, under any circumstances, comment publicly to criticisms of *Bared* right now? Those responses need to be carefully considered and run past several stakeholders at Simmons Corp. To be totally transparent with you, the brand looks juvenile. Will discuss further on Monday.

It was the most strongly worded message I'd ever received from him.

'I think I just need to be at home today,' I said. I could hear the familiar echoes of Westfield through the phone. Muffled music and chatty shoppers, Liv's impatient huffing as she scanned the jewellery display cases for something for herself. 'I'm too sensitive for Mum and Dad's. Can we just sing "Happy Birthday" to Mum over FaceTime and go over for lunch next week?'

A notification sprung up beneath my finger, and I clicked it.

I reacted to her name the way you react to seeing a spider on the wall.

My hands, clutching either side of my phone, were shaking. I could see nothing beyond the four metal edges of my phone, the brightness of the screen swallowing the rest of the dim, sleepy room.

It was a series of images, starting with a screenshot of the *Bared* homepage. I flicked through a screenshot of Cara Wong's post, a screenshot of my response, then several walls of white-on-black text. Here, in one place, Felicity Cartwright had distilled the sickness of what I'd done using the kind of intellectual, persuasive language she was famous for. I'd co-opted a tragedy for financial gain and been patently unable to listen respectfully when I was called out for it by a grieving relative. I was a media pariah, a transparently fake feminist, a parasite trying to attach myself to the national conversation around domestic violence.

Liv's voice was responding to me as I read Felicity's words.

'We're going. Seriously stop being so self-indulgent, it's getting really annoying.'

> It is so clear that Ruby Williams does not care about women. She doesn't even take the wishes of a dead woman's family seriously.

'You're worried about, like, three cranky people on the internet and you need to learn to ignore them.'

> She is the manifestation of white privilege. Entirely unable to see a perspective beyond her own. The lack of empathy is astounding.

'I honestly can't remember the last time we were both at Mum and Dad's, and I feel bad because I think they get really lonely.'

> How many times do we allow the same people to fuck up? What will it take for Ruby Williams' incompetence to be taken seriously?

'Anyway, can you get a cake on the way? And a card? And you owe me sixty-two dollars.'

> This is, frankly, exhausting.

My skin was crawling with unwanted adrenaline. I didn't know where to begin. My instinct was to climb back under the doona, to cover my face with it and block out all the light. To wake up again in a different life, one in which I had never chosen this career. In which I had never agreed for my mistakes and my miscommunications and my misjudgements to be in the public domain, rummaged through by people whose work days were full of failings, too, but failings they were allowed to quietly rectify in private.

'Is that a yes? Are we all good?' Liv said flatly.

I needed to be anywhere but here.

'Yes, fine. I'll see you at Mum and Dad's. Bye.'

Comments dropped under the post, like heavy stones sinking to the bottom of the ocean.

That woman is a fuckin cockroach.

Makes me sick.

I assume she won't engage with this because she's incapable of caring about anyone other than herself.

I fought the urge to throw my phone across the room, to let the glass shatter and the metal crack and the world inside it bleed out. *Why,* I thought, *would I be reading this on a Saturday morning if I didn't care? Why would I still be buried in my knotted sheets, stewing in the mustiness of my airless bedroom, tasting the bitterness of my furry, unbrushed teeth, if I was the monster they all thought I was?*

I squeezed my eyes shut, breathing in the sourness of the grey cotton shirt I'd worn to bed. This was not real. Felicity was not real. The version of me they were destroying was not real.

I dragged myself into the shower, scrubbing the filth of my nightmares from my pores. I would go to Mum and Dad's, and the infestation inside my phone would die from neglect.

But as I blow-dried my hair, pulled on a light, linen dress and went to buy Mum a cake, a thought nagged at me. If it was an effigy of me they were burning, an invented avatar, why did their image of me feel like a mirror? Why did a part of me fear that somehow, despite everything they had got wrong, they had managed to unearth the truth?

Chapter 26

When people ask me how many siblings I have, I never know how to answer. 'I have a sister,' I usually say, before telling them a quirky anecdote about Liv. She was once arrested for being a public nuisance. She put a tampon in and forgot about it for four days. She has a pet rabbit and walks him on a leash. That sort of thing. It gets the conversation moving, and no one ever circles back to the original question. To the part where 'I have a sister' is only half the answer. To the part where, if I was being entirely honest, I'd add: 'and I had a brother.'

His name was Max, but we called him Macky. As a two-year-old, he couldn't pronounce the 'ex' sound, referring to himself as Mack, so we did, too. He had a giggle that sounded like no one else's, more like a trill than a laugh. Liv and I would pretend to bite his feet and his thighs and his arms, and he would fling his head back in delight, making that distinctive noise. We would read him books in the morning while Mum was showering or making us breakfast, taking it in turns to put on silly voices. He'd listen in awe, staring at the pages in a trance, until he looked up to find one of our faces beaming back at him. His smile seemed to swallow his whole face. His eyes would disappear, his nose would crinkle, and he'd expose a row of tiny, white baby teeth, his gums pink and glistening in the wide spaces between them.

He never lost a baby tooth. That's how little he was when it happened.

I try to bury it, but that period of my life comes back to me in flashes, in uninvited images, in a haunting sense of shame, especially when I'm weak, when I'm vulnerable. It's like a demon who possesses you because it knows you don't have the strength to fight it. The pain inhabits my mind and my body and my soul, sometimes for days or weeks on end, cloaking my waking hours. Underneath it all is a voice, one that feels evil and foreign but is actually my own, that says: *It was your fault.*

Chapter 27

About halfway through year seven, I became friends with Kelsey.

We'd been paired together in science, sitting beside each other on two stools behind the blue-grey lab bench. For the first few lessons we had hardly spoken, just following instructions from the softly spoken teacher who insisted we learn how to label the parts of a laboratory accurately before we were allowed to touch anything. It was only then that we were allowed the privilege of examining a piece of hair under a microscope.

The hair was mine. Whoever had the finest hair had to break off a strand and place it on the slide. Kelsey's was the shade and texture of straw, so there was no question about whose hair would be sacrificed—I snapped a straight, mousy-brown piece and held it awkwardly between my fingers.

'Hair, please,' Kelsey said, a smirk on her face. She seemed to appreciate that I hadn't even asked whose hair we should use. There were other girls who might've tried to pull hers just to see how much it hurt, or joked that it wouldn't fit on the glass slide. But I thought Kelsey's hair was beautiful, bunched on top of her head in a messy bun like one of the carefree senior students.

She squinted through the eyepiece and adjusted the knob.
'Oh my God,' she said, recoiling.
'What?'

A part of me was certain she would be able to spot my weirdness, my wrongness, through the lens. Perhaps my hair was encrusted in a layer of filth, clearly visible when examined up close.

She was looking again, covering her mouth with one of her hands. With the other, she appeared to be zooming in. I was impressed by how confident she seemed with the microscope, given that I hadn't really been listening when our teacher explained how to use it.

Kelsey turned to me and, after first glancing behind us to check if anyone else was listening, whispered, 'I think you have nits.'

A surge of heat made its way up my body. She'd tell everyone, I knew. They'd need to disinfect the classroom. She was probably feeling itchy already just from touching an infected part of me, from making the mistake of thinking for a brief second that I was normal.

'I . . . I have a little brother, he's in day care, so maybe . . .'

Her expression broke and she gave a loud, warm cackle. She threw her head back and when she looked at me again, she was wiping tears from under her eyes.

'You should've seen your face,' she said, gasping for air. 'You were so scared. I have no idea how to use this thing, we haven't even turned on the light so literally all I can see is black. Were you listening when she told us what to do?'

The relief was like submerging my hot face in the cool ocean, the heat fizzling out immediately. From then on, Kelsey and I talked nonstop in science, about Max and our parents and her older sister who insisted Mrs Ryan always smelt like fish. After class one day, she casually asked me if I wanted to sit with her group at lunch, and suddenly I had six friends. It wasn't long before I was spending my weekends with them, on MSN or watching DVDs or going to the movies or ice-skating.

Ice-skating. That's what I'd been upset about on that Thursday during the school holidays. The day of the accident.

There was a rink at the local shopping centre where girls would hire slightly damp boots with scrunched up twenty-dollar notes from their parents, their ponytails swinging behind them as their blades left tracks in the ice.

They'd all been ice-skating since primary school. I'd only been twice, and spent both times clutching the side of the rink until my knuckles went white, terrified to let go in case I fell.

I had a recurring image in my head of slipping backward and having another skater run over my fingers, severing them, as I tried to get up.

The last time, Kelsey had invited two older boys to meet us after our parents dropped us off, and one of them was Marcus. He had deep brown eyes and a side-swept dark fringe, and he made me feel something in the pit of my stomach I'd never felt before. It was a mixture of sickness and excitement, of fear and desire. He wore tight black jeans that sat low on his narrow hips, with a bulky keychain poking out of a tiny pocket. He asked me my name when we were tying our boots.

I so badly wanted to become a different person when I stepped onto the ice. To stand tall and glide effortlessly like the others. For a moment, I thought I might. I took a few small steps, lifting one foot, then the other, but then I lost my balance, and a bolt of panic shot through my body. I didn't fall, but I had been close, and now my knees were locked, my arms frozen to my sides. I made my way to the edge of the ice by myself, wrapping my hands around the barrier and stayed there, unsteady and alone, surrounded by hard, unforgiving ice.

For the rest of the hour, everyone else skated together in a row, linking arms and building up speed so that when the person on the end let go, they went flying. A few of them checked on me, tried to pull me into the middle. Marcus went to take my hand but I jerked it away from him, knowing how sweaty it was, knowing it would expose my fundamental, ugly awkwardness.

Afterwards, I couldn't stop replaying it all in my head. The floating laughter of the rest of the group. The way they looked over at me and then whispered to each other, probably asking, *What's wrong with her?* I finally had friends and still I was like this, clutching the side like a praying mantis, hunched and skinny and weak.

On that Thursday, I wanted Mum to take me to the rink so I could practise alone. I needed to teach myself how to navigate the ice at my own pace, without my friends watching, taking small strides with my skates while knowing I could return to the edge when I needed to. That way, the next time I went, I'd be normal. Capable. Not a girl whose caution, whose anxiety, was just another sign I didn't belong.

Mum said no. It was too expensive, she told me. She had Macky at home, and housework to do, and we'd hardly sat still since the holidays started. Liv was at a party, so she couldn't bolster my argument, which I usually relied on her to do. She could convince Mum of anything. She would wear her down until Mum gave in, angry but too exasperated to shout. I didn't have that skill. When Mum said no to the ice-skating, I slammed my bedroom door, and then held my breath while I waited to see if she was going to come after me. Mum's discipline was scary because it was quiet. Her face would go red and she'd hiss, and you immediately wanted to take back whatever you'd done to make her look at you like that.

She didn't follow me.

It didn't take long for me to sheepishly creep back down the hall, hungry and bored. I went to the family computer and logged on to MSN, hoping that if I asked about ice-skating again in an hour, Mum might've changed her mind. Liv and Dad would be back then, so Dad could mind Max while the girls went to the rink. I wondered if Mum would let us have hot chips after. They always tasted better in the crisp, cold air, burning your tongue so that when you blew out there was a cloud of steam.

Not many people were online at this time. After dinner was MSN peak hour, where the bottom corner of your screen housed a constant stream of notifications.

Phoebe has just signed in.

Mike has just signed in.

Riley has just signed in.

Sometimes I waited all day for that feeling—the adrenaline of endless possibilities.

That afternoon, a couple of people from school were active, and I set my playlist to Avril Lavigne while I casually asked a girl from my homeroom, *hiii how r u?*

Our computer desk was pushed up against a wall near the kitchen, private enough that no one could see what you were typing unless they were hovering intentionally. It was timber, with a slide-out keyboard tray and a bottom shelf for the hot, humming beige tower that seemed to operate like a brain.

Beside me, with his back to the timber shutters, Max was playing with his racing-car mat. It had dark grey lanes and he pushed his toy trucks along them, every now and then abandoning the confines of the track altogether and launching the trucks across the floor. One hit me in the ankle and I shouted at him.

'Stop it, Macky! Play with your stupid cars somewhere else.'

I picked up the offending toy and put it on the desk beside me, which made him whine.

'Twuck! I want twuck.'

Mum appeared from the laundry, her top lip damp with perspiration even though it was cold and grey outside, the rain tapping softly on the windows. A strong breeze was flowing in from the side door attached to the kitchen, and I thought of asking her to shut it, but decided not to. I needed her to be in a good mood for when I broached the topic of ice-skating again.

'Can you please keep an eye on him?' she asked. 'I'm trying to sort the washing. And I can't find your netball skirt.'

I had a flash of the pile of clothes I'd stuffed under my bed when Mum told me to clean my room. I'd have to find a way to sneak them into the machine without her noticing where they came from.

'I'll find it. And I'll watch Macky. He just needs to stop being annoying.'

'He's not annoying,' Mum called over her shoulder as she returned to the laundry. 'He's two. Anyway, keep an eye on him. I've got a surprise for everyone later.'

Oh my God, I thought. *She's going to take us ice-skating.* I wondered if she would hire a pair of boots, too, and hold my hand while I tried to go further and further without needing to cling on to the edge.

I don't know if that was her plan, though. Because, of course, I never found out what the surprise was.

Chapter 28

Dad was painting the front gate when we arrived.

It was a narrow, wrought-iron gate built into the brick fence, separating the front yard from the street. The pavement beneath it was covered in several haphazard layers of newspaper. As we got closer, I noticed that drops of paint had seeped between the sheets of newspaper and onto the concrete. Mum would be furious.

'Hey, Dave,' Jamie said, as though this scene were the most normal thing in the world. 'Gate needed painting?'

Dad always seemed genuinely shocked when visitors arrived, like he'd been interrupted in the middle of his workday by people he wasn't expecting. Except that he was retired, and it was the weekend, and it was his wife's birthday, and we were his family.

I found it hard to look at Dad. While others might've seen a small, leathery man being useful with his hands because he was no longer as useful with his head, I saw something else. His soul, like his skin, was weathered by grief. He had never found the words for it, and so it had consumed him, from the inside out.

Selfishly, I wished he had been okay. That he had somehow found a way to cope, to show us all that what remained was enough, even in light of what we'd lost. But instead he went somewhere else. A reality where a front gate needed to be painted on your wife's birthday, at the exact moment your daughters were arriving for lunch.

Mum called out to us from inside, and I realised I'd left her cake in the car. I'd tried to buy her one from a fancy Italian patisserie on the way, but when we got there I saw it had closed down, so I'd had to settle for a bland vanilla cake from the supermarket. It reminded me of the cakes Mum used to make us when we were kids—plain, store-bought ones frantically decorated with as many colourful lollies as she could find. One year, when I was six or seven, she must've bought dozens of packets of Smarties, because she stuck only the purple ones to the entire layer of icing. It was my favourite colour, and I thought it was the most impressive thing I'd ever seen. So today, I'd done the same for her with yellow Smarties. It was lazy but thoughtful, which was the sentiment she appreciated the most.

I crossed the street to get the cake from the back seat. It was probably slightly melted now, the icing all soft and goopy. I unlocked the car and retrieved the cake—thankfully intact—and locked the car again. From here, I could see the whole front of the house. The liver-coloured bricks. The asymmetrical brown-tiled roof. The front verandah with its thick pylons, and the small, weed-choked yard bisected by the weather-worn path.

To the left was a wide driveway, the silver Toyota Tarago long replaced by a smaller white Subaru. Mum and Dad didn't need a car classified as a 'people mover' anymore. The driveway sloped down the length of the house, and at its base was a small set of steps leading to the kitchen door. On the other side of the driveway, along the fence, the crimson bottlebrush was twisted and overgrown. It looked dry, and I could see dead branches that needed to be pruned.

I wondered if people who walked down our street, past our house, knew what had happened here. If people still talked about us, or if they had forgotten.

Chapter 29

I was rolling Max's toy truck back towards him when I heard the MSN notification. I still remember that sound, the three ascending notes, the way it felt unfinished, full of anticipation. I learnt later that it's known as an arpeggio, a flowing melodic line that's more engaging than a static chord. I wonder if that particular one was specifically designed to trigger something in the brain—a rush of chemicals, a pull to attend immediately to the pop-up that accompanied it. Or maybe that association was just a result of conditioning, of Friday nights spent pairing that sound with the dopamine hit of social interactions, until the sound alone made you salivate, like one of Pavlov's dogs.

I turned to the screen and saw a flashing orange rectangle in the grey taskbar.

« ¤ » m.a.r.c.u.s « ¤ »

His name alone gave me a rolling sensation in my stomach, almost like I needed to pee. I sat perfectly still for a moment, staring at the blinking letters. The sound echoed around me again, and this time, I caught the square box that slid up from the right-hand corner.

« ¤ » m.a.r.c.u.s « ¤ »
heyyyy it's u

We had never chatted online before. He had added me after we'd both been part of a group conversation so chaotic that everyone left, and I thought it was a mistake. I wouldn't have expected him to remember me from ice-skating. We'd only interacted briefly, and I hadn't let him hold my hand.

Max was now facing the side wall of the kitchen, rolling his trucks across the floor until they hit the skirting board. He ran towards them, gathered them in his chubby hands, and placed them back in line with the bench, from where he'd start to roll them again. The side door was still open, the wind rapping the thin shutters against the window frames.

I waited a few seconds to reply, so that Marcus would think I was in the midst of several conversations, barely noticing a message from a boy whose angular face I could see so clearly it was like he was standing beside me.

`·.,.·´¯`·._.· rubesss `·.,.·´¯`·._.·
hiii yes its me hehe

He responded immediately.

« ¤ » m.a.r.c.u.s « ¤ »
wot u up 2?

I needed Liv. We had spent countless hours side by side in front of the computer, constructing the perfect messages to boys we liked or girls we wanted to impress or friends who were being mean for no reason. The truth was, I did strange things when she wasn't there to help. Once, she got up to get a snack and by the time she returned I had greeted our hottest family friend with: 'howdy!' She was horrified.

But this was an opportunity. If I waited for her to get home, Marcus might not be online anymore. Or he might start chatting to someone else.

`·.,.·´¯`·._.· rubesss `·.,.·´¯`·._.·
nuthin much, u?

« ¤ » m.a.r.c.u.s « ¤ »
so bored lol

« ¤ » m.a.r.c.u.s « ¤ »
wanna play a game?

I actually hated the MSN games. I preferred *The Sims*. Still, if it meant talking to him, I was prepared to pretend.

I was about to ask him what he liked to play, which would've been humiliating in hindsight, when he messaged again.

« ▫ » m.a.r.c.u.s « ▫ »
like truth or dare but its just truth lol

I swallowed, and felt my cheeks burn.

I knew what he meant. Girls at school had talked about this, the sorts of questions boys asked them online, and what they expected you to say. They referred to 'bases', which I only vaguely understood because of fleeting references in American movies.

One lunchtime Kelsey had regaled our group with a story about a boy who made her describe her body and who had touched it and what they'd done, before asking: 'do u no wether u can fit a cukumba in ur pus?' The absurdity of it hit us as she slowly spelt out the letters, and Laura spat out her water when she worked out what he was referring to. I laughed for so long that the corners of my mouth started to sting, and Kelsey became hysterical, too, her face red and her eyes watering as she kept repeating, 'Cukumba? What's a cukumba?'

Over the years, the joke became so embedded in the folklore of our friendship group that when we graduated, the description under Kelsey's yearbook photo read: *Kelsey Dermott will always be remembered for her love of cukumba.*

It's only now that I can see why we clung to that story, why we whispered, 'Can u fit a cukumba in ur pus?' to each other during mass, why it was so important that we kept laughing. To laugh was to strip the question of its shame. To refuse to reduce our bodies to mere objects of male titillation. None of us said out loud that the question itself felt so pornographic, so degrading, that it seemed almost violent, this idea that a boy might be interested in whether the green vegetable in his kitchen could fit inside us. It was instinctively scary in a way we couldn't yet articulate, just a feeling that popped up sometimes, in response to certain jokes on TV, or looks from men on the street, or behaviour from guys at parties.

A spark of that fear was probably ignited by Marcus's message. By the fact that I didn't know what he was going to ask, and I didn't know how I was meant to answer. By the fact that navigating your heterosexuality as a thirteen-year-old girl involved walking an impossible line, a tightrope between self-consciousness and desire, fear and exhilaration.

But was there something else?

When I think back to that Thursday afternoon, my little brother launching his toy cars along the cork lino while an unrecognisable version of myself stared at Marcus's words, I can hear the alarm bells. Like I could sense a wrongness in the air.

But maybe that only came later. When the memory was encoded with the haunting stain of what happened next, and all the moments that preceded it became significant in ways they wouldn't have been otherwise.

Chapter 30

'Have you heard anything else from Felicity Cartwright, Mum?'

Liv was sitting opposite me at the glass-topped table in the backyard. She'd arrived after Jamie and me, and made a show of taking the gift from her bag and handing it to Mum. I made a mental note to ask her later if I still needed to transfer the money to her, given how obvious she made it that I had nothing to do with its purchase. The earrings really were hideous, and Mum adored them.

'No, no, Ruby did a thing where I can't see any of her posts now,' Mum said, bringing out a handful of cutlery from the kitchen. 'Which is probably for the best. I can't help myself. I'd love to run into her in person. Actually have a conversation face-to-face about what she thinks she's achieving.'

Jamie smirked at me when Mum dished out the chicken. It looked slimy, like she'd used too much oil, and there were worrying flecks of pinkness in the flesh. Her salad, too, seemed inexplicably wet. It only had lettuce and tomatoes and a tiny bit of feta, and she beamed when she placed it in the centre of the table. She'd found the recipe online, she said.

It felt silly for her to be cooking her own birthday lunch, but she'd insisted. Dad struggled to hear in restaurants or cafes, so family gatherings were now held at home, and even though Mum had hated cooking when we were growing up, she said she enjoyed it now. It allowed her to be creative. Except that we all wished she'd be less creative and actually follow instructions, particularly when they pertained to meat.

'Okay, everyone has to shut up and listen to my new business idea,' Liv said through a mouthful of bread. 'It's called Rent Furn.'

'I hate it already,' I said, reaching to unlock my screen. I'd been checking my phone every few minutes, watching the comments on Felicity's post multiply. Two other creators with significant followings had shared it now, adding their own snark. *What a cow*, one of them had written. *I hope she loses her job.*

'No, it's really smart,' Liv said.

We'd been coming up with business ideas since we were kids and spent a weekend accidentally selling one-dollar Freddo Frogs for two dollars. We'd been fundraising for netball, and on discovering our mistake we'd realised we were, by our measure, filthy rich. It was the most entrepreneurial either of us had ever been, and so it became a running joke that we were always trying to claw our way back to that moment of glory. Our ideas were always appalling—brilliant in our heads but full of holes once we explained them out loud. I still thought my idea of Uber but for clothes was quite clever, with drivers going to shopping centres and delivering shoes and dresses and jewellery within the hour. Liv said there was no way it could make a profit. We'd gone back and forth over canned cocktails in her backyard one Friday night, Liv hammering me with questions about delivery fees and returns and why this elusive customer couldn't just order their clothes online and wait a few days for shipping. I'd ended up with hiccups from laughing and drinking, explaining that sometimes you have a wedding at noon and urgently need an outfit you forgot to buy. You'd pay anything, I insisted, and that's how the business traps you.

'So you know how there are more renters than ever because our economy is broken?' she went on now. 'Well, those renters need furniture. And when I was moving last time, I was like: wait. I genuinely don't want to buy stuff. I'm only going to be in this place for a couple of years, and whenever you move, you end up having to throw out furniture because it doesn't fit or it doesn't go with your aesthetic anymore or it turns out there's only room for a bar fridge in your kitchen.'

Jamie was giggling. He had been known to discard a lounge chair on a random street corner because we had nowhere to put it. We were both far too impatient to take the necessary steps to sell anything, and I couldn't bring myself to think about how much money we'd wasted over the years moving between rental properties, buying new bits and pieces each time.

'So, at Rent Furn, it's a warehouse full of second-hand furniture. And you *rent* it. For six months or two years or whatever. And there are handymen who work there to restore anything old or broken. Tell me it's not a gap in the market. Seriously.'

Jamie was on his third piece of bread, probably in an attempt to avoid the chicken.

'Okay, here are the big red flags for me,' he said, as though he were a potential investor. 'Furniture is relatively cheap anyway. So just buy it from IKEA and throw it away. It's fine.'

'But what about the environment?' Liv asked. 'It all ends up in landfill. We need to recycle our furniture just like we recycle our clothes. And maybe Rent Furn also has some other incentive, like people deliver the furniture to you and assemble it. And they disassemble it and take it away when you move out. My people can do that.'

Jamie shook his head, smiling. He took a gulp of the craft beer Dad had found in the fridge. I didn't want to know how long it had been there.

'You're forgetting the crucial point that no one cares about the environment. Everyone *pretends* to care, but when it comes to actually doing anything, we're wildly unmotivated. And if you've got staff running this warehouse, fixing the furniture, delivering it, assembling it, how are you making a profit, when the whole point is that you want to offer people a really cheap service?'

'Well . . .'

Dad looked up from his plate, a streak of oil running down his chin.

'Liv, if you need furniture, we've got some here. There's an old mattress and some dining chairs in the spare room.'

Liv was becoming irritated.

'No, Dad, I don't need furniture. I just have a business idea. Mum, what do you think?'

Mum was leaning over the table, piling a second serving of salad onto her plate. She dropped a piece of feta on the stained tablecloth, and didn't appear to notice.

'You know, Colleen's kids have all bought their own places. Her son has two investment properties. They must be very good at saving. I've always been hopeless with money and—'

'Colleen's husband owns a printing business!' Liv interjected. 'I don't even know what a printing business is or what it does or if they still exist, but that's why Colleen has a nice house and why her kids have money.'

Her voice was strained now, and she banged her elbows on the table and rested her forehead in her hands. She looked down at her plate as she spoke.

'Ruby, is there a reason why you're not part of this conversation? You keep checking your phone even though we're all sitting here right in front of you. It's Mum's birthday, for fuck's sake.'

The creator who had called me a 'cow' had seen that I'd viewed her post. She'd now shared a slab of text accusing me of being 'sneaky', and it occurred to me that she could see me looking at this, too.

I put my phone down.

'Sorry. I'm literally getting cancelled in real time. People are pissed about this story . . . ugh, it's too hard to explain. I think Rent Furn is great. If I had a cheeky one million I'd invest in a heartbeat.'

Liv didn't smile. She was silent, hunched forward.

'Are you okay, Liv?' Mum asked, rubbing Liv's back from the seat beside her. 'Is something wrong?'

I knew that if I asked, *Is it the chicken, sweetie?* Liv would burst out laughing. Even when we were sulking as cranky teenagers, there were always things we could say to break through the icy exterior. But I didn't want to make fun of Mum's cooking on her birthday. That seemed unnecessarily cruel. So we all sat there uncomfortably, Jamie picking up another piece of bread and lathering it in butter.

Eventually, Liv stood up and angled her head towards the gable-style awning above us. 'Sorry,' she said. 'It's just really hard to be here sometimes. Just give me a minute.'

She walked in the direction of the bottlebrush, following it until she was out of sight. No one spoke. I didn't dare make eye contact with Mum or Dad, because I couldn't stand to see what was written on their faces.

To say it was hard to be here, just metres from where it happened, was an understatement.

Chapter 31

For several weeks in year seven, we learnt about black holes. It was after we'd packed the microscopes away, Kelsey and I never quite figuring out how to focus the lens, how to study the cells in a strand of hair.

'They're not actually holes,' our teacher told us, smirking as though this was an exciting secret. 'They're huge concentrations of matter packed into tiny, tiny spaces.' She smelt like mothballs and had wiry hairs sticking out of her chin, and I had no idea what she was talking about.

The more I read about black holes, the less I seemed to understand. For the first time in my short life, it was as though I had no framework to which I could attach any of the information I ingested. I couldn't picture a black hole. I didn't know why one would exist. I had no sense of why they mattered.

In the exam at the end of that term, there was a question about how a black hole was created. I still remember the wave of panic, the way my eyes darted around the hall, clocking the pens around me dancing across pages while mine sat motionless in my hand. I looked down at the dotted lines again, empty where an answer should be, and felt a pang of failure. My mind was blank, and the lines remained blank, too.

It wasn't until quite recently that I realised I knew the answer. It came to me like an old piece of clothing turning up under the bed long after you've stopped looking. But once I found it, shaking the dust from the fabric and watching the fragments scatter through the air, they all seemed connected somehow. Like they meant something. Like they'd been telling me something all along.

That's when all the loose particles floating in the abyss of my memory suddenly fell into place.

• • •

A black hole is a corpse. It is created when a star dies.

Not just any star, but a very, very big star, one that is several times more massive than the sun. When it dies, it leaves behind a compact dense object, a region of space-time where gravity is so strong that nothing—not even light—can escape it. This cosmic body, identifiable only by the impact it has on the matter around it, is a black hole. It is sometimes described as 'the reverse of creation'.

Imagine you are floating in the terrifying vastness of space, and you accidentally slip over the invisible edge that surrounds a black hole. You feel a faint pull initially. Then it becomes stronger, more forceful than anything you can fathom, until everything, including you, falls inside. You can't have known, but when you crossed that edge, that boundary you couldn't even see was there, you passed a point of no return. A point beyond which you are trapped forever in infinite nothingness, where time and space and reality itself ceases to exist.

From the outside, any object falling into a black hole is frozen in time. In the eyes of an observer, you are eternally at the edge of the hole, unmoving, stuck in the exact moment your fate was determined.

When I picture that Thursday afternoon in the school holidays, rain slashing at the windows, plastic toy wheels squeaking along the lino, damp sponges piled behind the kitchen sink smelling vaguely of citrus, I see the corner where I'm sitting as a black hole. The gravitational pull is coming from a place beyond the screen, and I am both teetering on the edge of it and already inside, caught in a one-way exit from the universe. I cannot resist being swallowed by the abyss of the machine, the same way a bowling ball cannot help falling to the ground when it is dropped, the same way time cannot stop moving in the direction of the future.

I don't look away from the screen. Not at the world, the entire, magnificent world, that exists beyond it. Not at the paved courtyard behind me that glistens when it's wet, or at the crimson bottlebrush that grows alongside the driveway, weeping lazily over the fence. Not at the yellowing wall next to the cupboard where Dad has marked our heights in pencil since we were able to stand; three scribbled names marching restlessly towards the ceiling. Not at my brother and his wispy chestnut hair, his cheeks that still carry some of the chubbiness of his baby years, his little fingers that can now grasp crayons.

I stare at the screen because it is designed that way. To trap you inside it. To compress you. To stretch you so that you are no longer in one piece, so that the concepts of 'where' and 'when' disappear, so that the laws of physics break down.

On the screen, I am talking to someone who is not actually there. We are essentially communicating telepathically, he and I, transferring thoughts to each other via a portal. It's unclear whether we chose the portal or the portal chose us, these two teenagers whose brains are wired to process social stimuli unlike anything else. And this is the most social of stimuli.

Marcus was typing.

« ▫ » m.a.r.c.u.s « ▫ »
how far hv u gone? like wit a guy lol

I didn't know whether to lie. I worried that, if I did, I might find myself in a situation where I said the wrong thing, where it was obvious how inexperienced I was. I panicked and replied with a vague version of the truth.

> `·.¸¸.·´¯`·._.· rubesss `·.¸¸.·´¯`·._.·
> not very far lollll

> `·.¸¸.·´¯`·._.· rubesss `·.¸¸.·´¯`·._.·
> how bout u?

> « ¤ » m.a.r.c.u.s « ¤ »
> wot, like 1st?

First base, I was pretty sure, was kissing. At a school dance just a few weeks earlier, a guy wearing a Hawaiian shirt and baggy jeans had kissed me. For three songs, his hands grasped my waist while my arms were wrapped around his neck, and our bodies drifted closer and closer together until our bellies were touching. His warm cheek was pressed against mine and he smelt like Lynx body spray, like a chemical bomb of cheap, synthetic muskiness. When he lifted his face and turned towards my mouth, finding my tongue with his, I was surprised by how soft it was. How supple. Like sucking on a moist fruit that stroked you back, rhythmically pulsing inside you. Our tongues circled each other until the song was over, then he pulled away, the skin around his lips pink from where they'd rubbed against mine. I rushed to tell Kelsey, imagining how this boy—Ryan, I think his name was—might start calling my home, his voice breaking as he said my name, asking if I was there. But by the time I spotted him in the crowd to point him out to Kelsey, he was already dancing with another girl, his hands edging towards her arse. His mouth was open against hers before I'd even begun to speak. He kissed eleven girls that night. I don't know how we all knew that, but someone ensured that we did. It goes without saying that he never called my house. The kiss belonged to me, though, and I could still taste him, the heat of his tongue pounding into my own tender opening. The thought sent a weightlessness through my core.

> `·.,.·´¯`·._.· rubesss `·.,.·´¯`·._.·
> ok ive obviously kissed some1 lol
>
> « ¤ » m.a.r.c.u.s « ¤ »
> so 2nd? tell me hehe
>
> `·.,.·´¯`·._.· rubesss `·.,.·´¯`·._.·
> maybeee

I wasn't entirely certain what second base was. Some kind of touching, although I didn't know where. The question gave me a faint ache in my groin, like a heartbeat between my legs. Liv and I had discussed this sensation. We called it the 'funny feeling', and we got it sometimes when we jumped, or when we went down a roller-coaster, or when a friend found a porn channel on the TV at a sleepover.

> « ¤ » m.a.r.c.u.s « ¤ »
> or 3rd . . . like head?

I froze. I'd only ever heard about head from Kelsey, and it sounded complicated and unpleasant. She described trying to fit her boyfriend's fleshy penis—the size and shape of a deodorant can, she insisted—into her mouth, and how he shuddered when she gagged. I was stuck between sheer terror and curiosity, because I liked the idea of giving a guy what he wanted. Kelsey talked about how her boyfriend moaned, how he made her stop when it was too good. Was that what Marcus did, in a dark bedroom when his parents were away?

`·.,,.·´¯`·..._.·´ rubesss `·.,,.·´¯`·..._.·´
not yet

I didn't want to seem frigid, or for the conversation to go cold. So I fell deeper into the black hole, disappearing completely from the fractured afternoon light of the kitchen, the taps and rattles of the rain, the feathery, singsong voice speaking to his toy trucks. I no longer existed in this time or this space, but somewhere else, somewhere I didn't remember ever deciding to go, but that seemed inescapable all the same. I was surrounded by nothingness.

`·.,,.·´¯`·..._.·´ rubesss `·.,,.·´¯`·..._.·´
but close

« ¤ » m.a.r.c.u.s « ¤ »
like howww

`·.,,·´¯`··._.· rubesss `·.,,·´¯`··._.·
like close hahah

« ¤ » m.a.r.c.u.s « ¤ »
okkkk

« ¤ » m.a.r.c.u.s « ¤ »
do u lke 2 b touched?

The tingling was even lower now, in a part of me I couldn't quite identify. It was hot there, and it was spreading, like if I stood up there might be a puddle left behind.

`·.,,·´¯`··._.· rubesss `·.,,·´¯`··._.·
yesss lol

I couldn't tell if that was the right answer. Girls at school didn't really talk about their own pleasure, whether the things boys did to their bodies, the poking and rubbing and stretching, actually felt good. It was as though the question of what we liked was largely irrelevant. The established sequence of sexual acts was geared towards a boy ultimately being able to fit himself inside you, to tear a thin piece of your tissue, to take something from you. Perhaps I was breaking the unspoken rules by saying that I liked to be touched, particularly when I wasn't even sure if it was the truth. Maybe it made me slutty, dirty. Disgusting. Suddenly, I was convinced that Marcus was going to tell his friends, and my face burnt at the thought of them laughing at me, the sweaty, nervous girl, almost too shy to speak, who was secretly obsessed with sex.

A new message appeared.

> « ◘ » m.a.r.c.u.s « ◘ »
> i wanna touch u
>
> « ◘ » m.a.r.c.u.s « ◘ »
> lol
>
> « ◘ » m.a.r.c.u.s « ◘ »
> like realllll bad

I was no longer aware of the wind coming through the side door, of the chill it brought to the indoor air. My entire body was floating, suspended, unattached to anything around it.

Most physicists say you can't escape a black hole. It's a one-way trip, and once you're pulled in, there's no way out. You're trapped in the abyss for eternity.

But there's another theory.

It's messy and unstable, but it posits that black holes might take you to other galaxies, to another universe. That everything inside it might still exist, just not in a form that's recognisable to us. Not in a way that can be described using the existing laws of nature.

Perhaps that's what happened to me. I was spat back out in a different version of reality, one in which all the principles that had governed my life, all the fundamental beliefs I'd held about what was fair and right and possible, no longer applied.

I never responded to that message from Marcus, because that was when I heard the scream. The one that sent ripples of horror through the fabric of the universe.

Chapter 32

In hindsight, I should've known what was coming. It's so obvious, what the internet does once they have their gaze locked on their prey. They dig, searching for something that will utterly destroy you. And that's what they did.

On the morning it happened my phone was, as bizarre as it sounds, locked in a safe. Jamie had bought one online to use at school with kids' confiscated belongings, but he forgot about it. When we'd got home from Mum and Dad's—both of us quiet from the sadness that had briefly leaked through the gaps—he'd found it in the study, still in its packaging. A cheap, perspex box with a removable lid, topped with a built-in timer that could be set for minutes or hours or days. He thought it was the only way to stop me looking at my phone. To separate me from the shadow version of myself being crucified online. In order to remember that it wasn't real, that other self, I needed it to be inaccessible.

And so when I woke up on Sunday morning I didn't look at my phone. Your willpower, apparently, starts strong and erodes as the day goes on, so I safeguarded against my own fallibility. I put my phone at the base of the clear container, spun the dial until the small screen read *0 days 03 hrs 30 min 0 sec*, and heard the mechanical click of the lock. I searched my body for a reaction, and found that there was only relief.

It was just after 10 am, and I wondered for a moment what a person was supposed to do when they were untethered. My only memories of being truly free from the temptation of a screen were from when I was a child. MSN and *The Sims* and *RollerCoaster Tycoon* had knocked on my door to steal my time when I was entering my teens, and since then I'd been permanently caught between two realities: the one I woke up in, where I felt things I could not name and was paralysed by self-hatred, and the one I escaped into, where I could build mansions and fast-forward through time, where there were cheat codes for money and you designed your own face and if you made a mistake, you could simply start again. Now, I couldn't imagine a life without the escape hatch, even though there was a part of me that longed for it. A part of me that was certain it would be more satisfying.

As a child, I would spend days just thinking. Imagining. Inventing games with Liv. Why could I not go back to that?

As an adult, I hardly had an uninterrupted thought. Instead, they fought to be heard over the top of whatever podcast I was listening to or whatever video I was watching, like the soft strings of a violin fighting for attention in an orchestra.

Without my phone, the apartment was quiet. Jamie was at soccer, coaching an Under 14s team, and suddenly I wished I was there, too. I missed the smell of wet grass and rubber boots, of sweat-soaked jerseys and a dirt-stained, synthetic leather ball. I missed noticing what a Sunday smelt like.

I would go for a walk, I decided. Down the hill to the beach. My hands would be free and my mind would be present, and I would dive into the waves and hold my breath until it hurt.

I needed a coffee on the way, but as I dropped my keys in my pocket it occurred to me that I had no way to pay for it. I hadn't used my physical bank card in years, and cash now seemed like a historic artefact. I wasn't even sure the cafe would accept cash if I had it.

I rummaged through two handbags stuffed at the bottom of my wardrobe. One was forest green leather and one was neoprene, apparently machine washable—not that I had ever tested that claim. Both were lined with sand and hair elastics, and smelt like a mixture of gum and a perfume I hadn't used in months, and in the green bag I found my wallet.

As I walked down the main road, past crowds headed to the markets (did I enjoy the markets? I didn't think so), I sensed my missing phone like a missing limb. I wanted to message Liv. I wanted to know when Jamie would be home. I wanted to check my email and then all my messages and then scroll for no reason other than to pass the time, to mute the intensity of being alive.

At the bustling cafe on the corner, I smiled at the woman at the counter and hoped my unusual eye contact wouldn't be interpreted as an invitation for conversation. I ordered my latte, paying with the plastic card that still worked, thankfully, and waited outside in the heat. Around me, mothers chatted quietly to their babies, strangers stopped to pat dogs whose names they already knew, and couples stood together in silence, staring either at their screens or at the people walking by.

When my name was called by the barista, I heard it the first time—one of the benefits of not having a distraction in my hands—and thanked her as I reached for it. Paranoia made me think a voice nearby was whispering the word *Bared*, the familiar sound of it rising above unintelligible conversation. But when I turned around, no one was looking at me. I crossed the road feeling embarrassed by my self-obsession, that I'd become the kind of person who thinks the whole world is talking about them.

I was just outside the markets now, and a group of three girls in front of me had stopped and were blocking the footpath with their bodies, deciding out loud where they should go.

'I'm telling Izzy where to meet us,' said the tallest one, staring straight down, unaware of the steady queue of people growing behind her. 'Do we go to the candle stall closest to the street?'

'Nah, there's jewellery at the back and I want a chunky ring,' said the girl to her left, flicking through a social media app even though her friends, it appeared, were right there. 'I'm really into mixing metals at the moment. Like it's weird, I used to only wear gold but then I keep seeing people stacking bracelets and earrings that clash and I love it. How pretty is this?'

She extended her screen to the third girl, whose waist-length hair was styled in loose waves as though she was prepared for a photo shoot. She wore a tiny linen skirt that hung on her bony hips and a ribbed grey singlet that left a band of flesh exposed. It was all so flat. I felt a visceral sting of jealousy, and then I saw her face and realised she must've been fifteen. I never wanted to be fifteen again. Not even for the effortlessly skeletal frame.

A middle-aged man cleared his throat and, when they didn't move, he stepped theatrically into the bike lane to walk around them.

'People trying to get past here!' he boomed, and he kept looking back at them from further down the street, checking that they were sufficiently sheepish.

They were not.

The tall one hardly looked up, and the other two saw him and then exchanged looks and a stifled laugh.

I had been stuck behind them for a while, trying to find a polite way to pass, and now I was furious. The audacity of these girls—to entirely disregard every other person on the street, while they carried on an inane conversation. Izzy could meet them wherever the fuck they ended up, whether it was near the candles or the jewellery or the second-hand clothes.

I wanted to snatch their phones out of their hands and demand they look up. At me, at everyone around them, at anything other than the manufactured nothingness they had been sucked into.

It's funny, in hindsight. That I was so angry at them and whatever they were looking at, so certain that it was wrong and eroding the glue of a functioning society, even if that society was just a crowded footpath on a busy Sunday morning.

Because then I saw it.

Later, when I described to people how it all unfolded, no one believed me. They rolled their eyes and said there were simply too many people, too much content; that it wasn't possible. It would be too much of a coincidence.

But I have no reason to lie to you. I looked over the shoulder of the girl who wanted a chunky ring, and there was my face. I wasn't sure at first, I thought I might be losing my mind, but no, it was definitely my face. Strangely, though, it was my face from almost a decade ago. The photo was from my eighteenth, when my eyebrows were thinner and my hair was shorter, and I was wearing a dress I'd bought specifically for the party and never worn again. I vividly remembered my eighteenth. I'd really only had the party because I was obsessed with a guy from work and wanted him to come, but he'd arrived and promptly hooked up with someone else. By the end of my party I was vomiting vodka lemonades into a toilet bowl, Liv holding my hair back and promising not to tell Mum.

The girl in front of me was swiping through a series of images now, no longer of my face, but of posts from a social media platform I hadn't used in years. They were screenshots, with my name in bold at the top of every one. I clearly had some level of delusional optimism in that moment, because I recall thinking that perhaps this was a good thing. Maybe I was being applauded because I'd written something funny, or I'd shared an idea that was wildly ahead of its time. Someone might've unearthed a post that proved I was actually a good person, and now everyone would see the last week through that lens: that I had been unfairly targeted, unjustifiably torn apart, the latest sacrificial lamb for an ambiguous cause.

Then I registered some of the words.

They were the kind of slurs people had used without thinking back then. The terms you'd throw at your friends to make them laugh, even though no one really knew what they meant. Those same words had faced a reckoning in the intervening years, so that to say them now was unthinkable. The people who had once shouted them across a crowded playground, typed them, published them on a platform they didn't fully comprehend, had grown up. The wiring of their brains had changed, with higher-level cognitive abilities taking over the impulsivity and emotionality of adolescence.

But now the phrases of my teen years were printed in black and white in front of me, on the screen of a stranger who had been a small child when they'd been written. I didn't even know if they were real. I couldn't remember writing them, but I couldn't remember anything I wrote on the internet in those days, before I understood what the internet was. Would someone have gone to the effort of photoshopping my name onto offensive posts from ten years ago? Or was it more likely that they were my words, dug up by a person looking for the smoking gun—the conclusive evidence that I was as awful as I seemed?

I wanted to shout my defence at the girl swiping slowly through the images, her neat, chrome nails tapping against the screen. I wanted to demand an explanation of how she stumbled across them, whom she followed who had shared them, why she felt entitled to cast judgement on a series of out-of-context posts by someone she'd never met. But I had no air in my lungs. I was winded.

Then she swiped again, and I could've sworn she winced. My eyes lifted to study her expression, and landed back on the pixelated photo she was looking at. I recognised it immediately.

When I saw the photo on her screen, the scene played out like a movie. Our modern history class was huddled together on our last day of school, standing on the manicured grass outside the block that housed our classroom. Our wide-eyed young teacher held the camera, and Loretta dragged a log to the centre of the frame. 'We gotta pretend we're in the trenches,' she said, handing us tiny sticks to point as though they were guns. We laughed, and we crouched, and then Loretta shrieked, 'One more! One more!' She lined us up, fifteen girls in our too-short school uniforms, our blue socks faded to white, our skin tinged orange from unsophisticated formulations of fake tan. She didn't even tell us what to do; we just followed her lead. Everyone followed Loretta's lead. Straight faces, our left hands straight under our noses like a moustache, and our right hands extended in the air.

The Nazi regime had been part of our modern history syllabus. We'd seen countless photos of crowds doing the Nazi salute. I don't think any of us at seventeen, maybe eighteen, at a Catholic school in Sydney's north, had ever met a Jewish person.

But that didn't matter. Because there I was, on a stranger's phone, standing dead centre, the slightest smirk on my shiny face, doing a Nazi salute.

Above the photo, I could make out the name of the person who had shared it: Felicity Cartwright.

Chapter 33

By the time I found myself back in the thick heat of my living room, my coffee cold and my hands shaking, I still had 0 days 02 hrs 54 min 12 sec until I could access my phone. Without it, I needed my laptop. My personal one was long dead, and I hadn't bothered to replace it, instead using my slow-running work computer for everything from online shopping to streaming to checking site traffic, usually all at once.

But as soon as I opened my browser, I remembered I'd logged myself out of all my social accounts on my laptop, and needed a code from my phone to get back in. It was a security measure introduced by *Bared* because our personal accounts were linked to the company account, and I cursed the surly IT guy as I slammed my laptop shut.

The safe sat on the bleached timber coffee table. I could see my phone, facedown, switched off, no dings or vibrations to signify the invisible activity going on inside it. Not for the first time, I wondered if the old philosophical question about a tree falling in a forest was actually more relevant to the internet. Right now, did my own vilification only exist if I was there to witness it? Well, I knew there were *other* people seeing it, perceiving it, and therefore it was real. But what about the posts Felicity had shared? If a vile piece of content is floating around in the ether, sitting idly in such an obscure corner of the online world that no one, under normal circumstances, would see it, is it offensive? Or does it only become so when it's unearthed, the act of perception itself causing the offence, the way the human ear causes the sound of the tree?

I was getting impatient. I spotted the collapsed packaging for the safe by the door and searched inside for a manual. Instead, I found a single glossy sheet with a QR code for instructions. A QR code I couldn't use because my phone was locked inside the fucking safe. I knew it was unlikely there was a way to override the lock anyway. That's the point of a time-lock container, really. That you can't unlatch it just because you want to.

I grabbed the safe and brought it to the kitchen counter. The entire thing was plastic, and it surely hadn't cost Jamie more than fifty dollars. It had to be breakable. Ideally I could prise the lock open in a way that left the container intact, so Jamie wouldn't know that I'd only lasted forty minutes without my phone before discovering my entire professional reputation was at stake. Of course, technically, it had been the whole night and early morning *plus* forty minutes, which made me nauseous with the uncertainty of when Felicity had posted the screenshots and how many people had seen them.

I probably didn't need the serrated steak knife. A butter knife would've served the same purpose. But I thought the sharp point might reach inside the cavity, which appeared to house the lock. I stuck the tip inside and wiggled it around, but I couldn't feel any levers or pins, so I decided to try slicing through the tiny barbs attaching the lid to the box, one on each of the four corners.

Later, I discovered on Google you're actually meant to break the base. It's thinner, more susceptible to being fractured. But I couldn't see anything beyond that ugly, white lid, with its LED screen and fat wheel, like a menacing face that knew the power of the weapon it was holding.

I wrapped one arm around the safe to hold it steady, and with the knife in the other I thrust the blade at one of the curved corners.

But the knife missed, and the blade went straight into my arm.

It took me a moment to recognise the sound of my own scream.

I grabbed the nearest tea towel and wrapped my arm in it, holding my breath like it might stop the blaring pain. The blood soaked through the cotton.

I hated blood. I'd hated it since that Thursday when I was thirteen, when it had soaked into the gravel.

Maybe I should've gone outside. Knocked on our neighbour's door or run down the flight of stairs to the street, trying to find help. But anyone I approached would've asked how I did it, and whether they should call someone, and why I hadn't called anyone, and I didn't have the energy to explain. So I lowered myself onto the yellowing kitchen tiles, clutching the damp tea towel with white-knuckled fingers, and lay there. The side of my face rested against the cool, sticky floor, and salty tears slid diagonally into my mouth. They tasted familiar. Like the odd sense of peace, of calm, in knowing you are truly alone.

Jamie pointed out later that I could've sent an email from my laptop. Someone probably would've seen it and come rushing over, or contacted Jamie so he could've come straight home, instead of going to Westfield on the way back from soccer to get a new pair of runners. He'd sent me a message to let me know, but of course I hadn't seen it.

It didn't really matter. I would've chosen to lie there anyway, staring at the dusty legs of the coffee table, noticing the crumbs that had been swept beneath it. There was something sacred about the silence. The pain was almost meditative, demanding I listen to it, feel it surge and then soften. It made it hard to think about Felicity or the screenshots or the photo of me in my school uniform, committing a mortifying, disgraceful crime that I had no idea I'd be punished for a decade later.

When I finally heard the mechanical retraction of the lock, I didn't recognise it. It was like I'd given up on it ever opening, the way you can't imagine your name being called when you've been waiting a lifetime in a doctor's office. I slowly stood up and took my quiet phone out of the bloodstained safe, turning it on at the side and placing it on the bench. I unwrapped my injured arm, flinching as the fibres rubbed against the exposed flesh. My wrist and palm were painted in dried blood, and I gently tugged on some of the nearby skin to see where the edges of the wound began. I hissed at the sensation, a sharp burning, striking through layers of torn tissue. The cut was so deep the inside looked black, like it went beyond the tendons and the muscle, into whatever was left. Beside me, my phone screen was alive with activity—missed calls and messages and app notifications accumulating as I stood there. When I unlocked it, I didn't open any of them. I made a single phone call, sank back to the floor, and waited for Jamie.

Chapter 34

Mum had seen it all unfold from the window in the lounge room. Sometimes I think there's a shadow of her permanently etched into the curtains, like the Human Shadow of Death in Hiroshima; a ghost of her who still exists in that moment, the one where her little boy was still alive, playing in the driveway.

It was a sash window that had been painted shut by previous occupants before we moved in. On hot days, we had tried to open it, but there were too many layers of paint buried in the tracks, holding it all together like glue.

She was standing by the window folding the washing, sorting socks and undies and shirts into neat piles.

When she first saw Dad's car reversing into the driveway, she didn't know Max was down there. She thought he was in the kitchen with me, launching his multicoloured toy trucks into the skirting board. She watched the back of the silver Toyota Tarago edge down the gravel, the branches of the bottlebrush bending against the windows on the driver's side.

The rain meant the visibility was poor from the front seat. The rear window of the Tarago was covered in condensation, and when Dad had turned on the aircon to demist it, Liv shouted at him that she was freezing. He couldn't see the side mirrors clearly, either, the heavy water blurring the image in the reflection.

Neither of them knew the car was about to hit something until they felt it. At first Dad was worried that it was our cat. I know this because he wailed it when the paramedics arrived, as though the fact that he had thought it, in those few uncertain seconds, might make it true.

Mum was already screaming when it happened. She'd shouted and banged on the window to try to get Dad's attention, to get him to stop.

There's an image that sometimes comes to me in nightmares, or pops into my head as I'm trying to fall asleep. It's not a memory, because I didn't see it, so I guess it's an invention, although I'm certain it's real. I see Mum's face pressed up against the glass. I see her fists thumping it, her mouth making the shapes of empty screams. I see an animalistic instinct, a strength that might just shatter the window and contravene all the laws of space and time to get to Max and stop it all. But then I see the light go out in her eyes when she realises.

It's as though I was in more than one place that day, able to witness things I can't possibly have observed from the desk where I was sitting, tucked in the alcove near the kitchen. Because I can see Max, too. He's standing with his back to the reversing car, launching his toy trucks down the driveway. Our cat is weaving between his legs, so Max feels safe, like it's okay for him to be in the rain with no shoes on. But when the car comes, the cat slips underneath it, and he does not.

I don't think it's just Mum whose shadow was etched into that moment. Just like the man whose shadow was scorched into the stone by the intense energy of an atomic blast, a relic of me remains stuck there. The old, beige computer is gone now, replaced by smaller screens we can fit in our pockets. But I'm frozen in time. Staring into a black hole, feeling the gravitational pull of it, the inevitability that it will swallow me. The outline of the shadow makes it look like I'm on the edge, hunched over, my slack jaw just inches from the screen. But that's the thing about a black hole. You eternally appear to be in the midst of falling, when really, you're already inside.

Chapter 35

I ended up needing seven stitches. I was in hospital for almost as many hours. Sundays in an emergency room are full of concussions and dislocations, broken bones and lacerations. Then, of course, there are the quiet patients, the ones you watch as they sit blankly on plastic chairs, trying to tell from their body language whether they have an infection or a ruptured organ or are bleeding profusely from the anus.

The triage nurse directed several pointed questions at Jamie. It was clear that she suspected I'd inflicted the wound myself, and I was relieved when Jamie shook his head, concerned but entirely convinced I'd cut my arm open trying to access the safe.

'Now I feel sick that I made you put your phone in it,' he said, leaning forward with his elbows on his bare knees.

You could see the outline of his quad muscles under his skin, defined from decades of running. His body had muscles I simply didn't have, ones that were dormant inside me, never activated because I spent all my waking hours hunched over a screen.

A stocky man in a football jersey walked in through the automatic doors, his nose visibly misshapen. He approached the reception desk, holding a bloodied tissue to his face with one hand and searching for his Medicare card with the other. He was alone. Perhaps his partner had rolled her eyes when she heard about the injury, telling him that's what you get for playing a sport where grown men throw themselves at each other. A nose that no longer looks like a nose.

'I could've just hidden your phone and given you one without social media on it,' Jamie said. 'So you could call or message in an emergency.'

'It wouldn't have made a difference. I'm clinically insane. I needed to access the posts, so I needed my phone. And I didn't want to call anyone. I feel like a fucking idiot.'

The silence hung between us. Despite having sliced open my own arm in a desperate attempt to see Felicity's posts and the ensuing reaction, I still hadn't looked. The longer I went without seeing it, the less I wanted to. The initial urge to defend myself was gone, replaced by a lingering sense of despair. There was nothing I could do. The words I had written, regardless of how old I'd been when I'd written them, were wrong. The photo, of a group of naive, sheltered, dumb, dumb, dumb girls, was wrong. Anyone calling me a bigot or any kind of *-phobe* or *-ist* was justified, if they were judging me on my own behaviour, which was right there, staring at them from the palm of their hand.

They were right. But diving into the murky waters of Felicity's contempt and the outrage of those she'd galvanised would only serve to drown me. I thought of the lake I often swam in up the coast, stained a rich shade of rust from the oils of nearby tea-trees. As you waded in, the shallow waves were a transparent bronze, but as you sank deeper into the water, the colour deepened, too, to a thick red that resembled the blood left behind after a shark attack, then to black. I was always terrified once I reached the inky middle of the lake, haunted by the incomprehensible depth that drained every ray of light from the water, the creatures that lurked beneath me, the vastness of it all. Sometimes I'd be overwhelmed by an impending sense of doom, a certainty that something was going to grab me by the leg and pull me under, into the disorientating, never-ending darkness.

That's how I felt about looking at the posts. I knew that once I waded in, I wouldn't make it out.

I wanted to tell Liv about my arm, about the girls near the markets and the safe and the blood, so I opened my messages. There was one from her, sent hours ago.

> **Liv**: This is fucked. Call me asap.

So she'd seen the post. It must be bad if even she was panicking. There were no follow-up messages, which meant Jamie had probably called her and told her what had happened. I scanned the rest of them.

> **Yasmin**: Just saw Felicity's post, I'm so sorry. She really has it in for you, it's like a friggin witch-hunt. If it's any consolation, I once dressed as Osama bin Laden with a gunshot wound to the head for a party. The theme was 'infamous'. You don't want to know what other people were dressed as. I hope all the photos are wiped from the internet because otherwise I guess I'm just waiting to get cancelled, too. Normal, rational people will know you were just a teenager doing the stupid shit we all did as teenagers. This will blow over. I swear. xxxx

> **Ian**: Hi Ruby, have just been alerted to the posts shared by Felicity Cartwright. I understand this must be a very challenging time for you, and I want you to know your wellbeing is our main concern here. Please call me whenever you get a chance, I just want to check in. Ian.

> **Colleen**: Ruby, I've seen this silly thing going around about you and I'm thinking of you. I hope you know that the people who truly know you and love you do not take any of it seriously. I cannot see the point in judging someone for what they did years and years ago, and I can guarantee, your mum and I would be arrested if there was any evidence of our teenage years! Look after yourself, darl xx

Mum: Have been on the phone to Liv. This Felicity is a very strange person. How cruel. Call me whenever you can, I love you.

Jen: No.

Jen: Rubes. I can't. I'm so angry for you. Wtf.

Jen: I'm fuming. FUMING. So 17-year-old Ruby Williams deserves to be plastered all over the internet and called heinous names—many of which are worse than anything you posted—while there are ACTUAL people in this country doing ACTUAL bigoted shit who get a free pass? Let alone people with 'public platforms' who are 'instrumental in shaping the national agenda' (like I'm sorry, I love you, but you're an editor at a website, you're not the prime minister). How about Dan who has a weekly column in the Herald, even though he bashed a guy so severely that he will never walk again? I guess Felicity isn't interested in that story. Men are off limits, but if you're a woman who's posted a shitty thing on the internet ever, WATCH OUT. She's coming for ya.

Jen: What can I do, seriously, do you need a massage? A spa day? Whatever—I'm sending a voucher to your email it can be a surprise xo

My focus was interrupted by a hacking cough from a guy who sounded like he was trying to dislodge a stone from his throat. He was doubled over on one of the pale blue plastic chairs, shaking with the force of trying to breathe. A nurse rushed to him from behind the desk, and moments later he was gone, escorted through the double doors where, I imagined, someone would make sure he didn't die.

'Poor guy,' Jamie said, watching the nurse walk back through the waiting room and return to her seat at the triage desk, like nothing had happened. 'But I guess that puts you further down the line. Can you fake a seizure or something? I'm getting kind of hungry.'

He grinned and tapped me on the leg, then moved his hand to get his phone from his pocket. I stopped him.

'Have you seen it? All the Felicity stuff? Can you be honest about how bad it is? Because I genuinely don't know what to do. You'll say to ignore it but I can't have everyone thinking I don't care.'

He dropped his phone in his lap, the screen painted with green and grey and pink, an avalanche of notifications he hadn't yet opened. It felt like a lifetime while I watched him lean back, stretch his arms behind his head, and turn to face me.

'I had a quick look after I dropped you off, when I parked the car. She's brutal, this Felicity.'

Now his arms were crossed and he nodded his head at the phone. He shifted his feet on the vinyl floor, tucking his legs under the chair.

'Basically calling you a lot of names, saying your employment should be terminated immediately, ranting about how we need to hold people in positions of power to account, arguing that this is more evidence of your privilege and how you're self-interested and only care about women like you. The bow she's drawn from a few dumb posts to "Ruby Williams is a terrible person who deserves to be fired" makes absolutely no sense.'

It felt like he was talking about someone else. But hearing those accusations in Jamie's voice, even though I knew they weren't his own, was disturbing, and I suddenly had the distinct sense I was trapped in a nightmare. All my senses were muted, from the sound of beeping hospital devices to the smell of antiseptic and Jamie's sweat. It felt distant, like I was experiencing life through a screen. Like I wasn't truly here. I remembered hearing once that you can't feel pain when you're dreaming, so I lifted my arm, bandaged earlier by one of the paramedics, and pressed the wound. I recoiled immediately as what felt like a burning bolt of lightning shot through me. This was not a dream. This was really happening.

'So what do I do? Do I respond? Apologise? If I apologise, they'll tear that apart; if I don't apologise, I'm a monster; if I express how mortified I am, then I'm centring myself.' I was speaking too fast. I closed my eyes and took a deep breath, reaching for the familiar roughness of Jamie's hand beside me. 'I don't know who to ask, either, because at work they'll be thinking about Bared's reputation, not mine. If you were a normal person watching this unfold, what would you want the person who stuffed up to do?'

Jamie was watching as a doctor came through the double doors with a clipboard, repeating a name that wasn't mine.

Two girls in their twenties stood up. I'd decided hours ago that the pale one in the tracksuit pants, clutching her lower abdomen while her friend rubbed her back, probably had a ruptured ovarian cyst.

'It's weird,' said Jamie, 'because I hadn't even heard of Felicity Cartwright before all this. Like, for most people, this isn't on their radar. Most people don't care. But I guess, you know, once there are news articles about it publishing these photos that people are really offended by, it's a different story.'

I bolted forward and jerked my hand out of his.

'What?'

What news articles? How could there be news articles?

Jamie looked at me, his eyes wide. 'I . . . I thought you knew. I thought you would have seen it by now.'

'How would I know?' I hissed. 'You made me put my phone in a shitty plastic safe and then I hacked my fucking arm trying to open it. I haven't exactly been checking.'

Jamie was quiet, then he rested his head on my shoulder.

'Okay, well in that case, yeah, let's look at it together,' he said. 'Calmly. And we can work out what to do.'

Chapter 36

A small pop culture site wrote about it first: FELICITY CARTWRIGHT CALLS OUT PROMINENT FEMINIST'S CONTROVERSIAL PAST. The 'prominent feminist' was me.

When their post started gaining traction, the story was picked up by another media organisation, then another, then another. It was on the front page of gossip sites. Tabloids. Mainstream media outlets covered it, breaking up the copy with embeds of social media comments as though they were quotes from reputable sources.

I started reading the articles in the waiting room beside Jamie, him gripping my clammy hand while the extent of what was happening slowly dawned on me. A doctor called my name, and I followed her, my eyes still on my phone.

Even as she injected the inside of my gaping wound with a long needle, as she sewed the ragged edges of my flesh together, as she bandaged my wrist, I flicked between the windows on my screen. I didn't feel any pain, because I wasn't really present.

By then, I was studying Felicity's original post, the five photos that had somehow been unearthed from a place I didn't know still existed. The first was the one from my eighteenth, which, I could see now, had been shared because of a word I had used in the caption. It was a slur that made me wince. The next three were screenshots of similarly offensive language I had used in status updates—cringeworthy posts I had written thoughtlessly. Then, of course, there was the last image. Indefensible.

I wasn't stupid. I had worked online for long enough to know that people did this, that my digital footprint was public, that on the internet it was fair game to unearth what someone said when they were a different person, when the world was a different place.

A part of me had known that there was sludge from my past floating in the ether. I hadn't trawled through my own history, like other people might. It was a form of avoidance. I once logged on to an old social networking account, one I'd used when I was a teenager, and when I saw the profile image, I couldn't breathe. It was a version of me I never wanted to look at again. She was drawn and pale and wore the anguish of what had happened on every inch of her. I knew how she lived in a house that no longer felt like home, how there was no joy left at school, how she couldn't sleep by herself, craving a cuddle from a mum who didn't have the capacity to give it.

The reason I hadn't combed through whatever I'd posted when I was fifteen or sixteen or seventeen or eighteen was because it hurt. It was a time in my life I was desperate to forget. But I'd been naive in thinking that the hidden corners of my mind equated to hidden corners online. The truth was that it was all still there, and now it had followed me into the future.

When someone shows you who they are, believe them, Felicity began her caption underneath the photos.

> Ruby Williams is vile. The fact that the editor-in-chief of a major media organisation never thought to delete these speaks volumes. It's been clear to me for some time that this person is a truly reprehensible human being. First, she used a story about 'coercive control' as a Trojan horse to suggest women shouldn't have access to abortion. Then, she splashed photos of a woman who had been brutally murdered across her website, without the family's consent, and pretended to take accountability. Now, we know that according to HER OWN WORDS and HER OWN PHOTOS, she's racist, bigoted, homophobic, misogynistic and anti-semitic. This is how broken media is in this country—that THIS person has risen to the top. And I'm entirely unsurprised. Well done, Bared. Keep pretending you care about women, when you've chosen to employ someone who actively hates them.

I should've been stunned. Horrified. Furious, perhaps. But Felicity's words felt eerily true. Comforting, almost. Like I had been waiting for them all along.

Beth wrote a post of her own, with a carousel of screenshots. She said she'd tried to reason with me, had tried to make her voice heard at *Bared*, but I was such a narcissist that she'd been silenced.

> I'm sorry I couldn't have done more. I'm a writer at Bared and Ruby Williams is my boss. She has fostered an unsafe work environment that I've tried relentlessly to challenge. I have attempted to call out her incompetence and blatant self-interest, but have been ignored.

I tapped on the comments on Felicity's post, no longer frightened of what they might do to me. I was already torn open.

> Yuck I hate her. She's everything that's wrong with media in this country. Bitch needs to get a job stacking shelves and learn that she's not special. Something about her has always irritated me, she has this weird expression like she doesn't think she has to behave like an adult. I know women like that. Women who get called out and are then like 'meee??? But I'm just a little babbbbby?' That's her.

> Wow. Always thought her writing was bad but this is disgusting.

> You are brave, Felicity. Thank you for the work you do. The world is a better place for it. This woman is an absolute

disgrace, and deserves to be challenged on her shortcomings not only in her job but as a human being. I hope she reads your words and wakes up to herself.

I started to draft an apology in my Notes app, knowing as I wrote it how easily it would be dissected by someone who hated me. When we got home, my arm and every other part of me still numb, I asked Jamie to read it. He said it was perfect, even though we both knew it could never be.

I posted it to all my followers, and didn't feel a thing.

> Earlier today, screenshots surfaced from an old social media account of mine where I posted deeply offensive language, and engaged in an act which is such an unequivocal symbol of hate that it is recognised as a criminal offence in this country. I was seventeen at the time, which is not an excuse, because I should have known better. I am ashamed and embarrassed by my actions, and know that for a lot of people, there is nothing I can do or say to deserve your forgiveness.
>
> In recent weeks, I have also made a series of missteps in my role as editor-in-chief. These have understandably been called out, and I have handled them terribly. I have let down the Bared audience, my audience, and a number of women who were at their most vulnerable.
>
> I am going to open the comments on this post, and will not be moderating them, so that I can hear anything you want to express to me about the harm I have caused.
>
> I owe you that.

Then, from tomorrow, I will be having a break from social media while I take the time to listen, learn and prepare to do better.

Thank you, and I want you to know that I unconditionally apologise for the hurt I have caused. I am profoundly sorry.

Ruby

My injured arm was throbbing now, while I refreshed the comments. There were hundreds.

> Wow. This might be the worst apology I have ever seen from a public figure. Says she's going to 'take on' feedback but that she's ALSO taking a break from social media? What a privilege. She can switch off the people holding her accountable when she feels like it, but the people hurt by HER words and HER actions can't switch off that pain.

> Do you think it's somehow noble to leave your comments on? Like that makes up for being a really, really shitty person? Newsflash: it doesn't.

> Would we call EXPLOITING a murdered woman and FURTHER TRAUMATISING her grieving family a 'misstep'??

> I have started a petition for @baredmedia to fire her, if anyone would like to sign it. This simply isn't good enough.

Chapter 37

'Your mum is here,' Jamie said, poking his head through the crack in the bedroom door.

I was awake, although I hadn't moved. I didn't know what day it was, or what time it was. The hours had started to blend into each other, not identifiable by the sun or the moon or the colour of the sky, because I now lived inside a world that fit in the grasp of my fingers.

Jamie had called Ian on the way back from the hospital to tell him I wouldn't be coming in this week, and to give me some space from *Bared* until the vitriol died down. But it wasn't dying. It seemed to be spreading. My smiling face was plastered across news sites, looking relaxed and lighthearted, as though I was laughing carelessly at the people who were angry. I wanted to take a photo of myself now—unwashed, grey—and demand they use that image for their stories. *The woman you're villainising isn't some delusional cow*, I'd write. *She's just pathetic.*

Mum was sitting on our two-seater faded blue lounge, on top of the blanket that had been draped there to cover a wine stain. When I walked into the living room, she stood to hug me, and I breathed in her shampoo, the musky White Linen that was stuck to her clothes. It was the scent I had longed for as a teenager, imagining it when I couldn't get to sleep. I wanted to cry into her chest. To lie with my head in her lap and have her stroke my hair, whispering in my ear that everything would be okay. But I was too old now. It was too late.

'Are you all right?' she asked, her warm breath on my ear. 'You don't deserve any of this. I hope you know that. None of it.'

I pulled away and curled up on the lounge. I could only stare blankly at the coffee table, my arm stinging with the vivid recollection of how I'd plunged the knife into it, how I'd bled while I lay still on the kitchen tiles.

I said it quietly, before I even realised what I meant.

'I'm sorry.'

'For what? This whole thing is just silly people on the internet pretending to be offended because it gives them something to talk about. You don't have anything to be sorry for.'

'No. Not that. Mum, I'm sorry.'

I turned to her. She had the same colouring as Liv and me, although she'd started to sprinkle her greying hair with ash-blonde highlights. Her mouth was similar, too, a slightly crooked smile, thin lips, a barely perceptible dimple in her chin.

'I'm sorry,' I whispered, 'for Max.'

In the split second it took for her to register his name, I saw her eyes change. She did not cry—she hadn't cried in years—but a cloudiness came over her gaze. She reached out for me, gripping my forearm tightly.

'You don't need to say sorry for Max. You never need to say sorry for Max.'

I watched her mouth make the sound of my little brother. The grief had blasted a hole through my memories of him, of our family when he had been a part of it. It hurt too much to think of how deeply I loved him, of how excited I was for him to grow up. So I distracted myself. Perhaps I could've gone on distracting myself for a lifetime.

There was no moisture in the back of my throat, a rock where my tongue should've been.

'I was meant to be watching him,' I said, watching for a twitch of anger on her face, the sign that would betray the truth. 'You asked me to watch him, and I wasn't watching. Why wasn't I watching?'

My voice was louder now, cracking under the weight of the question.

'Why wasn't I watching? How could I have not been watching?'

Mum has always maintained she never asked me to watch Max that day. But I believe she's telling the kind of lie mothers tell to protect their children.

After the accident, we went to weekly therapy as a family. It was in a poky building in the city, up a narrow flight of stairs that I tripped up more than once. The man who ran the sessions looked like he was permanently in pain, and he closed his eyes when he nodded, which irrationally annoyed Liv and me. We did impersonations of him, contorting our expressions until we no longer looked like ourselves. It took a while for us to test out the impersonations on Mum and Dad. We were worried we weren't allowed to joke anymore, particularly when it was related to grief—grief that felt so deep and so raw that none of us knew what to do with it. But once Liv and I openly started mocking therapy, it gave us all something we could talk about that wasn't Max, but was still close.

I have forgotten a lot of what was said in those sessions, but I know we each blamed ourselves. We had each written our own story.

Dad was behind the wheel, it was his foot on the accelerator, his eyes on the blurry mirrors.

Liv was in the front seat, having shouted at Dad when he tried to demist the windows. She was the one who needed to be picked up, who was the entire reason for the car reversing into the driveway.

Mum was at home, trying to do too many things with not enough limbs. She was folding washing, darting between rooms, managing cleaning and cooking and tiny, fragile lives.

And I was behind the computer, not watching. Selfishly talking to a boy whose name now made me want to vomit. Distracted by some disgusting, animalistic instinct, letting my brother, my beautiful sweet-smelling brother, drift out of my reach.

But I couldn't tell Mum or Dad or Liv or the therapist what I was doing on MSN. It was too humiliating, too trivial. They had all been grounded in the real, messy, chaotic world, where rain and metal and wheels and bricks conspired to make the worst thing happen. It had been out of their control—every action of theirs was forgivable. But mine wasn't. Mine was the symptom of an innate flaw, something about me that could never change.

I was shaking now, tears soaking through Mum's cotton t-shirt.

'I hate myself,' I heaved. 'I wasn't watching him. I let it happen because I wasn't watching.'

She didn't say anything for a long while, just holding me so tightly I couldn't let go. Then she took me by the shoulders and, her eyes boring into mine, said, 'I hated so many things after that day. I hated cars and roads and driveways and rain. I hated myself. I briefly hated your father, which he knows. I howled. I screamed. I hated anyone who claimed to believe in God, because how dare they? But I never, *ever* hated you. Loving you and Liv was what sewed me up again.'

I imagined her skin, thin as paper, torn through that day. But somehow, instead of allowing grief to claim her, Mum had returned to us. Eventually she stopped taking long showers and retreating to her bedroom. She was there when I graduated high school, beaming with pride. She picked me up from my university exams when I'd had an all-nighter. She read every article I'd ever written. In the study, she had a box where she kept the handful of my stories that had been republished in the newspaper. Liv complained that she didn't have her own box, and Mum reminded her that she had almost an entire bedroom full of them. Every medal we'd won, every award we'd received, every assignment we were proud of, Mum had kept.

'You know what I think sometimes?' Mum said. 'Losing Max taught me to love in a different way. In a truer way, a deeper way.' She shook my shoulders gently. 'Ruby, you have access to something other people don't, and it's for a cruel reason, and I know you don't want it, but it's there.'

Our arms stayed wrapped around each other as it got dark. I didn't reach for my phone because my hands were holding my mother.

Before she left, Mum told me something I hadn't thought about for fifteen years.

'God, Max used to love sleeping in your bed. It would drive me crazy because he'd wake you up, and I'd have a house full of kids who hadn't slept. But some mornings I'd find you both fast asleep, facing each other, and he was so content.'

I remembered his sticky skin, how it smelt of milk. The sweetness of his breath when he woke up. Liv and I taught him to high-five and his hands were so small, collapsing inside ours.

That night, for the first time in as long as I could remember, I dreamt of his giggle. He was running from the hose, his feet slapping the concrete of the courtyard, looking back at me with the smile that made his eyes disappear.

When I woke up, I saw my palm was wide open in front of me. Like I had been holding his hand in my sleep. Or he had been holding mine.

Chapter 38

When I worked at *The Daily*, there was a recent graduate called Morgan who started a new role in our team, turned up for two shifts, and then disappeared. We were concerned, initially. What if she'd passed away in her sleep, or been in a car accident, and we were the ones who were meant to alert the authorities? Surely someone doesn't just *ghost* their job? Not after a painstaking recruitment process, and two full days of training?

But eventually we learnt that's exactly what had happened. My boss at the time heard through the grapevine that Morgan had hated the culture so intensely that she'd decided never to come back. Even though I hadn't been the one onboarding her, I was slightly offended. I'd taken her to the pub for lunch on her first day, and I'd paid, and I thought I'd made a good impression. She seemed fascinated by my stories of press junkets and red carpets, of breaking news and viral personal essays, of the breadth of digital media.

I saw her again about a year later. It was Kelsey's hens', her maid of honour demanding we actively participate in a life-drawing class, sketching a male model whose body looked like it had been moulded from clay. Kelsey and I weren't particularly close anymore, the fibres that tied us together as teenagers broken by different career paths, new friendships and, if I'm entirely honest, my constant cancelling of plans because I had an over-inflated sense of the importance of my work. Still, our core group were reunited for her hens', gulping champagne while our pencils tried and failed to draw a penis that was somewhat in proportion.

I saw Morgan's face through the wide-open legs of the man whose name was allegedly 'Carlos'. The attendees of Kelsey's hens' took up a majority of the class, but there were others, too—a pair of older women, a lone guy who didn't smile, and Morgan's corner of quiet, grungy types. She had a fringe now, finishing halfway down her forehead, her jeans and shirt and jacket all varying shades of black.

At the end of the session, emboldened by alcohol, I walked towards her. She grinned with her mouth closed, and presented her sketch as an icebreaker.

'I spent too long on the dick and forgot to include hands,' she said, shrugging at the thick charcoal lines. 'Where's yours?'

We exchanged light banter about Carlos, about the shrieking women who were about to get on a stripper-filled party bus, about the guy who was still perfecting his shading, clearly annoyed by the chatter of non-artists who had crashed his very serious session.

The conversation lulled for a moment—Kelsey's maid-of-honour was clearly about to rally the troops.

'I couldn't do *The Daily*,' Morgan said quickly, unable to look me in the eye. 'Everyone seemed really nice but I went home after that first day and it was like an elephant was sitting on my chest. The pressure of having to work that fast and be across that much and publish stuff that you don't, like, believe? I swear I had like a week-long panic attack. And by the time I felt like I could string a sentence together to properly resign, I was too embarrassed.'

Perhaps it was Morgan who gave me the idea. Because when Monday morning came, my online apology smothered with comments, my arm still pounding, my phone filled with missed calls and messages from people who needed me to say I was okay because they didn't know what to do if I wasn't, I didn't go to work. I didn't contact Ian, or Yasmin. At first, I didn't even tell Jamie. I just got in my car and drove.

Chapter 39

Dense bushland floated past my window, all skeletal trees with their limbs wrapped around each other, the ground covered in thick undergrowth like a layer of hair. With my phone switched off and shut away in the glove box, I had nothing to do but watch the road and the changing scenery on either side of it: apartment buildings giving way to leafy suburban houses, high rock walls opening up into flat, green paddocks, bustling service stations and packed fast-food drive-throughs replaced by the peacefulness of country towns.

I had been driving for six hours in silence, the only noise coming from the hum of the car's engine and the whistle of wind through the seal of my window. It was the most consecutive waking hours I'd gone without some kind of artificial stimulus for what might've been years. No podcast to focus on, no music, no videos or photos or messages or calls or articles or miscellaneous alerts. Just my own bottomless mind.

For a while I heaved at the wheel, gulping the air and sucking salty tears from the corners of my mouth. I grunted. I swore. I shouted. I thought it would never end, all these years of unprocessed living making their way out, stewing in this box of metal, flying at 110 km/h down the freeway.

Then the numbness. Almost like there was nothing left. My anger and my grief so exhausted from peddling fiercely in the background, from following me everywhere, from screaming at me to pay attention while I drowned them out with this device that shrunk my world into something I thought I could control.

My mind, I realised, had bled into my phone. They had become one and the same. Every thought I had now led me back to the prospect of waking that dark screen, of asking it questions I didn't have the answers to. I didn't know how to engage in the world without the thing that had, without my consent, become an extension of my consciousness. My thoughts were scattered and unfinished. *I wonder what the temperature is outside* and *whether I have complex PTSD* and *can you get fired for not turning up to work without giving notice* and *jobs in media where you can be anonymous* and *where should I go* and *where should I stay* and *who should I tell.*

It turned out I didn't need directions to get to Crescent Head. We'd gone there for holidays when I was a kid, and all

I could recall was that it was north. A green and white sign told me where the turn-off was, and then before I reached the main street, I saw an arrow pointing to Beachside Cabins. That's how I ended up with bushland on either side of me, bouncing on an unpaved road that my Toyota Yaris was not designed for.

I imagined how my destruction was playing out. I knew there would be opinion pieces being pitched in newsrooms, energetic, non-moderated comment sections bringing traffic to websites, an avalanche of misrepresentations burying my name, going completely unchallenged. The facts of what had happened would become a mere source of inspiration for a greater story, one where truth and lies were tangled together like a clump of badly matted hair. I knew that in the end, no one had time to undo the knots, to extract every lock and keep it intact, so instead they just chopped it all off. The cemented mass sat in a bin somewhere, attracting bugs and flies and eventually decomposing, and the person who cut it never wondered whether there had been some beauty inside, if they'd just approached it with a comb instead of a blade.

I slowed at a clearing that revealed a deserted beach to my left, and a narrow, dirt road to my right. Down the road, I could see the outline of a worn, weatherboard cottage, and two cabins beyond it. Parking the car, I felt like I'd arrived at the place you go when the world is ending. An isolated retreat to wait out the complete obliteration of mankind.

I thought I might stay for the night, make the arduous drive home tomorrow, call Ian, confront whatever difficult conversations were awaiting me at work. In the end, though, I never went back to *Bared*.

Chapter 40

I found *GossipGate* at 4 am. I remember what time it was because I had started playing a game with myself, promising I'd put my phone down at midnight, then 1 am, then 2.30 am, then 4 am. I'd exercised my willpower for the entire drive, and when I finally turned it on to call a sickeningly worried Jamie, I couldn't detach from it. I was alone, hours from home, after scaring my partner and my family so much they had called the police. Just the sound of Jamie's voice was too much to bear. I promised him I was okay, that I had only needed some space, a break from it all. He was coming to meet me tomorrow.

As soon as I opened the thread, I knew it was over. It was liberating, almost, to realise I couldn't do it anymore. That I had reached the limit of what I could withstand.

On Felicity's post, I re-read a comment that referenced a gossip site. I googled it, along with my name, and found ninety-seven pages of anonymous commentary about me.

The thread had been created when I worked at *The Daily*, on the day I wrote the story about the royal toddler. Someone had decided I was embarrassing enough to warrant an entire landing page, and I read every single thing that had been written about me for years. These people had formed a community by mocking me, by sharing quotes from my articles and stills from my TV appearances, by updating each other when I got a promotion or when I spoke at an event. On a few occasions, one of the users had been in the audience when I was onstage, and they provided detailed recaps in the thread.

> I was at the Convention Centre today and HAD to see our girl talk on the panel about women in media. Wow. Where to start. Her outfit was hideous, why is she never dressed appropriately for these things?! It's like nothing fits. She was onstage for an hour and didn't say anything of substance. You could tell that the other women were like . . . sorry, who is she? Why is she here? At one point she tried to make a joke and it didn't land and I wanted to die. She's like that kid at school who no one likes but the teacher forces you to be nice to. By the end, she also had sweat patches under her arms, which was disgusting. Has she heard of deodorant? It will never not be a shock to me that this person has fallen so far upward. She's dumb, inarticulate, unlikeable and not even pretty.

I saw myself through the eyes of that nameless woman in the audience and truly hated myself. I *had* been sweating that day. And I'd wanted to change my outfit that morning, but I was in a rush and convinced myself no one would be looking at me anyway. They were. And they were keeping a record.

Parts of what I read on *GossipGate* instantly became folded into my memories. I believed that everyone at *Bared* had hated me from the beginning, that they were talking about me behind my back, that they thought I hadn't deserved my role.

I stiffened when I saw a blurry photo of myself on the thread, taken when I didn't know anyone was looking. It was on one of the most recent pages, where the activity had ramped up since Felicity was 'finally' saying what needed to be said.

I was pale and bare-faced, my unwashed hair scraped back in a ponytail, wearing unflattering shorts and a baggy t-shirt. It was taken in the emergency room on Sunday. Jamie was beside me, his head in his hands. The photo had triggered a flurry of commentary.

> Holy shit, what's the bet she's going to claim self-harm? Like, 'people are being mean to me on the internet so look what I did to myself!' She's unhinged. Genuinely, I'd put money on the fact that she'll turn this into a mental health crisis where she's the victim.
>
> Are we going to talk about the partner who looks like he wants to run for the hills? Poor guy. He's also actually quite

good-looking lol he must be realising that he's wasting his time with her and could do so much better.

It's like a trainwreck! I can't look away. I am so happy she's finally being called out for the horrible, disgusting person she is. Good work unearthing those posts, team. She's an absolute disgrace and this just goes to show that bullies don't always win.

By that point I had already learnt that it was the people on that thread who had dug through every word and every image I'd ever posted to find the very worst things and then sent them to Felicity Cartwright. They adored her. They praised her like she was a freedom fighter, some kind of saviour for the disenfranchised. And in facilitating my destruction, she became even more special. A god.

They loved Beth, too. They needed the binary: good people and bad people, justice and injustice, kindness and cruelty. Once they had placed you in one of those categories, anything you did only served to further confirm your status.

I fell into a dreamless sleep in the early hours of that morning, the sun peeping through the dusty curtains of my lonely cabin. When I woke up, I knew I had to delete every social media app, from everywhere, and I knew I couldn't return to *Bared*. They weren't choices like any I'd made before. They actually weren't choices at all. They were necessary steps in order to ensure my survival.

Chapter 41

When you stop looking at your phone, a few strange things happen.

First, time slows down. You're more aware of the seconds, the hours, the days. You're not losing them, having them disappear into a place you cannot name.

This is equal parts rewarding and frustrating. You become acutely aware of your impatience. For a while, nothing is happening fast enough. The kettle boils in slow motion and the post office line is an abomination and every book and movie *drags on and on* and a walk down the street is utterly unbearable. You're enraged. You want to file a complaint with the manager of modern society. Every single person is incompetent and every system is broken.

You start to blame the problem on everyone else's phone use. They're wasting their lives away! They're distracted! They're not looking! You want to grab the devices that are stealing the precious attention of the human race and flush them all down the toilet. How has no one else realised the cost of this? How can no one else see what we've become?

You are, with all due respect, insufferable. But only for a bit. Then you enter the next stage.

You're high. Enlightened. You've discovered dopamine again—the kind that doesn't exclusively come from a screen. You crave good food and wild sex and new experiences, and you're bursting with energy to *live*. You think this might be the person you were meant to be all along, the person you would've been if you hadn't spent the last fifteen years staring dead-faced at the inside of your hand. But this isn't permanent, either.

You come back to a baseline that feels familiar.

You listen when your partner talks about work, or when Mum calls to tell you about Colleen's holiday to Vietnam, or when Liv has a truly terrible business idea.

You notice things. The wilted frangipanis squashed into the pavement. You pick one up by the stem and run your finger along its velvet petal, smelling the burst of yellow in the centre, hoping no one's watching you and thinking you're a freak.

No one is watching.

The smell brings you back to Christmas Day at your nana's house, the frangipani tree in the front yard wrapping your childhood in sweetness.

You see a toddler in the street one day, and you cry. It happens again. And again. You've started to talk about it, now. All of it.

For you, the online outrage was never really what it seemed, either. It was about shame. And for so long, you've been so deeply, profoundly ashamed.

...

The healing didn't happen in a single moment, in any dramatic discovery. It happened slowly and quietly, in zigzags, in stilted conversations and re-examined memories.

I thought about how, when I was at *The Daily*, I'd written a viral article about an influencer who was an anti-vaxxer. I'd been so proud of the traffic, of how I could represent my values by defining them in opposition to someone else. Then she'd written me an email. Three years prior, her friend had died after receiving a vaccination. It was one of the very, very rare but medically substantiated instances of someone developing a serious—and ultimately fatal—side effect linked to the vaccine. She was being abused online, she said, which was re-traumatising after the loss of her friend. She wanted to speak to me in person, to explain her experiences, so I might understand, so I might remove the article. I didn't. I told her I was sorry, but that I was very passionate about the public health benefits of vaccination. How had I been so cold? What had I been trying to prove?

I started having coffee catch-ups with Yasmin, who had become a friend once we'd stopped being colleagues. She was the editor-in-chief at *Bared* now, and I was relieved to find I had no sense of jealousy about her promotion. I was, however, still curious about the gossip. Yasmin told me Beth was gone, after the head of the IT department noticed that her login was being used on several different devices, sometimes in multiple places at once. He investigated further and found she had shared her details with people outside the company—people who were accessing *Bared*'s analytics and trawling through the unpublished stories in the back end of the site. Ian had already picked up on Beth's contempt for *Bared*, and her close friendships with several people in the industry who seemed to be leading the charge against the brand.

It was enough, Yasmin told me, to threaten her with charges of 'corporate espionage'. Beth agreed to resign quietly, without a fuss.

Weeks turned into months, and every now and then I'd see the looks. The waitress who stopped to stare on her way back into the cafe, the new mother pushing a pram who was too tired to disguise her curiosity. Maybe they didn't even know where they recognised me from. Soon, surely, they'd forget.

I'd picked up some copywriting work when I'd left *Bared*, and discovered that people were mostly fine to employ me to write, so long as my name didn't appear alongside the copy. Then I did some freelance consulting, which paid a lot better. I was offered a role at a large consulting firm providing clients with media solutions, and Liv joked that now I was the one who couldn't explain my job at dinner parties. For the first time in my life, work was just work.

Months turned into a year, and I surprised myself by feeling thankful that I'd been forced to step off the destructive treadmill I'd been trapped on. But the thing about healing is that, despite how it looks on the internet, it's perpetually incomplete. Sometimes all you need is a tug for all the stitches to come apart.

Chapter 42

Two years later

My water broke because of a storm. That's what a chatty midwife told me the day after the birth, when it had all gone so horribly wrong that I must've asked why.

It had been the worst storm in a decade. While I laboured at home, the winds were so fierce that they ripped the flyscreen from our bedroom window and flung the glass open. Then the wind grasped the curtain and pulled it through the gap with such force the curtain rod cracked under the weight. Jamie and I ran in when we heard the bang. I looked down at the dark clump of curtain on the footpath, my huge bump pressed against the window frame, and thought: *It's not meant to be like this.*

The drop in barometric pressure, I told myself later, had ruptured the amniotic fluid around my baby before he was ready. That's why his tiny body wouldn't descend down the birth canal, why he flopped into a position where he was facing my stomach instead of my back, why my cervix never fully dilated.

The first sign of my little boy was the watery, pale yellow leak in my grey underpants. It was tinged with pink, a streak of blood mixed with mucus, and I knew it was him. An hour later, in a tightly made hospital bed with Jamie's face pressed against mine, two rubber-coated fingers pushed so far into my vagina that I thought they would tear me in half. We were sent home to wait for labour to start, and it did, and then the sky began to roar and the building began to shake and an angry giant reached through the bedroom window and snatched our curtain.

In the early hours of the next morning, the contractions changed. Dull, shapeless waves were replaced with the sharp, hot sensation of being stabbed in the anus with a poker. I woke Jamie and we drove to the hospital through quiet streets covered in fallen branches.

A gentle midwife dressed me in a pale blue hospital gown and strapped a belt around my belly. On the screen beside me, a thin white line rose with my pain, and with each crest

I begged for an anaesthetist who did not come. He was on his way, I was next in line, he would be here soon, he would be here soon, he would be here soon. I inhaled the gas attached to the wall, not because it relieved the agony of the weapon sawing at the deepest layers of my flesh, but because it made me feel drunk.

I could not speak. My eyes were squeezed shut. At some point my mind left the room and went somewhere else. I was not in a hospital but in the house where I grew up, sitting on the floor with my back to the shutters, laughing as Liv tried to prise the last chip from my mouth.

I was cuddled up to Mum as she read to me, my hair still wet from the bath. We were reading *The Witches* and I was scared. I wanted to sleep in her bed, to spend all my days with her, so she could tell me who the witches were, so she could make sure I didn't get tricked.

I was walking home from school with Liv, the straps of our heavy schoolbags digging into our shoulders. I was telling her about what happened in drama, that we had to choose partners for our duologue, that no one picked me. She looked at me and said I was her favourite person in the whole world, that no one understood how brilliant I was, that being underestimated was my superpower. I believed her.

I was hunched in front of the TV, cross-legged on the rough, patterned carpet that disguised the stains from spilt soft drink and pasta sauce. Mum and Dad were lying on the lounge behind me, and Liv was near the heater with Macky, wearing a t-shirt but no pants. Dad was telling her to put warm clothes on and turn the heater off, that the electricity bill would send us broke, that she'd burn herself if she got any closer. She was ignoring him because we were all watching this movie, the one where the boy gets stung by the bees and he's allergic. I had the overwhelming sense that everything I'd ever needed was in this room, that if we could all just be together, if we could lock all the doors, I would be okay.

Then I was back in the hospital room, the cold lights pointed towards me, the rhythmic sound of a monitor or an alarm overpowering my voice. I vomited before anyone heard me ask for a bag, and the bile soaked through my gown, sticking to my clammy skin. My baby was in distress, the midwife said. The doctor was coming to deliver him.

I couldn't, I said. I needed an epidural. They had to wait.

When the doctor entered, followed by two others holding trays of sterile metal instruments, I howled. I turned to Jamie and begged him to take me to the car park to be shot. I don't know why I thought that was possible, that he had access to a gun or could get me downstairs, but at the time it seemed entirely rational.

The doctor looked like he had just woken up, his thin, white hair uncombed. He put my legs in stirrups and said my name firmly, drilling his gaze into mine. He asked me if I could push, if I was strong enough, if I had enough energy, and I shouted that I needed the baby out. He showed me the vacuum that would assist the delivery, and told me I had three pushes or there would be significant risks to me and my baby.

I pushed the first time and thought my eyes were going to pop out of their sockets. I imagined my pelvic floor tearing from the bone, obliterated by the force of a machine inside me, pulling a human head through tight tissue.

I pushed the second time and the baby was coming, the opening of my body not wide enough to let him through. The doctor asked the question like it was not a question. He needed to make a controlled incision to get the baby out.

I would've said yes to anything at that point. A chainsaw. A cricket bat. If it would end this torture, I wanted it.

But something about the monotone of his voice, about how the scalpel was hidden in his hand, about how two men stared at a part of me I could not see, while my legs were splayed open and my gown was covered in vomit, felt menacing. It felt cold and predatory and violent.

And so when my son was born, I did not react.

And when he did not cry, I did not react.

And this—the fact that I lacked the instinct for love in those first, most vulnerable moments of my baby's life—made me feel like a monster.

Chapter 43

I lay with my back to the plastic bassinet. The baby's head would heal, the doctor said. It was a subgaleal haemorrhage, a term I still don't fully understand, but from what my exhausted brain could piece together after four days of no sleep, it meant that the trauma from the vacuum had been so severe that my baby was bleeding on the surface of his skull.

I couldn't look at him. The swelling was in the shape of a cone, and the top of his scalp had started to scab, with flakes of blood attaching to his fine, brown hair. When I'd held him earlier, I'd brushed my finger along his ear and felt that there was fluid there, too, contorting the side of his face and under his eye. I recoiled. I didn't want to see the marks of his brutal birth on his tiny body, just like I didn't want to see the stitches between my legs. I had noticed in the shower—that first glorious but degrading opportunity to wash the fluids of birth from your skin—that the entire front of my pubic bone was bruised, as was the skin at the top of my thighs. 'You'll be amazed by how quickly it all heals,' the midwife told me, busying herself so as not to stare at the pale woman sitting in a shower chair watching clots of blood from her uterus disappear down the drain.

I was still facing the door, and not my baby, when I heard footsteps approaching on the sickly grey lino. Mum and Liv poked their heads in, holding flowers and an oversized teddy and a bag of snacks. They both came to me first, Mum squeezing me tight, then Jamie, and then went to our baby.

'Oh, Ruby.' Mum's lips were trembling, and she covered them with her hand. She squinted briefly, to absorb her tears, and reopened her eyes to study the contours of the sleeping boy in front of her. She stroked his foot, his leg, his cheek.

Mum didn't like to display emotion. I imagined she had trained herself not to, for fear that if she started, she might never stop. I wondered what this was like for her, to stand in a hospital room and peer down at a baby boy who might've resembled her own. To know that Max had been this small, this precious, this helpless, and that he never got to grow up.

• • •

'The reverse of creation.' That's how some people describe a black hole. A place that destroys the very laws that allow the universe to exist. A place so warped that there are no exits, no avenues of escape.

An old colleague of mine, Rachel, had told me that when she gave birth a few months before I did, it was like looking into the universe. It was the most transformative experience of her life, she said, and in my last days of pregnancy, she messaged me to say she couldn't wait for me to understand. She said nothing would ever be the same again, that I would become a fundamentally different person.

Now, I watched my mother cuddle the human I had created, and I felt nothing. I had looked into the universe, exactly as Rachel had promised, but I hadn't seen what she saw. My universe had an irreparable defect, a gash where the stars should be, and I was both teetering on the edge of it and already inside. I had been swallowed by a black hole long ago—a black hole that was the corpse of the brightest star I had ever known.

The hole itself was a rupture in space-time, so once it consumed me, there ceased to be a past or a future, there was no such thing as physical reality, just emptiness. Without the laws of physics to govern me, I was not only here, in a hospital bed, having just given birth. I was also in front of the beige computer in the kitchen, on the day Max died. I was in the cafe with Jo, about to write the story that destroyed me. I was the shadow version of myself who had been assembled online, and I was all the pieces that composed it. I was every terrible thing anyone had ever called me. *Vile, heartless, disgusting, reprehensible, shameful, ugly, undeserving, cruel, narcissistic, embarrassing.*

There were infinite dimensions and infinite timelines and infinite incarnations of me, but within infinity is nothingness. The void.

And it was my emptiness that haunted me. My knowledge of what I was not and could never be. My lack. Because if I was capable of creating a tiny, baby boy, I knew I was capable of destroying him, too.

Chapter 44

It was the morning of his hearing test. The one where they put little headphones on your newborn, so it looks like they're listening to a podcast. Most people take a cute photo, maybe send it to their families, joking that their little girl or boy is going to be a DJ. We didn't take a photo.

Every examination, every check, I was certain, was the one where the truth would come out. Where the respiratory rate or the heart rate or the temperature or the reflexes or the muscle tone or the auditory brainstem response would be outside the bounds of normality, and I would learn that this deep feeling inside me that I was about to be pushed off a cliff, clutching my tiny baby in my arms, had been a warning.

That morning, he wouldn't latch. The midwives had told me to keep his pink, wrinkled body against my bare chest for as many hours as possible, so that his instincts might kick in. 'Well, he didn't get breastfed immediately, so that's probably confused him,' an older midwife said, her rubber shoes squeaking while she wheeled the blood-pressure machine to my bedside. 'There's a reason they call those first few hours after birth the golden hours—they're so critical for skin-to-skin contact and early breastfeeding. Crucial hormones for mum, baby feels safe and secure to seek out the breast. But you can't wind back the clock now, can you?'

I waited until she left the room to fall apart. I sobbed, my whole body shaking with the force of it. The shame. The anger. The irresolvable pain of regretting something you weren't able to control, of wishing that it had been different, that I had been able to give my child what he deserved. Jamie gently lifted the sleeping baby off my chest, put him in his bassinet, and crawled into bed beside me. He held me, letting me heave into his chest, and said only, 'I know, I know.'

The hearing test was in a tiny exam room at the end of the ward. A tired-looking woman sat behind what looked like a computer from the 1980s and ran the screening in silence. I stared at my baby, his head still misshapen, his eyes closed, his body wrapped tightly in a striped blanket. My vision was blurry, like I was trying to see underwater without goggles, and I could sense my heart beating rapidly in my chest. I knew with certainty that there was a piece of me that was utterly broken. My soul, if there is such a thing, had been exposed and torn apart. Birth had made me feel vulnerable and helpless in a way I only ever had once before. It had eroded my trust in the universe, in my own safety.

'It's fine, he passed,' said the woman, standing up and removing the equipment from our baby's head.

'He's going to be a classical musician, aren't you, buddy?' Jamie said, smiling at me, his eyes bloodshot from sleep deprivation.

I nodded. I couldn't speak, because I knew if I spoke I would cry. I leant over our little boy's face and stroked his cheek. It was warm and softer than anything I had ever touched in my life. If I was weak and ultimately defenceless, what about him? With his heart the size of a walnut. With his skull not yet fused together, and his head, his poor head, filled with a bloodied bruise.

Jamie pushed the bassinet out of the exam room, and I looked down at the white card stuck on the back. I didn't remember who had filled it in, but in thick black texta someone had written his date of birth, the time of his birth, his birth weight and length. At the very top, the space for his name was blank.

I wondered if the midwives had talked about it. If they'd whispered about that exhausted-looking couple with the sleepy baby who wouldn't latch, who hadn't even bothered to name him.

The lump in my throat was there when I saw her. Walking out of one of the rooms, turning down the hallway. I recognised her immediately. Her shiny auburn hair, her distinctive teeth, the pitch of her voice as she said goodbye to whomever she was visiting, the shape of her mouth as the sound came out. I stopped. I must've made a noise because Jamie turned around, and when he saw my face he stepped away from the bassinet and towards me. He was probably going to ask me if I was okay, if I needed to sit down. One midwife had said women sometimes faint in the days after birth, and it could be a sign of postpartum haemorrhage. I was, of course, convinced that it would happen to me.

I imagine I looked terrible. But Jamie didn't have a chance to ask if I was dizzy. By the time he grabbed me, I was already screaming.

PART THREE

Chapter 45

I didn't recognise her, initially. She was so pale, her face rounder than I remembered. I thought this poor woman must be having one of those postpartum mental breakdowns. Then I recognised that expression. That quintessential Ruby Williams look, the one that made her seem so bloody innocent and fragile, the one that had irritated me since the moment I'd first laid eyes on her.

She kept shouting the words, 'GET OUT!' in my direction, pointing at me with an aggressive finger. Her husband was facing her, trying to get her to calm down, but she kept wailing, 'Why is she here? Why is she here?' over and over again, as though I wasn't just as entitled to be in the maternity ward of a public hospital as her.

My sister, Kelly, had just had a baby. At forty-one. Entirely on her own. An unmedicated water birth because she's that sort of person. And I was her bath partner, watching her moan and shake and go to someplace deep within herself to push out a five-kilo baby boy. 'Felicity?' she'd said afterwards, her voice almost gone from the strain of the last several hours. I'd thought she was asleep while I sat beside her, the pink, sticky newborn resting against my chest. 'You know, he's yours, too,' she said, the words muffled by the starchy hospital sheet. The room was dark and quiet, apart from the squeaks of the miracle in my arms. 'He's ours.'

I silently wiped the tears from my cheeks and wondered, if she really meant what she said, whether we could properly discuss his name, then. She'd named him Zeus, meaning 'the supreme god', which I thought took a lot of audacity. I didn't say anything, of course, but I couldn't imagine ever calling him that. Maybe I'd nickname him 'Z'.

Now, finally, I was going home to sleep for the first time in almost two days, and here I was getting shouted at by someone I loathed.

I kept waiting for the midwives to intervene. Surely things like this happened all the time, and they knew how to diffuse a situation and send distressed new mothers on their way. But for a good while they just stood there awkwardly, watching us, like this one-sided fight might resolve itself.

Her husband attempted to stop her from approaching me. He grabbed her by the arm but promptly dropped it, because

I guess you're not really meant to put your hands on a woman, especially when she's still bleeding from delivering your baby. He watched helplessly as she came within an inch of my face, so close that bits of her spit landed on my lips. There was a wildness in her eyes. 'My baby almost died,' she hissed. 'My body was torn apart. And in the back of my head, I still have your words and the words of all the people you encouraged playing on repeat. You know what I thought of when they took a scalpel to my vagina? I thought of how many times I've been called a cunt. And what the fuck that even meant. I thought of the rape threats I got after you posted that video. I thought of how you so confidently told half-a-million people that I don't care about anyone other than myself, and there I was, willing to die so this baby—'

Her voice cracked on that last word, echoing through the hall. I had no idea what any of that had to do with me. Why on earth would you be thinking about social media in hospital, when you're vulnerable and sensitive? It wasn't my fault that she'd behaved badly, and that people had told her so. It also wasn't my fault she'd had a brutal birth. That was just nature: cruel and violent and unjust.

'We will never get this time back, me and him,' she spat. 'The days after he was born. It's ruined. It's broken. *I* am broken.'

Suddenly, her expression changed. Her brows narrowed and she sucked her bottom lip, glancing at an older midwife who had appeared at the nurses' station.

'Can I . . . can I just know why?' she said slowly, between uneven breaths. 'Why do you hate me? What did I do? What is it about me?'

I studied her face. Her hair was oily, and a few strands were stuck to her forehead. Without make-up on, her features were washed out, her lips almost the same pallor as her skin, her eyelashes almost invisible. How on earth could I answer that question? We weren't teenage girls who didn't get along—she was a former editor whose actions had come with consequences.

The midwife was beside her now. She made Ruby look like a child, wrapping her arm around her back and rubbing it, beckoning the husband over.

'Why don't we go back to our bed and have a rest, hey? It's been a big couple of days.'

I saw the baby being wheeled towards her, fast asleep in the plastic bassinet. His head was misshapen, swollen, and there was a bloodied scab on his hairline. He was so small.

'This one here is tougher than she looks,' the midwife said, gesturing to Ruby. She leant over to encourage a nod from the husband. It was as though she was speaking to me, which was bizarre given that I still hadn't said anything. I'd just been shouted at in a public place, a few metres from where my sister was resting beside her newborn, and apparently I now had to hear how special this woman was—the one best known online for making a series of truly appalling decisions.

The midwife appeared to be in her sixties, and now that she was in front of me, I noticed she looked eerily like my mother. She had the same wispy hair, grey at the roots despite obvious attempts to dye it brown. Her eyes were like Mum's, too, gentle and softened with age, the expression lines so embedded that whatever she was feeling was written plainly across her face. Then there was the voice. A huskiness that made you trust everything she said. A steadiness. Just like Mum, I'm sure anyone who had ever worked with her would describe her as 'tough but fair'.

She turned to Ruby. 'Probably one of the biggest experiences you'll ever go through and you're doing so well. Look at this little guy—how comfortable is he? But we have to be gentle with ourselves. Give ourselves some grace. All of this is new and there's no perfect way to do it. We just do our best. Isn't that right?'

She looked at me now. I thought she might mouth an apology, or roll her eyes. Some acknowledgement of the weirdness of the confrontation. But she just smiled, as though she expected me to understand. As though accosting someone was totally fine so long as you'd given birth recently, and your baby had a sore head.

They shuffled back down the hall, the midwife rattling on about the cake selection at the cafe downstairs. I turned to watch them disappear into their room, the slow, unsteady woman, the tall, exhausted man, the sleeping baby, and the animated ball of energy moving them along.

I was still stunned by it when I got to my car. The combination of a lack of sleep and being confronted with both an unexpected burst of aggression and the ghost of my mother was so overwhelming that I just sat there, frozen, staring at the steering wheel. I had tried not to think about Mum over the last few days. I knew if I did, I'd fall apart, and Kelly needed me to distract her and make her laugh and help her with nappy changes—both hers and the baby's. In those hours after the birth, though, while Kelly dozed with Zeus on her chest and I laid on the recliner beside her, I felt something. A squeeze on my shoulder. Firm, reassuring. Like a thank you. And even though I'm not woo-woo, and I don't believe in any of that stuff, I had the fleeting thought that it was Mum. She was there, proud of both of us, probably winking at me about the name.

Then it was as if I'd seen her. Heard her voice. She'd smiled at me with the same eyes, her arm wrapped around a person who did not deserve it.

I turned on the car, and the music came on automatically. It was the playlist I'd put together for Kelly's birth, full of our favourite songs, ones that meant something, had made us feel something, through all the different eras of our lives. We'd got about four songs in before Kelly shouted at me, mid-contraction, to turn it off. It wasn't the right mood, she said, and for the rest of her six-hour labour she screamed into a music-less room.

Now, in the car park, one of the songs was playing. I heard the first few melancholy bars, and laughed. Kelly was right. I'd misjudged the mood entirely. But then the lyrics started, and I was right back there. Fifteen. In the car with Mum. Her steady voice singing along, her hand squeezing my leg, trying desperately, with every bit of her magic, to make it okay.

Chapter 46

There is perhaps no sense of repulsion as strong as that which a teenage girl feels towards herself. Especially when she is ostracised, alienated, rejected, so that she's sure others see something even more hideous than what she sees in the mirror.

That day, Mum had dropped me off out the front of the shopping centre, pulling over in a bus zone. She wanted to come in and do some shopping herself, but I begged her not to. The idea of running into Mum while I was with my friends was mortifying, and I knew they'd think I had her hanging around on purpose. Because I was immature. Weird. A fucking loser. So I jumped out of the car with a twenty-dollar note buried in the pocket of my white, three-quarter-length cargo pants, and told her to pick me up at five, absolutely no later.

The Worst Thing I've Ever Done

We were meant to be meeting at two, but by a quarter past I was still standing alone in the food court above the movies. Hayley had told the four of us to meet at Donut King, and as I stood in front of the glass display cabinet, I caught the familiar smell of warm cinnamon that always reminded me of going to the orthodontist with Mum. At my most recent appointment, I'd asked for fluoro pink and green bands on my braces, and was so excited to show everyone at school. Then Hayley had pointed out that it looked like I had food permanently stuck in my teeth, and they were gross colours anyway, and now every time I saw them I was embarrassed by my boldness. I should've just got black. They were meant to make your teeth look less yellow.

It was almost half past now, and I was trying to look relaxed, even though the movie was starting soon. I never knew what to do when I was by myself. My hands hung awkwardly by my sides in a way no one else's seemed to. My waistband dug into my hips, forcing white flesh to poke out over the top of my pants. I'd recently come across the term 'love handles' in a magazine and realised that's exactly what I had—pockets of fat on my sides, above my hip bones, that swelled over whatever I wore. The tight pink t-shirt I'd grabbed from the washing basket didn't quite reach the top of my pants, and so the softness of my belly was exposed, an almost translucent band of skin around my middle. The scrawniness of my arms and legs seemed only to emphasise my shapeless tummy and growing bust. My proportions also meant that nothing fit, and I was never wearing the right fashion on weekends or plain clothes days at school.

I would never have admitted it to my friends, but this was my first time being in a shopping centre alone. Before, I was always with Mum or Kelly or Nan, but I was fifteen now, and I was old enough to meet people and not have Mum wait with me. But without anyone to ask, I wasn't sure what you were meant to do if the people you were meeting hadn't shown up. This was a time before mobile phones, so there was no way to check if there had been some confusion. If there was another version of reality where we were meant to meet at Muffin Break or Gloria Jean's, and the others had been waiting there, wondering where Felicity was.

I checked my watch again—the one I'd got from a showbag a few months before. It was now after half past, and the movie would be starting soon. I kept thinking I could see Hayley, only to realise it was another girl with straight brown hair. Someone with their mum or a friend, who had no reason to look over at the tall, freckly, lonely figure standing too close to the doughnut display. People kept asking if I was in line and I had to keep saying no.

I thought about walking around the food court to look for them, but I was worried that if I left where I was standing, everyone would turn up and be annoyed with me for not waiting where we'd planned to meet. At the same time, I was certain the others were together, because they couldn't all be this late. Rhiannon was never late.

I decided to go to the bathroom. That way I could get a view of the cinema foyer down the escalators. If I found them, I'd just casually explain I was going to the loo—not that I'd been waiting for forty minutes on my own and had almost cried when a middle-aged woman had stopped to ask if I was all right.

I heard Hayley before I saw her. She was laughing, and the sound pierced through the Saturday afternoon hum of disembodied voices and passing pop music. I looked down to the level below to see the three of them—Rhiannon, Kaati and Hayley—at the bottom of the escalators, holding McDonald's cups. They must have eaten together, I realised, feeling a sudden pang of hunger. I hadn't let Mum make lunch because the plan was for me to meet my friends, eat and then see the movie.

Part of me wanted to continue on to the bathroom and never come out. To sit there alone and cry, kicking myself for every minute I had stood alone, paralysed by my own awkwardness and uncertainty. But if I went downstairs and met the others, I could tell them I hadn't eaten yet and maybe get a frozen Coke and some popcorn. I pictured myself in the dark, air-conditioned cinema, laughing at Rhiannon's silly quips, the anxiety of the afternoon replaced by the warm glow of being included.

Rhiannon spotted me when I was halfway down the escalator. I smiled and waved, but she avoided my gaze, nudging

Kaati to get her attention. Kaati's eyes brushed over me, and then she turned back to Rhiannon and giggled.

I was in front of them now, at the bottom of the escalators, trying to move out of the way of the people behind me.

'Hey,' I said, sensing the word had come out louder than I'd meant it to. 'I was waiting at Donut King. I couldn't find you guys.'

Hayley looked at me for the first time, and I saw her glance at my cargo pants, then at my t-shirt. It was stained with sweat patches I was clumsily trying to hide with my arms.

'Wait, why were you at Donut King?' she asked. 'Who goes to Donut King?'

They all laughed. From the way they looked at each other, I could tell they'd been talking about me. Predicting what I'd say so that when I said it, it was mortifying. A confirmation of my weirdness.

'We agreed to meet at Donut King and then get food before the movie,' I said, glancing at their matching cups. 'Did you guys get McDonald's?'

But they weren't listening to me; they were looking at each other. I was about to ask if they'd bought their tickets yet when Hayley, and maybe Rhiannon, too, yelled, 'GO!'

For a moment, I didn't realise what was going on. They shrieked and ran, their shoes squeaking on the shopping centre's shiny floors, heading towards a nearby department store, away from the cinema and away from me.

I can still hear the echo of their laughter. The intensity of it. The glee of those three girls as they ran away. I can see the smirks on their faces. The acknowledgement that they knew something I didn't.

I'm not sure how long I waited. Maybe five minutes, maybe fifteen.

Then, with a sense of heaviness, no longer hungry and no longer wanting to be anywhere I could be seen, I walked outside to the payphones. I only had my twenty-dollar note so had to buy a can of Solo to get change to call home.

I waited in the gutter, near the buses. A homeless man asked if I had any money and I gave him ten dollars. *I might not have friends*, I thought, *but at least I am a good person*. Generous. Compassionate to those less fortunate.

When I got in the car, I couldn't speak. Mum shook her head and said Hayley was a bitch, but that left bigger, silent questions. Why was she only that way towards me? Why had Rhiannon and Kaati gone along with it? Why had they bothered to invite me in the first place?

Mum rubbed my leg, and I looked down at the cargo pants. I never wanted to wear them again. The other girls had all been in jeans, with the same brand of white sneakers that I didn't own. Why didn't I have a pair of jeans? Why didn't Mum ever take me to the right shops? My shoes were a cheap knock-off of the brand everyone else wore, with four stripes instead of three.

One of Mum's favourite songs came on the radio, and she turned it up and sang along. It was a sombre ballad, one that made me stare out the window pretending I was in a film clip, the afternoon sun sprinkled artfully on my face. Maybe I'd be a singer one day, or an actress, and everyone who had ever been cruel to me would regret it. They'd realise I was beautiful, in that quirky, model-esque way, where the right haircut and make-up reveals you had uniquely stunning features all along.

When we pulled into the driveway, Mum switched off the ignition and told me that people like Hayley always get what they deserve in the end. They're stuck with their meanness while the girls who care about justice and equality and integrity get the gift of a truly fulfilling life. Of course, at fifteen, I didn't want a fulfilling life. I wanted friends who didn't run away from me.

• • •

By Monday morning, I'd prepared what I was going to say. I was going to stand up for myself and make them understand how they'd made me feel. They would see how wrong their behaviour had been, that they were bullies, that they were heartless and cold, and they'd be horrified. I was a real person, and they'd done something unthinkable.

But when I said as much to Hayley, she seemed confused.

'It was clearly a joke!' she said. 'We didn't know where you went. How did you get home? We waited for you and even missed the first bit of the movie.'

I couldn't believe what I was hearing.

'You told me to wait at Donut King,' I said, my voice already shaking. 'I waited there for forty minutes and none of you showed up. Then I found you and you all ran away. It was really mean.'

Hayley just laughed. 'Okay, no offence, Felicity, but you're *obsessed* with Donut King. And it's not my fault if you can't take a joke.'

• • •

At a sleepover towards the end of high school, the truth came out. We were going around in a circle, everyone sharing one good thing and one bad thing about each other. When it was Kaati's turn, no one could think of anything bad to say. She was so pretty, with her big white smile, her chestnut hair, her almond-shaped eyes, her golden brown skin. Every teacher adored her, as did all the boys we hung out with, because she laughed at them, even when what they said wasn't very funny. When it was my turn, the bad things tumbled out like wooden pieces at the end of a game of Jenga.

I was annoying, they said. My voice, my hobbies, my retainer (which I'd had to wear after my braces), my taste in music, the way I quoted movies, the books I read at lunchtime. My breath smelt. I was too competitive, too emotional, too sensitive. I took everything too seriously.

Then Hayley remembered how 'dramatic' I'd been after that day at the shopping centre. Leading up to it, I'd kept suggesting we meet at Donut King, apparently. Probably because I knew where it was, and I didn't want to get lost. So Hayley had agreed we'd meet there, but then told the other girls to meet at McDonald's, where they had watched me from across the food court, talking about my 'cringe' pants and my shoes. They *were* going to meet me eventually, but I had chosen the movie and they wanted to check if there was anything better on, because I always wanted to watch something 'lame'.

'We ran away because, in our defence, we didn't know how to tell you to stop being annoying,' Hayley said.

The other girls, sitting on the floor of Rhiannon's bedroom, all nodded.

'And we wanted to be your friend because, like, you're smart and stuff, and sometimes you're funny, but we didn't want you to be so weird. Like, Kaati wanted to invite these guys to come, but she couldn't do that if you were going to make us look like a loser group who were still into *The Simpsons*, yeah?'

• • •

After school, I wasn't friends with those girls anymore. Once, when I first started going viral on social media, I noticed Kaati had liked one of my posts. It didn't feel how I thought it would, in that it didn't feel like anything at all. None of the pain was really about them as individuals, it was about what it did to me. What it still does to me. For the last decade, I've built a significant following—mostly of women. Hundreds of thousands of them. They think I'm funny and clever, and when they see me in public they want photos with me to post to all their friends. But despite all of it—the likes, the comments, the messages, the brand deals—I haven't really changed. I'm still that teenage girl standing outside Donut King, certain I'm being laughed at.

Chapter 47

I remember the first time I saw the name Ruby Williams. It was printed under a headline about beauty hacks, where she'd asked a dozen women to share details about their eyebrow pencils and their slicked buns and something called slugging, which involves putting Vaseline over your skincare before you go to bed at night, so, I suppose, you look like a slug. I almost laughed. I was working at *The Daily*, the same publication that had commissioned this absurd story, and I was appalled that my journalism and whatever this was could possibly be grouped under the same masthead. But apparently it was crucial that women be taught how to make themselves look like non-sentient creatures best known for secreting a disturbing amount of mucus.

I noticed Ruby in the office after that. She had just started as part of the digital team and sat with all the other junior writers, who looked like they could feasibly still be in high school. I didn't have much to do with digital, crossing paths only in soul-destroying company-wide meetings, where their eyes glazed over whenever the agenda didn't directly concern them. Once, the editor-in-chief announced that I'd won a national journalism award for my political reporting, and when I scanned the cheering room with a self-conscious smile, I spotted Ruby. She was standing beside the door, her head bent over her phone, chewing her nails. The guy next to her whispered something in her ear and she turned to him and laughed. She didn't clap. She didn't even seem to notice what was going on. Which said it all, really. People like her don't care about anyone other than themselves.

Ruby was tall and lean, her sinewy arms and narrow hips clearly the result of early-morning Pilates and ocean swimming. She had thick, dark hair and enormous brown eyes that gave her a startled look, like she was perpetually scared of getting into trouble. Her voice was high and giggly and baby-like, the voice of a child who was too innocent to engage in critical thought or challenge authority.

I started seeing her by-line more and more on *The Daily*'s homepage. On stories about vacuous celebrities and insufferable influencers and the fucking royals and 'viral' trends. The newsroom was disproportionately male, and now, apparently, they had a woman to give a long-awaited 'female' perspective.

It seemed to be her job to select the dumbest, most shallow entertainment and lifestyle stories from the news cycle and convince people that's what the silly ladies really cared about. She clearly wasn't interested in politics or public policy or social justice or the economy or innovation. Instead, her dull, creaseless face appeared above an article about butthole sunning, a practice that involved exposing one's bare arse to sunlight because it had (entirely unproven) health benefits. That was another thing writers like her loved to do. They reported extensively on dangerous wellness advice while pretending they were being critical of it. *Don't do this!* they shouted. *But for content purposes I'm going to tell you exactly how to do it!*

We spent years in the same office, and she never spoke to me. She never asked me about my work or congratulated me when my stories brought about legitimate political change. Sometimes we'd be standing beside each other at the cafe in the lobby and her nose would be buried in her phone, like she was just *so* busy with her ridiculous job she couldn't possibly be offline. And whatever, that was fine. She was a nobody.

Then, over the course of a few months, two things happened. First, I was made redundant, and second, Mum got sick.

I had been at *The Daily* for eight years. Almost a decade of award-winning political journalism. I was determined to establish myself as the most balanced, well-researched, tenacious political journalist in the country, and according to both the trophies on my desk and the following I'd built on social media, a lot of people would say I'd succeeded. You might be familiar with the video of me in the prime minister's courtyard, confronting the leader of our country with demeaning texts he'd sent about a female cabinet member. Or the one under the budget tree, where the treasurer announced that most workers' wages would fall over the coming years and, with a single pointed question, I got him to admit that politicians had just been granted a significant pay rise. I uncovered a parliamentary affair that got a cabinet minister sacked. I broke the news of an impending leadership coup.

But *The Daily* was divesting specialised roles, they told me, and growing the social and digital teams. I was being made redundant, while a twelve-year-old writer called Ruby Williams was doing the urgent work of asking influencers what they fed their toddlers.

I told Mum on a Saturday morning at her house, while she tended to the vines and the plants in the back garden. She had always been proud of my work, telling her friends to look out for my face in the paper. She'd once told me that if she could have her time again, without a husband who insisted they start a family young then left her to raise two little girls on her own, she would've been a journalist, too.

She held me in her arms as I blinked back tears. She smelt of floral hand cream and powder foundation, and I breathed her in, thinking that she was the most familiar smell in the world.

That day she mentioned the weakness on her left side. I dismissed it. She was ageing, I reminded her, and she didn't exercise, so it was no wonder she didn't feel strong. She agreed to start swimming at the local pool again, like she had when we were kids.

She never did go swimming, though. Kelly noticed her speech was slurred and took her to hospital, which led to tests and follow-up appointments and eventually a neurologist's office in Westmead. The three of us sat on hard plastic chairs while he told us it was motor neurone disease. He started to explain what that meant, what they had found when they analysed Mum's neural function and muscle activity, but I wasn't listening. I knew about it already from late-night Google searches. That the nerves in her spine and brain would deteriorate, and she would lose control of her limbs and her speech and eventually her ability to breathe. She was only fifty-seven.

I had no income and a dying mother, so at thirty-two I moved back home. I used all my savings to ensure Mum could stay in the house where we grew up, with our old school assignments still in crates in the spare bedroom and jars of expired Vegemite at the back of the pantry. She wanted the dignity of being surrounded by the life she'd built, of seeing the frangipani flowers on the tree in her front yard bloom in summer, of pulling her familiar doona over her weakening body at night. Of knowing she would at least lose everything in the same place where she had once felt like she had it all.

We had all the doorways widened to accommodate her wheelchair and replaced the stairs with ramps. We lowered the doorknobs and the light switches and the window handles, and raised the electrical outlets. We redesigned and renovated the kitchen and the bathroom, and at every step, I saw myself trapped inside the Greek myth of Sisyphus—the king sentenced to spend eternity pushing a boulder up a hill, only to watch it immediately roll back down. By the time we'd made the space accessible for Mum, her disease had progressed so that the changes we'd made were useless. A light switch beside your chair means nothing when you've lost the coordination to flick it.

Kelly and I argued most days about whether to move Mum to a hospice where she could receive round-the-clock palliative care. The guilt of the decision was compounded by the fact that, even though Mum was aware of what was happening, she could no longer fight for what she wanted. There are no words for the unfairness of it. That a disease could allow the mind to stay alive while the physical body slowly and painfully died around it, rendering the patient unable to communicate their consciousness. I imagined Mum stuck behind a pane of glass, knowing she would die there, but not unable to say or write or type, *I'm scared*.

• • •

Ruby Williams had started appearing on TV as a regular guest on a panel show. One Thursday night they were debating whether mothers had access to more empathy, a greater depth of emotion, than people without kids. It was an inane conversation sparked by a viral video in which a woman insisted that the world became a fundamentally different place once you were a mother. You started seeing criminals as someone's son, missing kids as someone's daughter, the idea of your own mortality as more confronting, because you had birthed a helpless infant who only wanted you. It was ridiculous. To literally project the idea that women with children were worth more than women without them into people's homes during prime time. Would the same comparison ever be made about men? When it was Ruby's turn to comment, she laughed and said there were probably things she would only understand once she had kids. She was the only child-free woman on the panel, and that was her response. I shouted at the television that night. *You have no idea*, I thought, *that I am mothering my mother. That I am changing her nappies. That I am feeding her. Bathing her. Keeping her alive. You have no idea that life can demand you become a parent without ever having a child.*

It had been eighteen months since my redundancy, and apart from infrequent freelance work, I was mostly unemployed. According to every hiring manager who would answer my calls, I was disastrously overqualified. They sighed and tapped on their keyboards while they explained they couldn't offer me anything that would be 'appropriately challenging' or offer me a salary 'commensurate' with my 'extensive experience'. To be employable, I needed to be several years younger and willing to be paid so little that I'd have to rely on my non-existent wealthy parents for support. It was never said explicitly, of course, but that was the implication.

Over time, my contempt for Ruby became motivating. I was so infuriated by the hole *The Daily* had created by getting rid of me and platforming her, that I had an insatiable desire to fill it. I started to direct my knowledge and my commentary into my own social media, where I posted videos weighing in on current events and whichever debates were dominating the public discourse. It occurred to me, incidentally at first and then purposefully, ambitiously, that if no media organisation would hire me, then I would become the media organisation.

The week of the rugby league grand final, I recorded a video about how, historically, rates of domestic violence spike after major sporting events. This wasn't new information—it's a well-documented phenomenon—but for reasons known only to a volatile algorithm, it circulated unlike anything I'd posted before. Snippets of my voice and my face were played on the news. International publications covered it. Ruby Williams wrote around it for *The Daily*, which made me laugh, then seethe. She was being paid to report on my content, which was yet to make me any money.

Thankfully, the hordes of followers I gained from that video got me on the radar of several brands—menstrual products, skin care, teeth whitening, bedding—and soon I had a manager to negotiate partnership deals on my behalf. With the promise of a healthy, five-figure 'influencer agreement' on the horizon, I set up a makeshift studio in one corner of Mum's study. I scrubbed the dirty walls with Ajax and steel wool, and ordered a ring light and a minimalist, pastel artwork online. I pushed an old bookcase that had been gathering dust in the living room down the carpeted hallway and into my corner, and I filled it with every book I could find, arranging their spines by colour.

Opposite the bookcase was a double-hung window that looked out to the overgrown backyard, unpruned trees and vines forming almost a canopy from this angle. The Saturday I'd visited Mum, almost two years ago, when she'd held me after I lost my job, was one of the last times she'd tended to the garden. I couldn't bring myself to go out there or to hire someone. I wanted to let it become completely wild, a physical reminder of what we had already lost; of how the things she loved became untamed without her.

I cleaned the glass, wiping thick grime and rust from the hinges, and manoeuvred the desk to face it. Soft natural light poured in from outside, and when I mounted my phone and flipped the camera towards me, the effect was a flattering, diffused image. There were no shadows in the hollow parts of my face or under my chin, no unevenness in my complexion, just a warm, golden glow that brought out the green in my eyes and the richness of my hair.

Sometimes I'd glance over at the tower of incontinence pads by the study door, at the long-abandoned walking sticks, at the rails we never had a chance to install, and think that no one would guess by watching my videos what was happening just outside the frame.

We never officially made the decision to keep Mum at home, but it became clear she was going to die here, with me. I had fallen into a routine of recording a few videos while the nurse visited then spending the rest of my day lying beside her. I read to her for hours, avoiding anything about suffering or tragedy or grief. I played music. I filled her room with the sounds of an ordinary day, of chatter and gossip and phone calls and cutlery scraping on a single plate. Mum now had a feeding tube, but sometimes when I was cleaning it I'd wonder whether the tube—whether I—was extending a life she no longer wanted to live.

The friendships I formed online during that time were very real. I messaged regularly with people who found my perspective refreshing, who sought out my opinions on everything from ingrained sexism to influencer culture. Even though I promoted paid partnerships on my social media, I wasn't anything like the daft women flogging protein powders. I had a following based on what I said and what I stood for, not what my abs looked like after a six-week cleanse. I was added to a group chat with women like me—writers, creatives, freelancers—and for the first time I felt like I had the kind of friends I had never found at school. Ruby Williams got promoted at *The Daily* and we shared screenshots of her worst articles, lamenting the fact that these opportunities always went to the same group of private-school–educated, well-connected 'journalists' with straight teeth and shiny hair. One of the women sent a link to a thread on a site called *GossipGate*, where I discovered reams of commentary about Ruby. We all joined anonymously, and tried to guess each other's usernames based on the tone with which we wrote about her.

But it wasn't just that. I told those women about Mum. They sent me care packages and advice, they listened to the echoey voice notes I sent while hunched over on the toilet seat, when I didn't want Mum to hear me cry. They helped me navigate the nauseating moral question of when Kelly and I should let Mum go. If it would be kinder to stop the feeding or the medications, to give her the dignity of a painless death. One woman, Beth, had recently been through a similar experience with her dad, and she messaged me every single day to check how I was.

> **Beth**: How was today?? Thinking of you. I know how all-consuming it is. You walk around the world looking at people buying groceries and going to the gym and you're like . . . what is wrong with you? How can you mindlessly go about your day when life is so full of suffering? Even now, while I'm grieving, I think everyone's so full of shit. People get upset by things at work and I'm like, Oh. Just to clarify. I do not care. Shit happens and then you die.

You develop an intimacy when you can't see each other's faces. Like the boundaries melt away and you're able to seep into one another, merging until it's unclear whose thoughts are whose. The voice in your head is no longer just yours; sometimes it starts to sound like one of the people whose inner monologue you're continually plugged into. Those women's messages were the last words I read before I went to bed, and the first I saw when I woke up.

Then Beth sent a link to the group chat. Just months after her last promotion, Ruby Williams had been made the editor-in-chief at *Bared*, the women's media company where Beth had just been hired. It didn't make any sense. Beth, who was far more talented than Ruby, was going to be managed by the person we'd all spent years mocking. Suddenly, it wasn't funny. My life was almost entirely dedicated to social media, searching for content ideas and moderating comments and replying to messages from people who seemed to repeatedly, wilfully, misunderstand me. I didn't want to have to post ads for a drink called h20, which was literally just water but in a can, in order to earn an income. The brand guidelines had demanded I explicitly say h20 was 'hydrating' and I cringed every time I said it, thinking: *Of course it's hydrating. It's fucking water.*

I loathed Ruby Williams because she represented everything I hated. She was one of those people who just got chosen, over and over again. Someone, somewhere had decided she was special and that I wasn't.

Beth and I combed through every piece of information we could find about her online. I shouldn't have been surprised to discover she had the most basic of journalism degrees, most likely getting perfectly average marks while spending her time at exclusive college parties with the rest of Sydney's elite. Did I mention she went to a private school? She probably got the job in media through some kind of family connection, like a friend of her dad's or a distinguished godparent.

My qualifications, meanwhile, seemed to count for nothing. I had a first-class honours degree in journalism and a master's in politics from Oxford. *Oxford*, as in one of the world's leading universities; it's almost unheard of for a girl who grew up in Sydney's south-west to study there, but I did. People like Ruby Williams didn't understand what it was like to work hard, to defy the odds, to try and try and try even when the world kept wanting to put you back in your box, to shut you down. In another life, if Mum hadn't been so sick, I might've gone back to England after my redundancy. Built myself up there. Had a whole other career, bigger and broader and more stable.

But I wouldn't exchange that time with Mum, the privilege of caring for her, for anything.

Chapter 48

After that neurology appointment in Westmead, Mum, Kelly and I got in the car. For several minutes, none of us spoke. An annoying song blared on the radio and Kelly changed the station several times from the driver's seat before eventually turning it off. It was Mum's voice that broke the silence.

'I don't want to suffocate,' she whispered. 'What a horrific way to die.'

Four years later, in the early hours of a summer morning, that's what happened. The only thing that allowed me to live with the guilt was the fact that she was at home. As she strained for breath—I will never forget that awful, wet, crackling sound; the death rattle, it's called—Kelly and I lay beside her, holding a hand each, and spoke to her with salty tears running down our faces and into our mouths. I can't remember what I said. Probably just *I love you* over and over again. I do remember that I kept looking at the time. I wanted it to be over. These were the last moments I would ever spend with my mother, and I was checking my phone, wondering how long this could go on for.

Of course, once the rattle stopped, and her body was suddenly just a body with no more breaths left, it felt as if it had gone much too fast. In the quiet, her gone-ness was deafening. The frequency of the room had changed, the melody of the universe. Through blurry eyes I gazed at the wooden dresser with framed photos of us gathered on top, the material accumulation of a lifetime of memories. It struck me that the real memories, though, of two little girls dressing up in their mother's clothes and overcooked weeknight dinners and impassioned stories in the car after school—the moments the photos didn't capture—had died with Mum. A part of me, the part only she knew, was gone, too.

...

The day of Mum's funeral was oppressively hot. By 10 am the sun was already high and strong, one of those November days where you can feel the sting of it on the bridge of your nose. It seemed particularly cruel for the sky to be clear and the world to be bright, like it was taunting me, gaslighting me. *It's just a normal day*, the sunshine said. *Quite a nice one, actually. Maybe you should clock off at three and have a glass of wine on a rooftop terrace with some work colleagues. Oh. That's right. You don't have colleagues. And your mum is dead.*

Kelly and I were fighting that morning. She'd already started going through Mum's jewellery and putting aside what she wanted, which wasn't fair because she knew I was in no state to have that conversation. Then, when she picked me up to go to the church, I noticed the familiar gold Claddagh ring on her stumpy hand on the steering wheel. I knew from decades of having Kelly as a sister that once that ring was on her finger, it was never coming off. I shouted that I was the one who had moved in with Mum, I was the one who had gently slid the ring over her knuckle when she'd lost so much weight that it had become loose. I was the one who'd changed her nappies and cleaned her feeding tube and slept beside her, while Kelly was dating and then dumping an insufferable personal trainer named Steph. As we argued, I realised there would never be anyone to adjudicate anymore. No one to tell Kelly she was being unreasonable, that she had to share; no one to even listen as I articulated my case.

Kelly slammed the door when she got out of the car at the church. I sat in the front seat, pulsing with anger but unable to cry, and considered going home. I couldn't do it. I had never felt so entirely alone. I played out the rest of the day in my head like a film. I'd sit stony-faced through the service, which would make everyone think I was cold and callous instead of just emotionally dried up. Everyone would comfort Kelly afterwards, not only because she'd be crying, but also because she instinctively softened her edges so people could rub comfortably against her. I was the opposite. My edges were serrated. I didn't know how to be vulnerable, Mum had always told me. When I was sick or sad or scared, I defensively thrust venom into anyone who got too close, and then wondered why no one was stroking my forehead, telling me I was going to be okay. At the wake, I'd feel the eyes on me. Aunties and uncles and cousins and family friends who had never understood me and now either challenged me directly online or made fun of me among themselves. *I overheard you at Christmas last year,* I wanted to say to Aunty Meg. *Whispering to Dave about how my man-hating wasn't helpful to anyone. Why don't we talk about your son, then, and how he has three kids and a coke problem?*

I think I actually would've left. Missed my own mother's funeral and spent the rest of my life regretting it. But then there was a tap on the window.

It was Beth. I was confused at first. I hadn't expected her to come. We'd only met in person a handful of times, for coffee and walks and one boozy dinner. She'd asked about the funeral details but I thought she was just being polite, showing her support in the sanitised, modern way, through the glass of her screen.

I unlocked the car and she slipped into the back seat behind me. She leant forward, looped her arm around the headrest and squeezed my shoulder.

'I don't want to overstep.' She was whispering, as though we might be overheard. For a moment I thought she was going to say something very serious. 'But from my brief experience of them, it seems like your family might be really, really ... annoying.'

I burst out laughing. It felt strange, like the muscles had atrophied from underuse.

'I've spotted at least four haircuts that could be straight from a Karen meme,' she said, sensing from my laughter that she now had permission to be entirely honest. 'And I don't want to alarm you, but there's a six-year-old with a mullet. I believe he belongs to the tall man who also has a mullet, whose jaw is swinging like he's at a rave. Your mum needs you in the church to bring down the ratio of people who are currently high on meth.'

There was an intimacy to how she saw me. An outsider recognising that I didn't fit in and assuring me that it was a good thing. A strength. I looked at her in the rear-view mirror.

'Hey, Uncle Wally was in prison for dealing heroin, not meth. Don't be so judgemental.'

She nodded, chastened. 'Of course. That was unfair of me.'

We were quiet, then she started to giggle.

'I can't believe you have an Uncle Wally. I thought that was a made-up name. Like Boris. Or Don.'

I laughed again.

'I have an Uncle Don,' I said, trying to catch my breath. 'I always thought it was short for Donald but then I asked Mum and it's not, it's just Don.'

And then we were both laughing so hard we couldn't speak. After a while she sighed and slapped her hands on her thighs, like we both knew what we had to do. She opened her door, shut it, and opened mine. I walked into the church beside her, and she led me to the front pew, to a spot beside Kelly, and hugged me. I turned to watch her as she searched for a spot at the back. Her dress was beautiful. An A-line shape with cap sleeves, cinched in at the waist and pleated at the bottom, brushing the tops of her knees. I wondered whether she'd worn the same dress to her dad's funeral.

I did cry during the service, while watching the slideshow. A Wendy Matthews song played while photos of Kelly, Mum and me appeared and disappeared, our childhood now gone, resting with the woman who seemed so much smaller now that the length of her body was marked by the wooden ends of a casket.

Beth stayed for the wake. We sipped icy wine from glasses stained with old lipstick, in the dim, air-conditioned function space of the local bowling club. Every now and then, someone who had known me my whole life would come up and hug me, murmuring their condolences so they'd feel like they were allowed to go home. I would go right back to talking to Beth: about work and Mum and Kelly and the conservative male columnist who had recently described me as 'extreme and hysterical' in a national paper. She told me about *Bared*, about a new content series Ruby had come up with.

'She's so fucking dumb I can't deal. I haven't wanted to bitch, given you've got more important shit going on, but she's got me interviewing women who have experienced coercive control because she thinks it's really original to point out that often sexual and emotional and financial abuse comes before physical violence. Like, wow. Congrats on single-handedly solving the DV epidemic, babe.'

Beth usually gave me regular recaps of her days at work, with play-by-plays of Ruby's insufferable behaviour. Once, Ruby had tried to have a disciplinary conversation with Beth about an editing error and Beth had simply walked out of the room, returning to her desk and ignoring Ruby for the rest of the day. We laughed at how bewildered Ruby must've been, unsure of how to behave with a person who wasn't fawning over her, a person who didn't immediately grant her respect just because she happened to have fallen into a job she didn't deserve.

'I'm probably in trouble for having today off,' Beth said, reaching for the bottle of wine in the ice-filled bucket between us. 'Technically I'm out of personal leave days. But I've looked it up and it turns out there's actually nothing they can do about it. I considered telling them it was for a funeral but I was worried someone would ask whose it was, and they might get weird about you because of the time you described *Bared* as "a pile of meaningless drivel" that's "insulting to women". Which, in your defence, is absolutely true.'

I snorted.

I had asked Beth before I posted about *Bared*. I wondered whether, even though she was entirely disillusioned by the company and everyone who worked there, she still cared about their reputation. Whether she felt like an attack on *Bared* was an attack on her. She insisted she didn't. If anything, it was the opposite. She wanted to see their downfall, particularly under Ruby's editorship. Her job wasn't going anywhere, and it made her look better if the work of other writers or editors was being publicly criticised. She even shared her login with me, so I could look at what kind of stories drove traffic, which helped me decide what to post about. Sometimes, she sent me a link to a problematic *Bared* story before it was published, and we'd go back and forth articulating exactly what was wrong with it. I think my support made her feel sane.

'But yeah, I can tell they're pissed,' she said. 'When I called about being sick, Ruby was all passive aggressive about how she'll have to take over my workload herself and I'm, like, you forget I don't care.'

She tapped the side of her head with her forefinger as though she was a genius who had cracked an impenetrable code.

'Thank you for being here,' I said. I couldn't quite look her in the eye; being emotionally forthright wasn't exactly my forte. I took a swig from my glass, and set it back down. 'It just . . . it means a lot. So thank you.'

A cousin tapped me on the shoulder to tell me he was sorry for my loss, and when I turned back around, Beth was on her phone.

'The messages from work, my God. Ruby just wants everyone to know she's very busy and important doing an interview, but don't worry: she'll be back to save the day when it's done. Like, hun, the team is fine without you. I think they'll live without your shitty clickbait headlines.'

Obviously, it was Beth who sent me Ruby's deplorable story about coercive control and abortion. I was watching the words come up in the back end of the site as Ruby was writing them, and I couldn't believe how dumb she was. It didn't take me long to nail my argument. Tearing apart someone with a brain the size of an ant isn't particularly challenging.

It was also Beth who unearthed Ruby's old social media posts and saved them. We were both sceptical about whether they'd have any impact, whether people would excuse what she did because it was so long ago, but it turned out we just needed to wait for the right moment.

Thankfully, that moment came once she made such a mess of the Lucy Wong story. I didn't even need to orchestrate that one. Someone on *GossipGate*—I still don't know who—contacted Lucy Wong's cousin to rile her up about *Bared*'s use of private photos. Cara Wong was furious.

People like to have somewhere to direct their rage when they're grieving.

Epilogue

We named our little boy Oliver. His middle name is Max.

He was four weeks old when he smiled for the first time. It was just the two of us, the rest of the world asleep, and he looked up at me while he was feeding, and he smiled. For a split second, I saw Max. I still see it now in tiny moments, the way the light hits his face, the way his eyes disappear. Not always, but there's something. A glimmer of him.

The universe did open up when my baby was born, even if I couldn't see it immediately. There is nothing like his smell, like the way he buries his head into my neck when he wakes in the night. He is a ball of cells, passed from my grandmother to my mother to me, the dust of the universe turned into a person, a miracle I get to hold in my arms.

I've been thinking about the internet, about social media. I've been spending a lot of time on it again while I've been feeding, although I know I shouldn't. If someone were to ask me what I'm doing on it at any given time, what I'm actually looking at, I wouldn't know what to say. The closest answer, I suppose, is everything.

Words and images and stories and videos and all of human history and a video of a cat being scared of a cucumber. Live images from a currently unfolding world war, and a picture and a sentence that are making millions of people laugh. Conversations and advice and grief and an old schoolfriend's wedding day. How to cook a simple pasta and an old man being reminded of the woman he loved and a royal who is no longer a royal who people hate but can't quite articulate why. A promise that a robot which cleans your floors will change your life and an ad for those shoes you never told anyone you wanted and a woman who said the wrong thing being called names usually reserved for fascist dictators with blood on their hands.

Everything. I'm looking at everything.

And I think that's what makes the internet the ultimate illusion.

Because the internet makes us feel like we can be everywhere at once. That we can defy the very laws of physics. But the internet, and the devices that contain it, are the real black holes: the voids that rupture space-time. That pull you in and compress you, that stretch you so that you are no longer in one piece.

But there is so much that does not exist in the black hole of a phone screen. So much that cannot be expressed or represented.

Like the tenderness of sitting opposite a flesh and blood person whose experiences have challenged their politics. Who is asking, begging, to be seen. Who wants their story to mean something, so they can make sense of it, so they can fold it into a narrative that carries the hope of a happy ending.

Like the frustration of never having quite the right words to say what you mean. Of not reaching the potential of your ideas.

Like mess. Like unfinished books. Like a conversation where you're just on the verge of understanding. Like the act of truly listening. Like recognising yourself not in someone's words or someone's voice but in their soul, in the space between you, in the air.

Like seeing a person's skin up close, so close you could reach out and touch it, and realising that—no matter the history between you—you're unable to hate them. Because you're united by the shared complexities of your species, because deep down, you want the same things.

Like love. Like forceful, sickening, terrifying love, for people who do and say imperfect things, and who love you back, even when you believe they shouldn't.

Like tragedy and grief and the sense of truth that lies at the pit of loss.

And then there's you.

My little boy. The person I'm writing to. The person this story is for. Nothing about you can fit into the screen of a phone. You are the entire universe.

For so long, I was obsessed with my reputation. My career was based on it. When the masses came for me with their pitchforks, I wanted them to know the truth. I wanted redemption.

Then, I wanted to redeem myself to you. I didn't want you to grow up and learn that your mother was a monster, that she had hurt people, that she had made horrible mistakes and that she was hated. When I didn't feel the magic of you immediately, when your birth went wrong, I thought it was because some part of me was irreparably broken. What if I couldn't love you? What if that was my punishment?

But then you smiled. You saw me and you smiled. And I held you and recognised a soul that I knew I would love forever, no matter what mistakes you made, no matter what you achieved. It occurred to me that I had been held the same way. In my mother's arms, my father's, my grandmother's. Then by Liv, and by Jamie. The way all of us are held when we are truly loved, truly known.

And yet I had invented an avatar and asked the world to love her. I wanted redemption for her because I presumed it would mean redemption for myself.

But now that I've written this, now that I'm at the end, I've let go of that, too.

I am neither good nor evil, right nor wrong, an ideologue for justice or injustice, kindness or cruelty. I am all of those things and none of those things.

You will not find Ruby Williams on the internet. She doesn't exist there.

She exists here. The whole universe and a tiny speck of it. A beating heart in the darkness, with no eyes upon her.

Acknowledgements

It feels absurd to have my name on the cover of this book, when there are so many others whose names should be on there, too. I'm going to use subheadings, which I don't think is a thing in acknowledgements sections, but hey this is my book so you can't stop me (someone definitely has the power to stop me).

Publication-wise:

Cate Paterson, you are a force. Your honesty and wisdom were the engine driving this novel, and I am eternally grateful for your patience, your perceptiveness, your generosity and your incomparable skill. I have learnt so much from you about how to write a book, and I consider myself wildly lucky to have you in my corner.

Pippa Masson, thank you for 'getting' my idea from the very start, and also 'getting' my lack of manuscript when I was pregnant and miserable. Your guidance and encouragement convinced me I could actually do this. You navigated this entire process for me in a way I could never have done on my own.

Ali Lavau, my wondrous copyeditor, you solved one million problems that were keeping me up at night. NQR (not quite right) will always be my favourite note, and I apologise for all the NQRs. I hope you laugh about them at the end of a long work day.

Christa Munns, Ali Hampton and the rest of the Allen & Unwin team—thank you for your ridiculously hard work and for making me feel like a real, grown-up author.

Family-wise:

Mum, the best conversations of my life are with you, and they're the ones where I learn what I think. You once said you became an English teacher because you love ideas, and that's the simplest description of what you've ingrained in me. And sometimes an idea becomes a book! You fostered my love of reading and words and stories, and have always made me feel like what I have to say matters. Your walks and pies and other escapades with Matilda also made this book logistically possible—so thank you.

Julieann, whoever invented acknowledgements sections did so for the purpose of thanking their version of you. Without you, I might've completed this manuscript in 2045. Maybe. You're the greatest mother-in-law I could've asked for, and your support, child care, and lack of judgement have been the ultimate kindnesses.

Dad, your strong values and the way you see the world are endlessly fascinating. You've passed down your obsession with fairness and justice to me, and that's what inspired this novel. I'll warn you—there's a severe lack of golf in its pages. My bad.

Jack and Nick, you challenge the silliness of my little online microcosm, and remind me every day of what truly matters. I wish I could write a single line of dialogue that's anywhere near as funny as the way you speak.

Rory. Firstly, I am sorry. Secondly, no, seriously, I'm sorry. I have been an agent of chaos in service to this book, and have not followed any of the strategies you're meant to in terms of structure, time management, etc. If our marriage can survive the neurotic mess that is Clare In Book Mode, then we can survive anything. Thank you for your perfectly timed anecdotes about creativity and perfectionism, and for your unwavering faith in me. It is unfounded and yet it is the bedrock of my life.

Jessie, you're the only (non-contractually obligated) person I allowed to read this book early, because when I write, I am always writing with you in mind. You are the smartest, most creative person I know, and I still feel like we're five years old, with you leading the way because you're bolder than I am. I couldn't create anything without reassurance from you, which some might say is pathological, but I say is just common sense when your twin sister happens to be a genius. Thank you for all of it.

Matilda Mouse. There is nothing like having a child to remind you that time is finite, that life is magical but it is fleeting, and that if you want to write a book, you actually have to write the book. I missed you every moment I was typing this instead of holding you, but I hope you know that your smile was always the highlight of my day.

Life-wise:

Mia Freedman, you introduced me to the world of digital media and you are the most perceptive, wise person to talk to about it. You changed the course of my life when you stumbled across my (appalling, in hindsight) writing, and changed it again and again when you saw potential in a Gollum-like girl who, for some reason, wasn't wearing shoes in the office. Thank you for your humour and your brain, your generosity and your vulnerability.

To all the wonderful people I worked alongside at *Mamamia*, you gave me friendships and laughter and fascinating ideas and an ever-expanding vision of what a career as a 'writer' could look like. I always felt so quintessentially myself at *Mamamia*, and that was because I was surrounded by the most supportive network of women (and some excellent men!). Sorry this book seems cynical, and I promise none of you are Beth, you are all Yasmin. With that said, *Bared* is not *Mamamia*, so thank you to Lize, Bel and Keryn for your insights about how other media companies work.

There are so many people whom I reached out to in moments of crisis, or who offered advice and pep talks when I needed them most. Thank you to (in no particular order) the Stephens' and Coffeys', Holly, Charlotte, Naima, Andi, Larl, The Wild Gals, Luca, Jason, Tai, Charlie, Luke, Ellie, Greta, Andrea, Curt, Adrienne, Vinnie, Libby, Ronan, Lachie, Liv, Will, Mannon.

I spoke to a number of people throughout the writing of this book who helped me navigate ideas around the internet, attention and outrage culture—some of them in published interviews, and some of them off-mic. After going back and forth, I've decided not to name them here, so that their identities don't confuse the fictional nature of this story. But to everyone I've had these conversations with, thank you for your honesty and your vulnerability.

Finally, to the women who keep creating and working and showing up when, deep down, they're terrified.

Every woman I admire is hated for something.